Praise for Nancy Herndon's mysteries featuring Detective Elena Jarvis . . .

"FINELY CRAFTED . . . HARD TO PUT DOWN . . . EXCELLENT."
—*El Paso Herald-Post*

"[ELENA JARVIS] IS SMART, WITTY, AND CAPABLE . . . GREAT READING."
—*Mostly Murder*

"ELENA JARVIS IS TOUGH BUT APPEALING, AND HERNDON'S TONGUE IS FIRMLY IN HER CHEEK."
—*El Paso Times*

Don't miss any of the Elena Jarvis mysteries by Nancy Herndon . . .

ACID BATH

WIDOWS' WATCH

LETHAL STATUES

HUNTING GAME

TIME BOMBS

MORE MYSTERIES FROM THE BERKLEY PUBLISHING GROUP . . .

CAT CALIBAN MYSTERIES: She was married for thirty-eight years. Raised three kids. Compared to that, tracking down killers is easy . . .

by D. B. Borton

ONE FOR THE MONEY	TWO POINTS FOR MURDER
THREE IS A CROWD	FOUR ELEMENTS OF MURDER
FIVE ALARM FIRE	SIX FEET UNDER

ELENA JARVIS MYSTERIES: There are some pretty bizarre crimes deep in the heart of Texas—and a pretty gutsy police detective who rounds up the unusual suspects . . .

by Nancy Herndon

ACID BATH	WIDOW'S WATCH
LETHAL STATUES	HUNTING GAME
TIME BOMBS	

FREDDIE O'NEAL, P.I., MYSTERIES: You can bet that this appealing Reno private investigator will get her man . . . "A winner."   —Linda Grant

by Catherine Dain

LAY IT ON THE LINE	SING A SONG OF DEATH
WALK A CROOKED MILE	LAMENT FOR A DEAD COWBOY
BET AGAINST THE HOUSE	THE LUCK OF THE DRAW
DEAD MAN'S HAND	

BENNI HARPER MYSTERIES: Meet Benni Harper—a quilter and folk-art expert with an eye for murderous designs . . .

by Earlene Fowler

FOOL'S PUZZLE	IRISH CHAIN
KANSAS TROUBLES	GOOSE IN THE POND

HANNAH BARLOW MYSTERIES: For ex-cop and law student Hannah Barlow, justice isn't just a word in a textbook. Sometimes, it's a matter of life and death . . .

by Carroll Lachnit

MURDER IN BRIEF	A BLESSED DEATH

SAMANTHA HOLT MYSTERIES: Dogs, cats, and crooks are all part of a day's work for this veterinary technician . . . "delightful!" —Melissa Cleary

by Karen Ann Wilson

EIGHT DOGS FLYING	COPY CAT CRIMES
BEWARE SLEEPING DOGS	CIRCLE OF WOLVES

TIME BOMBS

Nancy Herndon

Nancy Herndon

BERKLEY PRIME CRIME, NEW YORK

TIME BOMBS

A Berkley Prime Crime Book / published by arrangement with the author

PRINTING HISTORY
Berkley Prime Crime edition / September 1997

The Putnam Berkley World Wide Web site address is
http://www.berkley.com

ISBN: 0-425-15965-5

Berkley Prime Crime Books are published
by The Berkley Publishing Group,
a member of Penguin Putnam Inc.,
200 Madison Avenue, New York, NY 10016.
The name BERKLEY PRIME CRIME and the BERKLEY PRIME CRIME design are trademarks belonging to Berkley Publishing Corporation.

PRINTED IN THE UNITED STATES OF AMERICA

10 9 8 7 6 5 4 3 2 1

For my husband, Bill

Acknowledgments

Many thanks to members of my critique group, Jean Miculka and Joan Coleman; to my agent, Richard Curtis; and to my editor at Berkley, Cindy Hwang; to Dan Williams of the *El Paso Times*, whose series about water on the border was an invaluable source of information; to Raul V. Munoz, Jr., associate director of the El Paso City-County Health and Environmental District; to Bonnie and Bill Whalen for the inspiration of their delightful period bathroom, which was never attacked by a hammer-wielding conservationist; to Sgt. Bill Pfeil of the chief's office; Sgt. Adolph E. Metcalfe of the El Paso Police Department Bomb Squad; Agent Frank Flores of the FBI; Douglas Rittman of El Paso Water Utilities; to Lt. Ricardo Guzman of the El Paso Citizens' Police Academy; and, among the many interesting speakers in the program: Lt. Brad Peevey of the Shooting Review Team, Director Al Varela of First Step Stress Management, Sgt. Pete Pacillas of SWAT, Officer Tom Grady and Jack (a German shepherd with a nose for narcotics) of the Canine Unit, and Detective Eoff, weapons training officer with the Police Academy.

N.R.H.

1

..

Saturday, May 18, 11:55 A.M.

Boom!

The first explosion stopped the university president in mid-prayer. Detective Leo Weizell lunged into the aisle and scooped his partner, Elena Jarvis, off the floor, where she had dived, rolling, coming up on all fours. "You saw the mountain lion again, didn't you?" Leo said, hauling her back into her chair.

Shaken, Elena nodded. She'd been having flashbacks and nightmares for over a month—the result of a particularly violent case she and Leo had worked in March. Her friend Sarah Tolland said it was post-traumatic stress and kept recommending clinical psychologists. Elena's lieutenant, who didn't even know about the flashbacks, had suggested, at the time of the mountain-lion incident, that she see the stress management company contracted to the Los Santos Police Department, but Elena had hoped the problem would go away if she gave it time.

"That palm tree just blew up," cried President Sunnydale.

"Get hold of yourself," Leo whispered to Elena. "Say, you're not carryin', are you?" He asked the question as if he thought she might go berserk and shoot him.

"Sure," she replied resentfully. "Under two layers of clothes."

1

Having been uncomfortably hot, she now felt chilled and slipped her shaking hands into the sleeves of her academic gown. "I'm fine," she assured him.

Leo was attending Herbert Hobart University's first graduation with his wife, Concepcion, because they had been designated the "university's adopted family," which meant that the Psychology Department had offered to pay the freight on the quintuplets they were expecting. In return an H.H.U. psychologist got the right to study the seven Weizells in their natural habitat.

Elena had just received H.H.U.'s first honorary doctorate. What a crock that was! H.H.U. didn't have doctoral programs. She was being rewarded for her "services" to the university, like catching a couple of campus murderers in timely fashion, but mostly for her last case, which the papers had facetiously called the "hot regalia caper."

"Sure, you're fine," said Leo, worry lines lengthening an already long face. "Your lips are blue."

"Well, I'm not fine," hissed his pregnant wife. "I just had a contraction."

"False labor number three?" Leo murmured.

"You'll be sorry if my water breaks in front of this mob of millionaires," Concepcion retorted, dark eyes snapping with the frayed temper of a woman too long and too heavily pregnant.

Once Elena had shaken off the flashback, she felt a stab of apprehension because she doubted that palm trees were given to spontaneous combustion. Several spectators, rich parents undoubtedly, were covered with globs of dirt and bits of palm leaf. Noisy dismay prevailed among the university administrators and faculty, who had, just seconds ago, been heat-dazed and somnolent during the long closing prayer.

Boom!

"That was an oleander bush!" exclaimed Dr. Harley Stanley, Vice President for Academic Affairs. Most of the distinguished party on the stage had risen, craning to see the shower of glossy green leaves and red petals. Could the exploding shrubbery be some weird graduation finale arranged by Hector Montes, the superintendent of buildings and grounds? Elena wondered.

"I just had another contraction," said Concepcion, wincing.

Boom!

Chief Clabb of the university police force rushed to the edge of the stage and cried, "Sir, the sprinkler system seems to be blowing up."

"Our palm trees? Our sprinkler system?" President Sunnydale looked as if he'd just heard Armageddon announced on the loudspeaker system.

Boom!

Three gardenia bushes under the salmon plastic graduation tent burst into a perfumed, green-and-white cloud. Plastered with gardenia petals, the nearby parents tried to escape down the rows toward the center aisle. An art deco tent support tilted, shedding turquoise and gold tiles, causing the salmon-colored ceiling to sag. Turquoise and salmon were the university colors.

The graduating class, bedecked in turquoise academic gowns, all stood up and cheered, flinging their color-coordinated mortarboards into the air.

Idiots, thought Elena.

Boom!

The green-and-rose fragments of four more bushes ballooned majestically into a tattered cloud. Shrieking and cursing, more parents scrambled into the crowded rows.

Without relinquishing the microphone, President Sunnydale fell to his knees and raised his face to heaven—as seen through a transparent plastic ceiling. The tent had been his idea. He'd told Elena at the pregraduation prayer and cocktail brunch that he wanted the parents to be able to admire H.H.U.'s beautiful art deco architecture and lush shrubbery set against the stark grandeur of the desert mountain on which the campus was built. "Oh, Lord," the ex-TV evangelist prayed, "if it be thy will—"

"There's another one," gasped Concepcion.

"—spare our palm trees," President Sunnydale beseeched his God.

Boom!

A second palm erupted.

"Spread the mantle of thy divine protection over our shrubbery, oh God of our fathers."

"Are you sure it's not another false alarm?" Elena asked Concepcion, who had gone into labor twice previously without producing any of the five children she was now thought to be carrying.

"Send forth battalions of angels to defend our trees."

Boom!

"How would I know?" said the expectant mother testily. "Leo, I told you I should have stayed home."

"Consider, oh Lord, our sprinkler system," begged Dr. Sunnydale into the microphone. "Without water, how can there be grass? Without grass, how can our students frolic on the greensward?"

"Hey," said Leo, "don't blame me. We need the money, and this was the public acknowledgment that we're going to get it."

Elena was still feeling dazed and shaky from the flashback and all the commotion when her father and mother, Sheriff Ruben Portillo and the beautiful Harmony, climbed the stairs at the side of the stage and made their way toward her. They had insisted on coming down from Chimayo, New Mexico, for Elena's hooding. "You'd better do something about this," advised the sheriff.

"I don't know how to deliver a baby," Elena protested.

"I do," said Harmony. "Are you in labor, dear?" She studied Concepcion. "Goodness, you look as if you should have delivered a month ago."

Boom!

More petals, leaves, and mud showered the fleeing crowd.

"Our enemies are legion, oh Lord, but we stand steadfast in thy strength." President Sunnydale looked close to tears.

"I'm talkin' about the explosions," said Elena's father.

"The campus police should be dealing with it," Elena

replied, lifting a fall of long black hair from her neck. She was sweating because the portable air conditioners that were meant to cool the tent couldn't contend with the rising temperatures of May in the desert. Desperately, she looked around for Chief Clabb. After his initial announcement, he had disappeared. "Of course, they usually run away when things get tough," she mumbled bitterly. Now that she was Detective Dr. Jarvis, she'd probably be expected to deal with every weird thing that happened here at H.H.U.

"Mom's had five kids," she told Leo's wife, who had groaned again.

"We are beset on all sides, oh Lord, by the enemies of art deco," complained the president.

Boom!

"Let us smite them hip and thigh!"

Wringing his hands, Vice President Harley Stanley bent down and murmured, "I'm not sure this is an architectural protest, sir."

Boom!

"Let us rise like Christian soldiers to defend our green and leafy ramparts."

The tent began to collapse, dropping transparent salmon plastic on the panic-stricken crowd. Pandemonium broke loose, but Elena was still rattled and slow to act. Her father stared at her in surprise, then turned to his wife. "Harmony, you an' Weizell get Miz Weizell out before the ceilin' falls on the stage." They left immediately, Leo and Harmony supporting Concepcion. *"Elena?"* Her father spoke so sharply that he caught her attention. "Start callin' for help." He thrust his cellular phone into her hands. "I'll see what I can do out there."

She blocked out the memory of the big cat's snarl, closed her mind to the savaged corpse in her bedroom, and made her first call—for the fire department and EMS units to take care of the tent and the casualties. At least one person had gone down under those tiled tent posts. She called the Westside Command for crowd-control officers and, last, the bomb squad because, inexplicably, someone had blown up a lot of Herbert Hobart University landscaping. Then she took a deep breath, cursed her hands because they were still shaking, and waded into the melee.

2
##

Saturday, May 18, 12:30 P.M.

Elena found that she had done Chief Clabb and the H.H.U.
police an injustice. The officers were without direction because
their chief had fallen beneath one of the mosaic tent posts.
After lifting the pole off him, the university cops stood around
looking befuddled in the midst of chaos, so Elena and her
father had detailed a man to guard the unconscious chief. Then
they set the shaken campus police to raising two fallen poles so
that the trapped portion of the graduation audience could
escape before they were asphyxiated by the equivalent of an
enormous, salmon-colored plastic bag.

The most difficult imperative was keeping the parents and
guests headed away from the area where the explosions had
occurred. For this sensitive task, the university force proved too
subservient to be effective. Elena and her father had to manage
traffic control, and a number of prosperous, middle-aged
gentlemen resisted taking orders from a young woman wearing
an academic gown banded on the sleeves with turquoise velvet,
hair flowing long and black over her shoulders, and a stocky,
middle-aged Hispanic male in Stetson, string tie, and Western
boots.

In a moment of extreme exasperation generated by a
particularly abrasive CEO, Elena actually drew her gun, no

mean feat since it was tucked in a holster under both her academic gown and her suit jacket. "You can't go that way," she shouted.

"Mah car is in that di-rection, li'l lady, an' no one tells Big Hank Spike he cain't go collect his Cadillac."

Oh Lord! She was tangling with the father of militant feminist Cadet Major Melody Spike, the most irritating coed at H.H.U. Elena had met her while investigating the killer statues case. Mr. Spike was the last straw. She pointed her 9-millimeter Glock straight up and shot a hole in the plastic ceiling while glaring at the uncooperative Houston millionaire. As her hand jumped and the hammer-blow sound of the shot rang out, the one moment of silence in the whole debacle ensued. Then, with renewed shrieking, the well-dressed spectators, including Big Hank Spike, stampeded in the right direction—away from the leveled landscaping.

"Git along little dogies," Elena murmured to their backs. Then she took a moment to realize that she really was losing it. Discharging her weapon meant she'd have to talk to the Shooting Review Team. What was she supposed to tell them? *I'm running on a short fuse lately?*

Still, there was justification. The shot had got the parents moving without more arguments. She reasoned that there might yet be unexploded bombs out there. Or land mines. God knows what. Unfortunately, the gunshot had also frightened some of the H.H.U. police, who dropped the tent supports they were holding, causing another collapse, which this time caught the slower members of the audience and the injured.

Led by Sergeant Vincent de la Rosa, Westside patrolmen roared onto campus in their blue-and-white cars and took over crowd control. De la Rosa muttered, "I hate this place, and I especially hate your cases, Jarvis." He had been first on the scene of Elena's last big investigation, when a wealthy garment manufacturer had been killed by an arrow, then attacked by his own falcon. While de la Rosa deployed his men, the fire department, sirens shrieking, rumbled onto the quadrangle in welcome red splendor, followed by several green EMS vehicles. The tent was raised a third time by firemen, and EMS began collecting the victims. Elena breathed a shaky sigh of relief, righted an overturned chair, and fell into it.

"Things seem to be gettin' under control," said her father, lifting his Stetson and running a square, brown hand through graying hair.

"The bomb squad's not here yet," said Elena, "but then they're part-time. They'll have to be pulled from other assignments." Thanking him for its loan, Elena handed the cellular phone back to her father.

"De nada," said Ruben Portillo and sat down to call his wife at the hospital, where she had gone with Leo and Concepcion. "False alarm," the sheriff told Elena after a brief conversation. "Reckon I better get on over there an' pick up Harmony. You O.K., *mi hija?"*

"Sure, Pop," said Elena. "And thanks for pitching in."

Ruben shrugged. "Makes a change. Don't get things like this happenin' in Rio Arriba County. Still, we gotta get back, your mama an' me."

"Right now?" asked Elena, disappointed. "I hoped you'd stay another night." Elena had about decided to talk the flashbacks over with her mother.

The sheriff shook his head somberly. "Not a good idea, *niña.* We got *real* trouble brewin' up home. Damn environmentalists are tryin' to keep us locals from takin' wood outa the national forests. Don' know how they think people are goin' to stay warm come winter. Likely they don't care." He patted various pockets in search of his truck keys, muttering, "Usual bunch of Anglo do-gooders runnin' over poor Hispanics so they can save the Mexican spotted owl or some damn thing. Nobody's seen a spotted owl in more'n a hundred years, but the environmentalists don't care about that, either."

"Mom didn't say anything in her letters."

"No? Well, some folks from Truchas an' the other towns, your mother included, went up to Santa Fe before Christmas an' hung a couple of the forest-lovers in effigy."

Elena grinned and said, "Where Mom's concerned, once a

rebel, always a rabble-rouser." Her mother had been a protester at Berkeley in the sixties.

"Well, you may laugh, Elena, but if the judge hadn't backed down, the forest conservation people mighta got hung for real. Folks don't like bein' without firewood, an' you know most of 'em can't afford to pay for heatin'. There's still a suit in court to stop wood gatherin' in the Carson an' Santa Fe Forests, so I gotta get on home before something else happens."

"O.K., Pop." Elena went on tiptoe to kiss his cheek. "You take care now."

"Always do, *niña*," her father replied. He looked around the campus. Although a lot of vegetation had been blown to bits, even more remained intact. "This place sure is green to be settin' on a mountainside in a bone dry desert town. Maybe you got your own environmentalists makin' trouble."

Elena nodded. There'd been tough talk lately from a group called Water Now. Could they have enforced water conservation on H.H.U.? The university had its own wells, but those wells drew on the same bolsons that supplied drinking water to Los Santos, not to mention towns in New Mexico and the much larger sister city across the border in Mexico. Everyone in Los Santos who didn't have a water allotment from the river or a private well had to follow the water conservation rules. H.H.U. didn't. "It's a thought," said Elena.

"Well, we're mighty proud of you, *niña*. Never figured you to be a doctor before your sister."

Elena laughed. "How'd she take the news?"

"Said honorary degrees don't count, an' no one was gonna let you do a heart transplant." The youngest Portillo daughter was studying medicine in Albuquerque.

A truck rolling to a stop at the edge of the quadrangle caught Elena's eye. "I think the bomb squad's here."

"Then I'll be sayin' adios. Be sure you write or call. Your mama frets when she doesn't hear from you. Starts tellin' me how you got an aura that worries her, an' you know how that aura talk bothers me. Man doesn't like to think his wife's seein' colors around people's heads."

Ruben gave Elena a brief, hard hug and clumped away to pick up his aura-sensitive, ex-hippie wife, while Elena walked toward a very large uniformed black man wearing sergeant's stripes and followed by two subordinates hauling equipment out of a truck marked Los Santos Police Department Bomb Squad.

3

Saturday, May 18, 1:30 P.M.

"Sergeant Washington?" Elena hurried toward a man who looked more like a linebacker for the Dallas Cowboys than an explosives expert. Well, a retired linebacker, she amended; he was probably in his late thirties.

"Ma'am," he replied politely.

"I'm Detective Jarvis."

He eyed her graduation gown, colorful hood, high heels, and long, loose hair, topped by the mortarboard. "I was told you were Crimes Against Persons. You undercover?"

Elena shook her head, relieved that he hadn't seen the article about her getting the honorary doctorate. She had been teased unmercifully in her own department since the news spread. "It's a long story," she replied evasively, and it was not one she planned to tell him unless she had to.

"My technicians, Otis Blevins an' Pete Amador." Washington gestured to a young Anglo with a half-inch gap between his front teeth and a Hispanic officer who had once arranged a bicycle lineup at headquarters for Elena.

"Pete," she responded, smiling at Amador. "Officer Blevins." Gap-toothed, cowlicked, and skinny, poor Blevins looked the quintessential redneck.

"Team's one short," said Washington. "He's doin' a hazard-

13

ous device course at Redstone Arsenal in Alabama. Where's the bomb site?"

Elena nodded toward the shredded greenery. "Bushes and palm trees exploded both in and outside the tent. I kind of lost track of how many." That confession embarrassed her; it was an indication of how poorly she'd been functioning the last month or so.

"Explodin' bushes?" Sergeant Washington produced a somber smile. "That's a new one."

"New to me," Blevins agreed.

"How do you know it was bombs?" asked Amador.

What else would it be? she thought. "Loud explosion sounds, then flying leaves and flower petals."

Sergeant Washington turned slowly in a circle. "Lots of bushes an' trees left," he observed. "Any one of 'em could be dangerous."

"Certainly could," said Blevins. "Shall I count the bushes, Sarge? Give us an idea of how many—"

"I want all civilians cleared off this campus," interrupted the sergeant. "Have the Westside officers take care of that, Detective. And no press. We don't like photographers around while we're workin'." He then focussed on a stocky man, wearing chino trousers and shirt, who was stamping from one fragmented bush to another. "Pete, fetch that fella."

Amador left to corral the greenery inspector while Elena, having passed Washington's instructions to Sergeant de la Rosa, returned with Vice President Harley Stanley.

"Am I to understand that we are being ordered off our own campus?" the vice president demanded.

Sergeant Washington rocked thoughtfully on his heels, calmly considering his answer. "Well, sir," he said, "where you got a number of explosions, you can figure there's some devices that didn't go off. That bein' the case, we like to establish perimeters. We'd like to avoid any *people* gettin' blown up. On the other hand, this bein', as you say, your university, you can insist on stayin' with as many of your staff as you see fit to keep in harm's way. I doubt your insurance company will cover injuries—"

"An excellent point," Dr. Stanley agreed and left to hurry the departure of the remaining faculty and graduates.

"You expect me to leave my trees? After some *hijo de puta* attacked 'em? Not likely," protested Hector Montes, chino-clad superintendent of buildings and grounds, as he was escorted into Sergeant Washington's circle. "I can't turn my back but some new attack's made on my bushes."

"This has happened before, has it, sir?" asked Washington.

"Damn right. A bunch of *mujeres locas*—"

"Crazy women," Elena translated, then introduced Hector, whom she had met on the acid bath case a year ago.

"—tore up my bushes an' used 'em to burn that naked statue." He pointed indignantly to the large, blackened statue of a Charleston dancer that marked the center of the campus. "An' now they're goin' after the palm trees. Look at 'em! Couldn't sell what's left for mulch. You got any idea what it costs to ship three full-grown palms here from Florida?"

"So you think these crazy women went after your palm trees, sir?" Sergeant Washington interrupted.

"I don't know. Am I a detective?" Hector Montes glanced at Elena. "*She's* the detective. Nice to see you, *niña*." He shook her hand.

Elena wished people would stop calling her *little girl*. That was twice today: first her father, then Hector Montes. Even her lieutenant called her *niña* when he wasn't mad at her.

"Who pulled up your shrubbery an' burned it?" asked Washington.

"The Anti-Fornication Brigade and the campus feminists," Elena told the sergeant.

"You think today's explosions are their work?"

That hadn't occurred to Elena, but it seemed unlikely. "They were pissed off about the naked statue. Half of them considered it an 'inducement to fornication'—their words. The other half said it made 'sex objects of women'. I don't see any connection to what happened today. Bushes and trees don't carry sexist messages."

"It's the people who want us to stop waterin'," Montes interrupted indignantly. "I got a note a couple a weeks back. 'Turn off the water or we will.' Words cut out an' pasted on a sheet of paper. If I turn off the water, the plants die, the trees die, the campus looks like shit, the head honchos start complainin'. Well, it's off now. The sprinkler system's busted."

"Blevins, check the sprinkler heads. And be careful!" Sergeant Washington bowed his head. "Oh Lord, let this man survive the dangers of the day. Amen. Was it signed?"

Blevins, who had dropped to one knee during the brief prayer, jumped up, flashed a gap-toothed grin, and sprinted away.

"Prayer and care, Blevins," the sergeant shouted after him. "It's the eager beavers who get blown up. Well, was the note signed?" He'd turned his attention back to Montes.

"And do you still have it?" asked Elena, recovering from her surprise. It seemed that, as well as university presidents, bomb squad leaders were given to impromptu prayer.

"Yeah, I've got it," Montes replied, "an' no, it wasn't signed."

"Mr. Montes!" With a wrench in one hand and a clipboard under his arm, a lanky kid came bicycling across the grass.

"What's that civilian doing in the secured area?" Washington boomed in the direction of Sergeant de la Rosa, who had been listening to his men as they reported on the evacuation.

"Mr. Montes, the wells have blown up!" cried the new arrival, braking and jumping off his H.H.U. bicycle, which was turquoise with a salmon stripe and a carrier behind the seat that sported the university seal in gold. "If I'd been checking the wells instead of inspecting the pump house, I'd a been red confetti by now," the kid announced dramatically. "I wouldn't be here to tell you what happened." He thumped his chest, looking tragic. "Or I'd a been dragging my bloodied carcass away from the scene, screaming in agony, but still game, still trying to carry the news to my leader."

Montes scowled at the messenger. "You tryin' out for another play, Billy Roy?"

"No sir, a movie."

"How many wells?"

"Two, sir."

"That's half, not all," snapped Montes.

"Unless the others are set to go off later," said Washington.

Elena shuddered. *What next?* She wasn't up to this. Maybe Sarah and Lieutenant Beltran had it right. Maybe she ought to see a psychologist. That stress management group that had debriefed her after the mountain lion attack claimed they didn't report to headquarters, but Elena didn't trust them to keep their mouths shut, and she didn't want anything on her record that might keep her from making sergeant. Then she remembered that she'd shot the tent. *That* would go on her record, and it wouldn't look good.

"Where are these wells?" Washington asked. "Here on campus?"

"Farther down the mountain and north," said Montes. "We pump from the Mesilla Bolson, then run water up to holdin' tanks. That way we're not stuck with city water regulations on anything but our drinkin' water."

"Hmm," said Washington.

No wonder someone had blown up the sprinkler system and wells, thought Elena. H.H.U. was deliberately ignoring the water shortage, circumventing the very regulations that sought to alleviate it. Or maybe people from New Mexico had mined the campus and wells. There was a time, not that long ago, when Los Santos wanted to use bolson water from New Mexico. Big court case. Los Santos lost.

"Well, we'd better help Otis check the sites," said Washington. "Detective, why don't you find out how many people were injured? Tell the hospitals to save any material they find embedded in the victims an' label it as to victim an' victim's location at the time of injury. Report your findin's to me in the field."

Looking out at the grassy quadrangle and all the bushes and

sprinkler heads that might be about to explode, not to mention the remaining wells, wherever they were, Elena decided to take her time with the victim count. When the first bomb went off, she'd hit the floor. God knows what she'd do to embarrass herself in front of this large, calm bomb squad leader if she had to witness any more explosions.

4

: :

Saturday, May 18, 3:00 P.M.

"A group called Water Now picketed us a couple of weeks ago," said Hector Montes as he went through his desk drawers looking for the note he'd received. "Anglos. Chicanos. Some, accordin' to their signs, from the *colonias*. You gotta feel sorry for someone who lives out where the water an' sewer lines don't go. But still, turnin' off the water here isn't gonna help 'em. Here it is." He handed the note to Elena. "That's a photocopy."

The note had been pieced together with words cut from headlines. "Turn off the water or we will," it said. Odd typefaces. Fancy, old-timey looking styles. She had taken off her academic robe and mortarboard but still felt hot in the summer suit she'd chosen for the pregraduation prayer and cocktail brunch given for parents and new graduates. She'd also tried to restore her hair to its French twist. The mortarboard hadn't fit over it very well, but she'd thought the style more appropriate than her usual braid.

Then Michael Futrell, her former lover, acting chair of the Department of Criminology, had pulled her hair loose while putting on her doctoral hood. Instant mess. "It took me five years to get my degree," he had muttered.

"Tough," she'd hissed back, both of them low-voiced so

Dean Vorten of the College of Arts and Sciences couldn't hear.
In March, Michael had blamed her when his brother was killed
in her house, and Elena had resented his attitude. End of
romance! But that was a couple of months ago, and his
condemnation had been unfair. She did a lot better with crime
than romance, she reflected, her failed marriage to Frank the
Narc being a case in point.

"Does that typeface look familiar to you, Hector?" she
asked.

"Kinda," said Hector Montes, "but I don't remember where
I've seen it."

"Wish we had the original."

"Well, Chief Clabb didn't seem to take the note seriously. He
probably threw it away. You could ask."

"He's in the hospital," said Elena. Clabb had a concussion,
caused by a falling tent post; another such post had broken the
shoulder of some graduate's mother. Various persons in the
audience had sustained minor injuries as a result of being
knocked over by fleeing parents. One man, who'd had a heart
attack, was in the ICU at Columbia West but was said to be
recovering. No one had been hit by any bomb fragments that
could be retrieved for Sergeant Washington.

"Could we get back now?" asked Montes. "I gotta see what
they found out."

Elena nodded and accompanied him. Landscaped areas
being suspect, both of them kept carefully to the sidewalks and
paved paths that crisscrossed the campus. They found Sergeant
Washington in a huddle on the quadrangle with two strangers.
Maybe the newcomers were from the Westside Regional
Command or else big wheels in the department who wanted to
get in on the action when crime appeared at Herbert Hobart
University, enclave of the less successful offspring of the rich
and famous.

"None of the injuries are life-threatening," Elena told Washington as she handed him the note. "Mr. Montes says the
university was picketed a couple of weeks ago by Water Now,
an organization that disapproves of H.H.U. water usage."

"Either of you takin' over this case?" Washington asked the two new men.

Elena bristled. This was *her* case. She had been the first officer on the scene, and with eight injured, it was certainly a crime against persons. So why was he offering it to strangers, an Anglo with red hair and pale, freckled skin and a good-looking, trim-bodied Hispanic?

"Gentlemen, this is Detective Jarvis of Crimes Against Persons, LSPD," said Washington. "Detective Jarvis, Agent Perry Melon, FBI, Agent Consuelo Amparan, ATF."

Both men acknowledged the introduction, Amparan with a wide grin, Melon looking stunned.

"Why'd you call in the feds?" she asked Washington.

Ticking points off on his fingers, he replied mildly, "Multiple bombing injuries, a university with several federal programs, possibly a case of domestic terrorism. Any one of those makes it federal if they want it."

"Domestic terrorism?" Elena grinned at him. "You're kidding, right?"

"You yourself mentioned a group called Water Now."

"Well, yes," stammered Elena, "but we don't *know* that."

"Tell you what," said Amparan, "I'm happy to leave you as primary investigator, Detective—you and G."

"Who?"

"I'm G.," said Sergeant Washington.

"As in G-E-E?" she asked.

"As in G period," said Washington.

G? The sergeant had only an initial? No name?

"And I'm Connie." The ATF man gave her a big smile and shook hands. "My mom named me after my Aunt Consuela. Since I can't beat up the whole world, I get called Connie."

"And I'm Perry," said the FBI agent. "Perry Melon." He grasped her hand and held it a little too long.

"Elena," she responded grudgingly. Was she crazy, or were these two guys showing a less-than-professional interest?

"The FBI can wait, too. We'll see how the case develops," said Melon. "No matter who becomes the primary investigating agency, we'll certainly need your input every step of the way, Detective—ah—Elena."

With an odd expression, G. looked from one fed to the other. "So I guess that means you'll check for pyrodex and dynamite purchases, Connie, and you'll send the debris off to the Bomb Data Center." He had turned to the FBI man.

"Absolutely," said Perry Melon. "Are we all agreed that the bomber used water to trigger the pyrodex?" The other two nodded.

"Figures," said Connie. "The water caused a short. The electricity flowed through the wires. Ka-boom!"

Elena had no idea what they were talking about.

"So that means the system across the quadrangle will blow if they turn the sprinklers on there," Melon concluded.

"Somebody planted explosives under every bush and tree on campus?" she asked.

"Just the middle," said Melon. "The wells had slurry sausages dropped in. The dynamite was probably triggered by the well pumps, but two containers are intact." He paused, then explained, "It's a device used for oil-well work. If you want to see one, I'd be glad to take you over."

"Ah—maybe later," said Elena. "This sounds like a lot of work—all this mining the bushes and wells. Someone must have seen them doing it."

"Had to have been done last night," said Hector Montes. "We had the sprinklers on yesterday most of the day."

Elena scowled. Her sprinklers had to be off by ten A.M. on the three days a week she could use them. If she wanted to water, she had to do it early or after dinner. As a result, she could almost sympathize with whoever blew up the watering equipment here. H.H.U. was a huge user from a disappearing supply.

"The wells were pumping yesterday, too," Montes added.

"So we better start asking who saw what," said Elena. "Gardeners, campus police—who else?" She looked at Montes.

He scratched his head. "There were guys here last night putting up the tent."

"We'll need names of H.H.U. employees who would have been on campus then. Also the tent company number," said Connie Amparan. "Elena and I will want to talk to them all." He gave Elena an exuberant look, as if talking to a bunch of gardeners, campus cops, and tent-raisers was going to be a real blast.

"What about me?" demanded Perry Melon.

"Right." Amparan snapped his fingers. "You and G. take the tent company. Elena and I will cover the campus."

"While we leave the explosives in place?" asked G. dryly. "Or did you want to call in EOD."

"Who?" Elena felt a headache coming on.

"Explosives Ordnance Disposal," said Perry. "That's a good idea. With their regular unit in Bosnia, they've got temporary detachments coming in on a monthly basis. They'd love to get in on the cleanup."

"How do you clean up?" asked Elena.

"Just blow the stuff in place," said the ATF agent breezily.

"What?" Hector Montes looked horrified. "You're going to blow up the rest of my sprinkler system?"

"Only the part on the quadrangle," said Perry. He whipped out a cellular phone and put through a call to Fort Bliss. "I'd like to speak to the head of the Explosives Ordnance detachment," he said.

Great, thought Elena. They were inviting another portion of the bomb community in on the fun.

"What about the wells?" asked Montes.

"Those, too," said Connie Amparan.

"This is Agent Perry Melon, Los Santos FBI. Who'm I talking to?"

"How are we supposed to keep the campus looking decent?" demanded Montes.

"Lieutenant Calzone, we've got a situation here. . . ."

"Believe me, the administration will never go for this," Montes assured them.

"That's right, two wells . . ."

Elena and G. exchanged glances. Both of them knew that

H.H.U. wasn't going authorize any further destruction of their precious Miami Beach shrubbery, mandated along with the art deco buildings by the will of the founder. "Isn't there any other way?" she asked Sergeant Washington.

"Great," said Melon. "We'll save them for you."

"Get out the bomb suit, I guess," Washington grumbled.

Otis Blevins, who had just rejoined the group, said, "Geez, Sarge. It's too hot for that."

"It'll be hotter in the suit," his sergeant replied.

5

"Absolutely not," said Vice President Stanley when informed that the bomb squad planned to blow up the rest of the booby-trapped sprinklers. He then called on the chief of police and the mayor to protect H.H.U.'s water system. When the wrangling ended, the feds and the bomb squad on one side, the politically inclined on the other, H.H.U. won.

"I guess you can't fight city hall," G. muttered and ordered his men to haul the Kevlar bomb suit from their truck. It weighed ninety pounds and, with its thick apron from waist to thigh, great fan collar, and Plexiglas helmet, made the wearer look like a space alien. However, the unprotected rear offered a bizarre contrast where the bomb tech appeared human from shoulders to feet.

From the window where she was interviewing gardeners and campus police, Elena could see them: Otis Blevins, Pete Amador, and G. himself. They took turns as the baking late afternoon heat assaulted them through layers of Kevlar. First one, then another lumbered from sprinkler to sprinkler, digging up devices, clipping wires, carrying the parts away.

It was a slow process, as were Elena's interviews. She, Amparan, and Melon had appropriated offices in the administration building to interview university employees, who plainly didn't want to give up Saturday afternoon. Midway through, tent company workers began to arrive, and they were even grumpier, except for short, muscular, and talkative Bonnie Murillo, who had run away with a circus at fourteen and returned to Los Santos twenty years later, which explained why she was an expert tent-raiser. Now a single mother, she worked full time in a convenience store, part time as crew foreman for the rent-a-tent company.

While raising the graduation tent, Bonnie had noticed a man, medium height and build, wearing an olive green uniform that bore the legend Morris Irrigation Services. He had been working on the sprinkler heads between eight-thirty and eleven-thirty Friday evening.

"Cute guy," said Murillo. "Had a bushy, black mustache, good skin, great buns, and a braid down his back. Oh, and a baseball cap that matched his uniform."

Elena asked Bonnie to cooperate with a computer artist on a picture of the fellow's face. Then she fished a telephone book from the bottom drawer of the desk she occupied and looked up Morris Irrigation Services. Either the company didn't exist, or it had no telephone.

Amparan hit pay dirt as well, a university cop who let the irrigation man onto the campus that night, and Perry turned up a gardener who had talked to the man. The ersatz sprinkler expert had claimed he was putting in an anticorrosion compound that extended the life of sprinkler heads by ten years. Hector Montes said he hadn't hired him.

The three witnesses were sent to headquarters while Elena and the feds went back to the quadrangle, where the Kevlar suit had been returned to the truck. Sweaty and exhausted, the bomb techs were sprawled on the grass. "Got 'em all," said G., wiping his face with a navy bandanna. "Two EOD men are gonna haul 'em over to the Fort Bliss firing range and blow 'em. Also, the bomber called to say the well bombs that didn't blow have secondary devices attached that make them tamper-proof."

"What does that mean?" Elena asked, noting the approach of an army officer and five soldiers.

"It means if we try to take the canisters from the wells, they'll blow up." The sergeant got to his feet. "This is Lieutenant Roman Calzone from EOD at Fort Bliss."

The lieutenant was a short, olive-skinned man with curly black hair and flirtatious eyes, which he directed toward Elena while pissing her off by saying, "What's a pretty girl like you doing on a homicide squad?"

She stared back and retorted, "What's a pretty boy like you doing on a bomb squad?"

Calzone, oblivious to sarcasm, all but preened.

"So, Mr. Montes," said Sergeant Washington, "your vice president won't let us blow the well bombs, and we can't fish 'em out. That means—"

Calzone interrupted by saying, "I'll get them out."

Washington eyed him with disfavor. "Chief Armando Gaitan has forbidden us to—"

"My responsibility, old man," said Calzone. He clapped Washington on the shoulder. "Let's go see these wells."

Reluctantly, Elena accompanied the bomb techs, now nine in number. Two of Calzone's soldiers had hauled off the explosives retrieved from the quadrangle in a trailer that held a bomb containment unit. The techs tossed around ideas about what kind of secondary device the bomber might have attached to the original slurry containers. Montes, who had joined the cavalcade, complained that if they blew up the other two wells, H.H.U. would have no water for irrigation.

"Plant desert stuff," said Amparan. "That's probably what the bomber wants you to do, anyway."

Along with about three-quarters of the city of Los Santos, Elena thought.

"Anyway, we'll catch him," said Melon. "Right, Detective?" He gave Elena a besotted smile.

"Beats me," she replied. "I've never hunted a bomber."

"Never fear," said Melon. "The rest of us have."

Billy Roy met them at the well site. "You've got the pump timers turned off, right?" asked Montes.

"Oh, yes sir," said Billy Roy. "Water, water everywhere, and not a drop shall flow."

"For God's sake," muttered Montes, "if you're quoting poetry, just stop it."

The nine men inspected the two shattered wells, gathering pieces of debris. Then they studied what they could see of the two remaining bombs. Elena stayed away from the site of possible explosion and talked to Billy Roy. "Any guards here at night?" she asked. The site wasn't on campus, so perhaps it didn't come under university security.

"No, ma'am," said Billy Roy. "You're sure pretty. Ever thought of becoming an actress?"

"Never," said Elena. "Have you seen any strangers around yesterday or today?"

"No, ma'am. Why don't you try out with my company, Border Players? I'd be happy to sponsor you."

"No thanks."

"Except the state inspector," Billy Roy added.

"What state inspector?"

"Yesterday afternoon. He came by to test the water quality. I told him we didn't use it for drinking, but he said, 'You put bad water in the ground, it soaks through and contaminates the aquifer.'"

Elena frowned. "The aquifer's way the hell underground. Only the shallow wells get contaminated. Did you watch him making the tests?"

"Sure. He said the water was too hard; it'd corrode our pipes. So he put in something to soften it. He gave me a card in case we wanted to get some more."

"The state inspector wanted to sell you a water-softening system?"

Billy Roy cocked his head. "I guess that *is* strange."

"Do you have the card?"

"I don't know. Maybe it's in the pump house."

"Let's go." She headed in that direction, asking over her shoulder, "What did he look like?"

"Five-ten. One sixty. Horn-rimmed glasses. Wearing a green uniform that said—I don't know—Texas Water Resources Commission or something." Billy Roy looked pleased with himself. "I study people, you know. We actors—"

"What color hair?"

"I couldn't see it. He was wearing a cap with a visor, but he had a light brown beard."

"Good looking?"

"Nothing special."

"Do you think if I got you together with a computer artist, you could help with a picture?"

"Wow, sure. What a cool idea." Billy Roy found the card in a trash basket.

Elena put the bomber's ID in a plastic evidence bag from her purse and tucked it into the breast pocket of her suit coat, which she was carrying over her arm because it was so damn hot. Then she sent Billy Roy off on his bicycle to catch a ride to headquarters at Five Points while she joined Hector Montes and showed him the card.

"Never heard of them," said Montes, who was infuriated when he discovered that his assistant had allowed a stranger to attach devices to the university wells. "That kid has the brains of a *flauta.*"

Elena felt a pang of hunger, having had nothing to eat since brunch and cocktails.

"I can get the slurry containers out," said Lieutenant Calzone. "Nothing to it."

The local and federal bomb men looked at him as if he were crazy. *So that's the way it is,* Elena thought. *Calzone is the new boy in town. Not trustworthy until he proves himself.* Connie Amparan reinforced her opinion by saying, "No way. I'm not going against orders."

"So move out of the way if you're scared," said Calzone. "What about you, Detective?" He put his arm around Elena's shoulders. "You'll stay with me, won't you?"

Elena glanced at her watch and exclaimed, "Look at the time! I'm off shift!"

An amused laugh rumbled out of G. Washington. "I knew you were undercover at that ceremony. No one on regular duty would wear those shoes."

Elena glanced down ruefully at her pointy-toed heels, which her sister had talked her into buying during a shoe sale in Albuquerque.

Washington turned to Calzone. "Sorry Lieutenant, but I can't risk Los Santos police officers in an operation I consider foolhardy." He took Elena's arm in one large hand, waving his two bomb techs after him, and started to walk away from the well site, calling over his shoulder, "Don't do a thing till we're two hundred yards away."

"No confidence at all," said Calzone. His own soldiers were looking pale.

"This is a mistake, man," said Connie Amparan.

"You people are the ones who said the local bigwigs don't want these wells blown, so I'm telling you how we can get the explosives out. I recognize that antitamper device."

"We know what you're telling us," said Melon, "but it won't work." Then he and Amparan followed the Los Santos contingent with Montes joining the retreat.

"Now we know why Calzone didn't get sent to Bosnia," Perry Melon murmured once they were all ensconced behind a stone wall, well away from the site of possible explosion.

Washington bowed his head. "Let us pray. Lord, spare the idiotic and the foolish, for they know not what they do. Amen." The others murmured "Amen" after him as if they were used to Washington's impromptu invocations.

"Likely, all the smart techs went off to Bosnia," said Amparan, picking up the conversation where it had stopped before the prayer.

"I think I'll see how many Water Now names I can dig up tonight," said Elena, trying to distract herself from thoughts of an incipient explosion. "I'll start interviewing tomorrow."

Washington said, "Unless there's an incident or I'm on duty, I don't work on the Lord's Day."

"That's O.K." Elena glanced at him sideways. "I can go out on my own."

"I'm flying up to Albuquerque to conduct a seminar for their police department," said Melon regretfully, "or I'd be glad to help."

"I can go with you," said Connie Amparan.

She turned to him, surprised. "You ATF guys do interviews?"

"Sure," said Amparan. "And I'll run any names you turn up through our computer."

"I can do that," said Perry Melon.

"Looks like you're gonna have all the help you need, Detective," said G. dryly.

Boom!

Elena dove sideways, stifling a cry of terror as she confronted the mountain lion once again. The others just hunched behind the stone wall while debris rained down. Then they popped up to see what had happened. Connie whispered to her, "Good instincts. You'd do great in the trenches."

Bad instincts, she thought. *Worse startle response, horrible flashbacks.* Elena bit down hard on her lip, unwilling to let him see how shaken she was. His voice had blotted out the image of the big cat and the mangled corpse in her bedroom. She rolled into a sitting position and inspected the damage, laddered stockings, skirt hiked up to her thighs. Trembling, she yanked it down.

Two round-eyed soldiers peeked from behind the pump house. Bits of cement, brick, and metal littered the ground under a cloud of dust. Lieutenant Calzone was down. Fifty feet away, one of his soldiers swayed on hands and knees, shaking his head and trying to rise.

"Anything else about to go off?" Connie Amparan shouted to the two soldiers at the pump house.

"No, sir," they replied and headed toward their fallen lieutenant.

"Well, some guys you can't tell anything," said Sergeant Washington and climbed over the wall to inspect the damage and casualties. Connie helped Elena over. While they were waiting for the ambulance to arrive, Calzone opened his eyes and mumbled, "It wasn't what I expected."

"What do we do about the fourth well?" asked Montes.

"We're gonna get permission. Then we're gonna rig it so we can turn on your pumps from farther away. And then we're gonna blow it," said Perry Melon. "After that you can hire someone to come in and repair what's left."

"Take him up on it, Hector," Elena advised, "before Harley Stanley gets us all killed." She brushed dirt off her suit. "You notice he wasn't here to get hit by falling well parts."

6

Elena was hurrying into the lobby of the university apartment house when Michael Futrell called to her. Although she tried to reach the sanctuary of the elevator, he cut her off both physically and with the words, "We really do need to talk."

"I'm having enough trouble dealing with what happened to your brother," Elena retorted. "Why would I want to talk to someone who thinks it was my fault?"

"But I admitted that I was wrong to blame you, Elena."

"Michael, let it go, will you?" Nonetheless, there was one wistful corner of her heart that still found Michael's light brown hair, hazel eyes, and earnest face appealing. She sighed, remembering the first time she'd seen him, at the bicycle race in Chimayo, where she'd thought he was a police groupie.

"At least, let me apologize for my remarks at graduation today. Truly, I'm pleased for you. About the degree, I mean."

"Uh-huh," said Elena, becoming annoyed all over again. "Is that why you knocked my hair loose when you yanked the hood over my head?"

"It was an accident," Michael protested.

"I had heavy duty pins in that French roll. You gave it a yank."

33

"I did not. The button attachment on the hood caught in your hair and—"

"Yeah, right. Try sitting through a graduation and an endless prayer on a hot day with three feet of hair hanging down your back, and see how much *you* like it."

Looking sad, Michael said, "Your hair's so beautiful."

"Absolutely. Just what you'd expect to see on someone getting an honorary degree—a ragtag hippie hairstyle." Then she was sorry she'd said that because her mother was a hippie of sorts, semiretired. Harmony still wore her hair long, but hers always looked good, while Elena's, let loose, turned into demon hair. At that moment the elevator arrived, and she stepped on, hitting the Close button immediately so that the door shut in his face. Sarah's apartment was only one floor up; but Michael couldn't possibly get to Sarah's door first.

"What have you done to yourself?" Sarah exclaimed when Elena let herself in. Dr. Sarah Tolland was the chairman of electrical engineering at H.H.U., a slender woman in her early forties with short, blond-gray hair. She was Elena's best friend. After the mountain lion attack at Elena's house, Sarah had taken her in and insisted that she stay long after she should have gotten her act together and gone home. "You have dirt on your suit, and your hose are in shreds!" Sarah herself never had so much as a hair out of place or a thread loose on any of her numerous, expensive, very conservative outfits.

"One of the university wells exploded while I was hiding behind a rock wall," Elena replied. She looked longingly at the pristine sofa and mumbled, "I guess I better go take a shower." Then she had a thought and went to the telephone to call *Times* reporter Paul Resendez. She needed to do research on Water Now. However, she couldn't reach Paul, and without his help, there'd be no access to the newspaper morgue. Nor was the public library open.

"Listen, Sarah." She turned to her friend and hostess. "Do you know whether the university library indexes the local newspapers?"

"I have no idea," said Sarah, "and you don't need to spend your evening working, if that's what you have in mind. You need a hot bath, something to eat, and a good night's sleep."

Elena grimaced. "I haven't been getting any good nights' sleep lately, so I might as well work."

"You might as well get some therapy," said Sarah.

"Come on," coaxed Elena. "I'll bet you could show me how to use the library files if they have them."

"Absolutely not," said her friend, then added grudgingly, "but I will put a TV dinner in the microwave for you while you shower."

"Gee, thanks," said Elena. She hated those TV dinners, but in Sarah's apartment nothing else was available unless they ate out or Elena cooked.

The H.H.U library did index the local papers; they also bound them, and every issue other than the last two weeks was at the bindery. The rest were on racks, which the periodicals librarian suggested Elena page through. There wasn't much on water conservation and water advocacy groups, but one article, she thought, was significant. She wondered whether, in giving an interview to the *Times*, Professor Simon Metusich hadn't inadvertently incited a group of local citizens to bomb the university.

Engineer Predicts
Thirst by 2010

At present rates of usage, the Hueco Bolson, from which Los Santos draws 35 percent of its water, will be depleted by the year 2010. This prediction was made by Dr. Simon Metusich, professor of hydrology, University of Arizona. Metusich has been studying the water resources of seven Western cities under a grant from the Environmental Protection Agency.

The professor also stated that "to expect Los Santos water usage to remain static in coming years,

> even given water conservation measures now in
> force, would be an exercise in insane optimism."

Elena shook her head, thinking that statement must have
upset those who read it. The man was saying things were going
to become critical, water-wise, in less than fifteen years. And
the water district's press handout wasn't all that reassuring.

> A spokesman for Los Santos Water Utilities, re-
> sponding to Metusich's remarks, said, "Doomsday
> predictions are not in the public interest. Our figures
> indicate that present sources will be adequate until at
> least 2025, by which time other options will have
> been exercised. We are addressing the problem and
> do not anticipate that our plans will prove wanting."

What other options? She knew the district had bought a
ranch with water under it, but the land was a hundred and fifty
miles away, and the ranchers who lived over the Ryan Flats
Aquifer were pretty pissed off at the idea of Los Santos
drawing on their water supplies. Not to mention the fact that
the price of water would shoot up if the city had to import it
from so far. The really interesting thing about the article was
that the reporter had contacted members of Water Now for their
comments. She began writing down names and taking notes.

> Members of the local advocacy group, Water Now,
> were quick to react:
> President of Water Now, Father Conrad Bratslowski:
> "The problem is with us today, not in the next century.
> Even as we speak, the poor go thirsty while the rich
> grow roses."

Very poetic. Father B. belonged to every pressure group in
town. Elena found it hard to believe that he'd have time to plant
all those bombs at the university.

Celestina Ortiz, mother of six: "In the *colonias* we
have to cart water to our houses in barrels, and now,
even if we get hooked up to the city water system,
there's gonna be no water in the pipes? Is that what
he's saying?"

Six kids, no toilets, no washing machine? That might be
enough to push you over the edge.

Gladys Furbow, Sierra Club liaison officer: "The
water district needs to find new sources before we
run out. If something isn't done, our children and
grandchildren won't be able to take baths."

Gladys was too optimistic. If Metusich was right and the
Sierra Club lady wasn't a senior citizen, her own bathrooms
would be running dry.

Efren Maruffo, Upper Valley cotton farmer: "I hope
no one thinks they can take away my Rio Grande
water allotment. If I don't irrigate, I go broke."

Would he bomb the university because he foresaw that in the
next decade or so the city might insist on taking his irrigation
allotment to water its lawns or just to keep the showers running
and the drinkable water available?

Magdalena Reyes, computer instructor, Pancho Villa
High School: "Water conservation measures haven't
solved the problem. The heavy water users, public
and private, have to curb their usage so that immi-
grant families in the *colonias* can stop living in the
Third World conditions they came to this country to
escape."

Well, H.H.U. had been one hell of a big user—until the
bombs went off. Elena wondered if they'd knuckle under and

opt for cactus to replace the palm trees, grass, and flowering
bushes. Or would they repair the wells and the sprinkler
system, replant the shredded greenery, and go on hogging
water?

> Sister Gertrudis Gregory, Convent of the Sacred
> Chamisa, secretary of Water Now: "No water in
> 2010? There's no water now in places like San
> Elizario and Socorro. Infectious hepatitis and other
> diseases bred by poor sanitation are endemic."

Elena knew Sister Gertrudis. She was an antiabortion activist, already out on bond and appealing a conviction for
attacking the H.H.U. Health and Reproductive Services Center.
The question was: Did she know how to make a bomb? And
could she reconcile her religious beliefs with the possibility of
killing someone?

> Gary Messner, Vice President, Water Now: "A lot of
> Anglos think it doesn't matter because some poor
> guy living in a cinder block house with an open
> cesspool in the backyard doesn't have city water or
> sewers. Think again. He's probably busing your table
> at that restaurant you go to on Saturday night. You'll
> be the next one to get hepatitis."

That had happened. Diseases came out of the *colonias* as
they did out of the rain forests. Elena had read a book about
AIDS and ebola coming up a new highway from the back
country to the villages and then to the cities in Africa. Scary
stuff. And here at home there had been the cholera alert in Los
Santos. And the hepatitis. And the TB.

> Contact Los Santos *Times* Roving Reporter, Sal
> Cruz, to give us your thoughts on the water crisis.

Los Santos Times, Monday, May 13

She stuffed the notes into her pocket and returned the newspapers to the librarian, from whom she borrowed a telephone book to look up addresses on the Water Now interviewees. When she got back to Sarah's apartment, it was eleven. Should she call Connie Amparan? The ATF agent had said he wanted to go with her, and he'd given her his home and beeper numbers, telling her "any time, day or night." If she called now, they could get an early start.

"This is Jarvis," she said when he answered. She could hear the television in the background. "I've got some names."

"Fine," said Amparan. "What time do we start?"

She glanced over her list. "How about eight?"

"Eight! Can we get breakfast before the first interview? I'm buying."

"Great," said Elena. "I'm eating. There's a place in Canutillo. Great *huevos rancheros*. We can start in the Upper Valley and work our way around the mountain."

"Ought to be a full day," he said, sounding suspiciously cheerful.

Just what she needed, thought Elena after they'd made the arrangement and she'd hung up—a federal agent with the hots for her. He *was* cute, but she didn't think dating someone she was working a case with would be too smart. Lieutenant Beltran wouldn't approve. On the other hand, she needed to forget Michael. What better way? Not that Amparan had asked her out. He'd just offered to buy her breakfast. Maybe he was married and had five kids.

Which made her think wistfully of Leo, her usual partner in Crimes Against Persons. With Concepcion going into labor every couple of days and refusing a cesarean section, he wasn't likely to be available for this case. And anyway, he'd been drafted for stakeouts on the border, where the bandits were coming over from Mexico and robbing whoever drove by. Los Santos was one of the few cities left in the country that was working to retain its Old West ambiance into the twenty-first century.

7
⠒

Sunday, May 19, 8:10 A.M.

Water Utility Reminds
Customers of Summer Rules

Although warm weather watering rules went into effect on April 1, not all Los Santos Water Utility customers are cooperating. The utility has had to send reminders that its six Conservation Enforcement inspectors are cruising the streets looking for violations and responding to calls.

Even-numbered addresses are allowed to water before 10 A.M. and after 6 P.M. on Tuesday, Thursday and Saturday; odd-numbered addresses on Wednesday, Friday and Sunday. Monday, Wednesday and Friday are the watering days for schools, parks, cemeteries, golf courses and industrial sites.

Cars may be washed at any time with buckets and brushes and rinsed quickly with positive on-off hose nozzles, but under no circumstances can water run in the streets.

Watch out readers! You can be fined between $50 and $500.

Los Santos *Times*, Sunday, May 19

Elena passed a fraying basket of hot flour tortillas to the ATF agent, Connie Amparan, who had ordered *menudo*. "You must be a native," she said, wondering if he had a hangover. Mexican tripe soup was reputed to be great for hangovers. Elena herself didn't care for tripe, which, in her opinion, had the consistency of a shredded inner tube.

"I was born and grew up in San Diego," said Amparan.

"Do they have water rationing, too?" she asked. An article in the Sunday paper had reminded her that she needed to drive by her house to see if the kid she'd hired was keeping her yard alive.

"Not unless they've started since I left," Amparan replied. "I've been gone a long time."

"How'd you happen to get into Alcohol, Tobacco, and Firearms?" She sipped her coffee appreciatively and took another bite of *huevos rancheros*.

"Came out of the army with a lot of experience in all three, so I joined up." He grinned at her. "Since I'm buying you breakfast, don't you want to know whether I'm married?"

"O.K.," said Elena. "Are you married?"

"No," said Connie Amparan. "But I got nothing against it. How about you?"

"Divorced," she replied.

"Yeah? Guess you're not Catholic."

Elena shrugged. "My father is; my mother kind of discovered New Age before it became popular."

Amparan looked confused.

"She was a hippie," Elena explained. "My dad's a sheriff in New Mexico. He met her while he was raiding her commune."

"No shit," said Amparan. "That's a great story. Romantic."

"They thought so," Elena agreed and cut another dripping, delicious bite.

"This is a terrific place," said Amparan, looking around the little café. "I never heard of it."

"Stick with me," said Elena, "and you'll discover all the hole-in-the-wall Mexican restaurants on both sides of the mountain."

"I'd love to."

His response was so enthusiastic that she wished she'd kept her mouth shut.

"So what did your ex do?" he asked.

"He's a narc in the LSPD."

"Oh, boy! Husband and wife in the same department?"

"Not me. I went straight into Crimes Against Persons from patrol."

"You like it?"

"It's interesting. How about you? You like ATF?"

Amparan paused with a spoon of *menudo* halfway to his mouth. "Well, yeah, pretty much, but I might as well tell you right off: I was at Waco. So if you want to yell 'child killer' and walk out, let's get it over with."

Elena shrugged. "I guess you're talking about the David Koresh business."

"That's it."

"Well, I think these wacko fringe groups are as dangerous as anyone around."

Amparan's smile flowered. "I liked you right off," he said, "even though I couldn't figure why you were wearing that black robe and mortarboard with all that long hair hanging down your back."

"I was getting an honorary doctorate in criminology," said Elena.

"You're a doctor?"

"Only if you count an honorary degree from a dingbat university," said Elena. "Believe me, it wasn't my idea."

"Well." He looked a somewhat bewildered. "It's nice to know the academic world is supporting law enforcement."

"That's right," she agreed. "When their poets get dissolved in bathtubs, I find out who did it. When their statues start killing people, I catch 'em." She grinned. "When their fraternity boys kidnap the academic regalia, I hunt them down."

"And that's what you got the doctorate for?" Amparan looked astounded.

"They probably figured I'm the only person who could be forced to accept one. My chief wouldn't let me say no."

"So what do I call you?"

"How about Detective Dr. Jarvis?" said Elena, grinning.

He looked disappointed.

"Oh, all right. Detective Dr. Elena will do."

"I'm making headway," said Amparan, "and we're not even through with breakfast."

From the Ocotillo Café, they took Elena's pickup onto the farm roads. "I've got five or six names," said Elena. "The first one's a cotton farmer here in the Upper Valley. Efren Maruffo."

"Sounds like one of *la raza*," said the ATF agent. "Sure is hot." Elena had been driving with the windows down instead of turning on the air conditioning.

"You're kidding. Later it will be hot. Right now it's only eighty."

"And it's only May," he added.

"Sometimes it's hot in February. Sometimes it snows in March. Keeps things interesting. I think that's our turnoff."

They swung right onto an unpaved farm road, and Amparan leaned out to read the name on the mailbox. "Maruffo," he confirmed. They bumped along until they came into the dirt yard of a long, low adobe farmhouse. Windbreaks of trees guarded the homestead to either side. Cotton fields spread out in every direction, planted and growing.

"All this is irrigated, right?" said Amparan.

Elena nodded. "He's got a water allotment from the river. Comes through canals. He gets to open the gates and let in so many inches from time to time. More some years than others. The valley farmers grow mostly cotton, chilies, onions, and pecans."

"They make much money?"

"Some do," said Elena. "This guy seems prosperous." A new Chevy pickup sat in front of the house and beside the pickup, a Dodge van, maybe three or four years old.

"So if the city takes more water from the river, he gets less," mused the ATF agent. Elena had explained the local water situation on the ride out.

"That would depend on how much they're holding in the dams upriver." They knocked on a heavy, carved door with hardware that looked as if it had been hand-forged by a blacksmith. The woman who answered was short and full-bodied, her dark hair shot through with gray streaks and pinned in an elaborate roll on her head. The coiffure demanded a fancy Spanish comb and maybe a mantilla draped over it. "Mrs. Maruffo?"

Within minutes they were talking to Efren Maruffo, who was built like a bull and had a combative disposition to match. Mrs. Maruffo sat listening to the conversation, hands folded in her lap.

"Damn right I belong to Water Now," said Maruffo in answer to the first question. "I gotta protect my interests, even if it means spending time with a bunch of bleeding-heart environmentalists and wetback immigrants. Everyone wants water, and there's only so much to go around, so I'm keeping an eye on my share."

"Efren's family's been farming this valley for over two hundred years," said Mrs. Maruffo.

Elena nodded understandingly. "My family's been in the Sangre de Cristos since colonial days," she said. "They're real careful about water, too."

Both Maruffos showed approval. "What's your family name?" asked Efren.

"Portillo."

"I know some Portillos up in Truchas."

"Likely they're my cousins," said Elena.

Amparan cleared his throat. "So Mr. Maruffo, maybe you heard about the explosions at Herbert Hobart University."

"I heard. Someone had the right idea, but it wasn't me, if that's why you're here."

"You keep explosives on your property?" asked Amparan.

"Why would I do that?"

"Efren's been out of town," said Mrs. Maruffo. "He wasn't

available to blow up anything in Los Santos, so you can just go talk to someone else."

"We plan to do that," said Elena. "Perhaps you can give us the names of other Water Now members."

Maruffo glared at her, the Hispanic camaraderie dissipating. "You want names, find them for yourself."

"That's not very cooperative," said Amparan.

"I know my rights. I don't have to tell you a thing."

"But you obviously think or know that Water Now was involved."

"I didn't say that."

"Where were you Friday night?"

"Albuquerque," said Maruffo. "Didn't get back till last night."

"I was with him," said his wife.

"So were a lot of Water Now members, so you're wasting your time looking at our organization," said Efren Maruffo.

"Oh? What were Water Now people doing in Albuquerque?" Elena asked.

"Attending a water resources conference, that's what."

"Why don't you go talk to Ollie Ray Ralph," said Mrs. Maruffo maliciously.

"Shut up," said her husband.

"Ralph wasn't in Albuquerque. His snobbish wife didn't want to go. Thinks Albuquerque isn't good enough for her."

"Shut up, Sylvia."

"Shut up yourself. You know I can't stand that Anglo woman. Thinks her salsa's as good as mine. She wouldn't know salsa from corn syrup."

"That name was Ollie Ray Ralph?" asked Amparan. "The last name's Ralph?"

"Right," said Mrs. Maruffo. "A tall, skinny redneck."

"Your problem, Sylvia, is you can't stand it when Ollie and me go off hunting and fishing together," snapped the husband.

"'Cause you're left to run the farm for a few days. You'd rather get your hair done or eat lunch with some woman whose daughter's Fiesta de las Flores Queen or Maid of Cotton or some damn thing."

"The trouble with me is I don't like tall, skinny rednecks," she snapped back.

Maruffo had risen from his recliner. "The interview's over. Why don't you two leave?" He glared at Elena and Amparan.

"Why don't you tell me whether you've got papers on your field-workers?" retorted the ATF agent. "I got friends on the border patrol who'd like to know."

Maruffo cursed him in Spanish. Elena said placatingly, "Thank you for your time, Mr. and Mrs. Maruffo," and dragged her new colleague out. "For Pete's sake," she protested, "what were you going to do? Get in a fight with the man?"

"He's a pain in the ass," said Connie, climbing into the passenger seat of her pickup. "We should have got an address on this Ralph character."

"We can call the sheriff's department and get that. With a name like Ollie Ray Ralph, someone's bound to know him."

Although they found the Ralph farm, a brick ranch-style structure that looked as if it had been plucked out of Midwestern suburbia and dropped into a cotton field, the Ralphs were nowhere in evidence. A tobacco-chewing farmworker ambled out of a flat-roofed adobe building about two hundred yards from the main house and informed them in Spanish that the *patron* had gone to church and then into Los Santos for Sunday dinner; he wasn't expected back until late afternoon.

The man was hard to talk to because he was either spitting tobacco or coughing a harsh, phlegmy cough that wrenched his narrow chest. During the middle of his last spasm, he spotted Elena's gun when she reached for a business card. Turning pale, he shouted, *"La Migra,"* and took to his heels. The two officers watched as three more men emerged from the back of the dormitory and ran away.

"Was it something I said?" asked Amparan wryly.

Elena shook her head. "I hope that cough doesn't mean he has TB. I don't need to spend six months on antibiotics. Oh yeah," she added when she saw her colleague's questioning glance, "we've got lots of TB here. Plague, too. You read in the paper where they found a cat up in Las Cruces infected with plague?"

"Bubonic plague?" asked Amparan, gaping.

"Sure. How long you been here?"

"Couple of months."

"Well, then you've got all sorts of neat things to learn about the area."

8

"Who's next?" asked Amparan.

"Gladys Furbow, the Sierra Club liaison. She lives in Mission Hills." As they made the trip, they discussed whether either of the two farmers could have been the bomber.

"If Sylvia Maruffo's description of Ollie Ray Ralph is worth anything," said Elena, "he's too tall to be one of our suspects."

"Yeah, but she's real short. Ralph could be medium height and look tall to her. The bomber was described as medium build, but a skinny guy wearing the right clothes could create that impression. You know how much eyewitness testimony's worth."

Elena nodded. "What about Maruffo? You think he could be our man? He's medium height, but I sure wouldn't call him medium build. He reminds me of the water buffalo at the zoo. Saw it during a recent case."

"Murder at the zoo?"

"Well, actually it was the elephant who—"

"Murder by elephant?" Connie Amparan started laughing. "I read about that." Then he wiped the humor from his face and said, "Of course the poor guy who got trampled probably didn't think it was funny."

49

"His family didn't, either," said Elena. "So could Maruffo fit the description?"

"Maybe, but he says he was in Albuquerque."

"They're all going to say that. Alibi each other." Elena swung down from her side of the pickup. The woman who answered the door was a skinny, wrinkled, white-haired individual using a cane and wearing Sunday clothes, including a hat. She didn't look capable of planting a dozen or so bombs next to sprinkler heads or dropping slurry canisters down wells. "Mrs. Gladys Furbow?" Elena asked.

"I carry a personal alarm," was the response, "so don't get any ideas about mugging a helpless old lady."

Elena introduced herself and Connie Amparan.

"And you expect me to forgo church in order to talk to you? I have no knowledge of any crime or—"

"You belong to Water Now, don't you?" Amparan interrupted.

"That's right, young man. I belong to Water Now. And the Sierra Club. And a number of conservation groups. Is that against the law? You said you were with Alcohol, Tobacco, and Firearms?" She squinted at him disapprovingly. "That's the group burned up those children in Waco, isn't it? Well, come in. I have a thing or two to say about that."

Connie winced. Mrs. Furbow, sensible black lace-up shoes and cane tapping, led the way into her severely furnished living room. Elena felt sorry for Connie. He looked like a man on the verge of bolting. "Sit down," ordered Mrs. Furbow as if he were a naughty grandchild instead of an ATF agent. They took seats as instructed on a piece of furniture that seemed to be half church pew, half storage chest and wholly uncomfortable. "And don't expect refreshments," snapped Mrs. Furbow. "I consider you federal agents spawn of the devil."

Elena blinked and said, "I'm with the Los Santos Police Department."

"Humph," said Mrs. Furbow. "At your age, you should be home having children."

"I'm not married," said Elena.

"Then you should get married. I don't approve of unwed motherhood or single-parent families. Time enough for public service when you're my age."

"I'm afraid the LSPD discriminates against senior citizens in the hiring realm," said Elena dryly.

Mrs. Furbow refocused on Amparan. "Did it ever occur to you, when you were storming that religious community in Waco, that David Koresh might be the Second Coming of Our Lord Jesus Christ? Mind you, I don't say he was, but with the second millennium at hand, we need to be alert. You may have killed the Son of God."

"As far as I know, I didn't kill anyone," said Connie resentfully. "And I felt real bad about the kids."

"So you should," said Mrs. Furbow.

"Actually, we're here about the bombing at Herbert Hobart University," Elena intervened hastily.

"What bombing?"

"Yesterday's bombing of their watering system and wells."

The old lady's eyes lit up. "I'm sorry I missed it. I was in Albuquerque."

"Let me guess," said Connie. "At the water conservation conference."

"Well, if you know that, why are you bothering me? Obviously I wasn't in Los Santos setting off bombs. And how did you know where I was? Are you people spying on me? Tapping my phone?"

"We just interviewed Efren Maruffo," said Elena hastily.

"Well, there's an unpleasant man. However, you take your allies where you can find them. If you're thinking I had anything to do with a bombing, you're wrong. But I can't say as I don't applaud the effort."

"Eight people were injured," said Elena.

"Don't bombers usually give notice when they're going to blow something up? I'd check with that university. They probably failed to heed a warning."

"And what would you know about the warning, Mrs. Furbow?" asked Amparan.

"Nothing," said Gladys Furbow. "But I read the newspapers. I know how bombers operate. The IRA. And all those terrorists. The world's potable water supplies are disappearing at an alarming rate. When enough people get thirsty, you can be sure there'll be more bombings of the haves by the have-nots. There's always a lunatic fringe that turns to violence."

The clock on her mantel began to chime, announcing the quarter hour, and Mrs. Furbow, who had been leaning forward intently with both hands on the head of her cane, struggled to her feet, saying, "However, there are no lunatics in Water Now. I have to get to church, so I'll say good day to you."

Since she was leaving, they had to follow. Their next call took them to Crazy Cat Mountain, past a gate where a guard, even after examining their credentials, was reluctant to let them in and called ahead to announce their arrival. As they drove up the steep slope of a private road, Connie said, "Do you think that old woman could have been right? That Koresh was the Second Coming?"

"No way," Elena assured him. "The man was a megalomaniac gun nut and child abuser. You ever hear that Jesus stockpiled weapons or even went armed?"

"No," said Connie, "and those were violent times, too."

"That Waco business really bothers you, doesn't it?"

"Yes," said Connie. "I have bad dreams about it. The fire. And the kids."

Elena patted his arm. "I know what you mean about bad dreams," she murmured. Hers started with the snarl of a mountain lion coming from under her dining room table. Even thinking about it raised the hair on her arms. She swung the pickup into the driveway of a huge structure that appeared to be composed of balcony rooms tacked onto an old water tower. A riotous variety of blooming cacti surrounded the house.

"I've never actually been up here," said Elena, wondering what a house like that cost and how scary things got when the wind was swooping over the top of the mountain, bearing down like a runaway train on the exposed homes that clung to the steep slopes of Crazy Cat.

9

Their quarry was Gary Messner, vice president of Water Now, who had told the newspaper that disease came out of the *colonias* and endangered everyone in town, a sensible remark, in Elena's opinion.

A maid answered the door to the water-tower mansion and led them up a spiral see-through stairway that made Elena very nervous. The inside of the cement tower had columns of rooms rising three stories, connected by the stairways and by walkways that crossed the open center space. A great round skylight at the top let in sunshine and nourished the trees below in an enclosed courtyard that had made the investigators feel as if they were standing at the bottom of a huge well. Vines grew up along the stairways and hung off the crosswalks.

It was one weird place, and Elena couldn't imagine actually living there. All that stair climbing and walking across open space when you could see down through the iron walkway into the pit. She visualized lugging a vacuum cleaner up the spiral staircases, but of course the owner had maids to do that. Glancing at the young woman ahead of them on the stairs, Elena felt profound sympathy for her if she had to clean this place.

At the second level, the maid knocked and led them into a

room that cut through the wall of the tower to overhang the downslope of the mountain. A picture window overlooked the whole Westside. Even with the stacks of the smelter bisecting the horizon, Messner had an impressive view. It must be spectacular at night.

Reclining in a suede and black metal chair with his feet up on a matching ottoman, the vice president of Water Now took his attention away from a tennis match on an enormous TV screen—as big as those in sports bars—and rose to greet them. He was a middle-aged man with pale receding hair and a ruddy face. *Sunburn from too much golf or tennis?* she wondered. *Or is he a heavy drinker?* He wore perfectly pressed trousers and a knit shirt with an armadillo embroidered on the pocket.

"You said Alcohol, Tobacco, and Firearms?" he asked Connie and laughed heartily. "Can't think of anything I've done that might bring me to your attention, unless you're spreading the word that Cuban cigars are about to become legal again. I'd be happy to hear it."

"We're here about Water Now," said Elena.

"Right," said Messner. "I'm the V.P. Great organization. You want to join?" He grabbed a pad of paper and a pen from the table beside his chair. "I'm not the membership chairman, but I'd be glad to sign you up. Dues are one hundred a year for those who can afford it, down to zero for those who can't. We've got members in all walks of life. Poor suckers living out in the *colonias* without any water at all, right on up to me, living in a three-million-dollar converted water tower. I'm president of Messner Advertising. Sit down. Can I offer you a drink?"

"Maybe some water," said Connie, who had grumbled about the sun's heat while they made the climb to Messner's television eyrie.

The maid was dispatched to bring cold drinks. Then Messner said expansively, "Have you seen our public service announcements on TV? Came out of my agency. Clever stuff if I do say so myself. Really eye-catching. I do a lot of work for public interest groups—PACs, environmental groups of all kinds, pro- and antiabortion. We're a public-spirited agency. Wouldn't touch tobacco advertising, for instance. Nothing too heavy on the sex. Don't want to give the kiddies any ideas they don't already have. Know what I mean? I can tell you, I picked up some good accounts in Albuquerque over the last two days."

Elena was listening to all this hype with interest. She wondered whether the man had any philosophical attachment to Water Now beyond the business contacts it provided. Maybe he joined all sorts of groups so that he could garner ad accounts.

"People donate a lot of money to organizations like Water Now, and I'm a whiz at fund-raising. Course, what goes around comes around," he said, confirming her suspicions. "They all need publicity."

"I'm sure," said Elena. "You said you were in Albuquerque?"

"Sure was. Ah, here's the refreshments. Nonalcoholic, since you two are evidently on duty. Say, ATF could use some good public relations work. We do PR," he said to Connie. "After that mess at Waco, you folks need all the good press you can get."

"Look Mr. Messner, we're here—"

"And you, miss. Detective? That what you said? How about the police union? Maybe—"

"Mr. Messner, we're here on official business—investigating the bombing yesterday at H.H.U."

"Well, that's got nothing to do with Water Now." He looked astounded. "Good Lord, you think we'd do something like that? That would *not* generate good publicity. If anyone even suggested a bombing, I'd have them drummed right out of the corps." He smiled ingenuously.

"No, ma'am. We don't put up with violence of any kind. I've always got my finger on the public pulse, and that sort of thing does not go over well. I heard the news reports when I got home. Eight people injured. No way to put a positive spin on that."

Elena thought about what he'd said and asked, "So, have you drummed anyone out of the organization for violent tendencies?"

"Of course not. We're interested in water, not violence. It's a good group. Good citizens, every one. Come to one of our meetings, why don't you? You'll be impressed."

Elena doubted that she'd be as impressed with the meetings as Gary Messner was with himself, but she smiled politely and joined Connie Amparan in more questions, none of which produced any helpful answers.

"Do you happen to have a membership list?" Connie asked.

"Can't say that I do," said Messner. His attention by that time had wandered back to the tennis game. "By God, did you see that backhand? He's gonna take the tournament. And I've got money on him." His eyes darted toward Elena and Connie. "Just a bet between friends. Nothing illegal." He cleared his throat.

"The president might have a list. That's Father Bratslowski. He's a priest. Very active in causes. One of my best business contacts. Or maybe Sister Gertrudis Gregory. She's the secretary. She'd for certain have the list. Though I'd have to say I've never got a commission for the Church per se. I suggested to the bishop once that they might try advertising, but he didn't take to the idea at all. Maybe that Polish pope wouldn't approve. They take orders from Rome, you know."

"Do they?" murmured Elena. "Well, thanks for your assistance, sir. Here's my card if you think of anything."

Connie gave him a card as well, and both officers received Messner's card in return. "Now, you folks call if you feel the need of some good PR." He plunked his highball glass down and sprawled out again in his comfy suede chair. Exclaiming "Way to go!" in response to some tennis move on television, he hardly noticed their departure.

As they were descending the wrought-iron stairs, Elena being very careful not to look down, she wondered why anyone would want to spend time watching a tennis match. Bonk bonk

bonk bonk. That was the extent of it. About as exciting as singing along with a bouncing ball.

"Who's next?" asked Connie after the maid had let them out of the water tower.

"The very people he mentioned, Sister Gertrudis Gregory and Father Conrad Bratslowski."

Amparan groaned. "I hope the sister's one of the nice ones. I went to school with nuns, and it was no picnic, I can tell you."

"Well, she's no gentle spirited bride-of-Christ type," said Elena. "The woman's already been convicted for attacking someone going into an abortion clinic."

Amparan groaned again. "Why don't we get some lunch first. Maybe you know another hole-in-the-wall Mexican place where I can fortify myself for an afternoon with the Church."

10
##

"I couldn't get an address on the one member who might live in the *colonias*," said Elena. "No telephone. No listing in the city directory, here or in any of the surrounding towns." She glanced down at her notes. "So these are our last two for today unless we can get a membership list."

They parked in the church lot and headed for San Ysidro del Valle, Father Bratslowski's Lower Valley church. Before they reached the door, Connie and Elena met the priest himself coming out with a group of parishioners. Since Elena doubted that he had been holding mass this late in the day, she assumed that he had been stirring up good Catholics for some new rebellion against the establishment.

Father Bratslowski glared at them when they introduced themselves. "If you've come to arrest me, let me warn you that I have the full power of the Church and the Catholic community behind me. You'll never—"

"We wanted to interview you, sir, not arrest you." Elena interrupted to reassure the people surrounding him, who were muttering among themselves, looking as if they were ready to take up arms in his defense.

"Ha! Dragging me down to some police interrogation room. Is that your plan?"

"No, Father," said Connie respectfully. "We can sit in the church or wherever it's convenient for you. As Detective Jarvis said, this is just an interview."

Looking a little disappointed, the priest said to his followers, "Don't worry about me. God's protective hand is on my shoulder." Then he turned and strode back into his church, a mission-style structure with carved *vigas,* uncomfortable looking wooden pews, brightly decorated Stations of the Cross, and an amazing religious fresco behind the altar. The mural looked as if it might be the product of some well-meaning project to turn gang graffiti artists into the Diego Riveras of Los Santos.

Elena and Connie took seats on the front pew as directed while Father Bratslowski climbed two steps and sat down in a great carved wooden chair, obviously intended for visits from the bishop. "Well?" he said challengingly.

"We're investigating the bombing at Herbert Hobart University," said Connie.

"And you think it was a plot by the Roman Catholic Church?" demanded the priest.

"Actually, we're more concerned with the Water Now connection," said Elena.

"There is none," was the reply. "But because I am the president of Water Now and a Roman Catholic—"

"Look, Father," said Elena irritably, "I'm a Roman Catholic, too."

"So am I," said Connie Amparan.

"Are you observant Catholics? Do you attend mass? Make confessions regularly, take communion—"

"Could we talk about Water Now?" Connie looked flushed and nervous.

"I take it that the answers to my questions are no. Very well, Water Now. We did not bomb Herbert Hobart University. We are a peaceful group whose purpose is to see that water and sewer services are brought to poor, devout Catholics in the *colonias.*"

Elena wondered whether he was hoping to get those services for poor non-Catholics as well.

"Are you aware of the situation there? The unsanitary conditions? The disease? The birth defects? The poverty? Are you aware that eighty percent of pregnant women from the *colonias* test positive for hepatitis antibodies? *If* they can get prenatal care and tests at all. The Anglo establishment thinks that because poor Catholic women don't practice birth control, they don't deserve prenatal care."

"Come on, Father," said Elena. "Most of the local politicians are Hispanic, and it was those politicians who refused to fund cancer screening for poor Hispanic women because they were afraid Planned Parenthood might slip the women condoms or mention abortion."

"You're no Catholic," said the priest angrily.

"I'm no advocate of poor Hispanic women dying of breast cancer," she retorted, "and they are."

Ignoring her, he turned to Connie. "Are you aware that all the children in the *colonias* get hepatitis? Most of the time they're not even treated."

"No, Father," said Connie, "I wasn't aware of that."

"Look," said Elena, "we want to know if you've heard of any bomb plots among your members or noticed any tendencies toward violence."

"I repeat: we are a peaceful advocacy group."

"Where were you on Friday and Friday night?" asked Elena, thinking that he had the right build to be the bomber, although she found it hard to imagine a priest discarding his collar, donning a fake uniform, and planting bombs by sprinkler heads at a campus overrun by tent crew members and security guards.

"I was in Albuquerque," said the priest triumphantly, "addressing a water conservation conference."

"You and everyone else we've talked to." She resented having to shout because of the distance he'd put between them. The only time he came close enough for ordinary conversation was to stalk over and lecture them about the *colonias*. When asked a question, he returned to his bishop's chair.

"So if your bomber did his work Friday night or Saturday, you can't accuse me. Hundreds of people heard me speak and talked to me between sessions. The whole Water Now contingent from Los Santos knows that I was there."

"All right," said Elena. "We'd like a membership list of the organization."

"So you can harass well-intentioned citizens? Not from me."

"We can get a court order," Connie pointed out. "Federal judges frown on bombings."

"We're not bombers," retorted the priest. "Get your court order. Let them find me in contempt and jail me."

Martyr complex, Elena thought and wondered why he hadn't ended up in a cell before now if his attitude was the same for all his many projects.

"Thank you for your time, Father," she said, rising.

As they walked down the aisle toward the church entrance, he shouted after them, "Have you considered that in harassing us, you're placing yourselves firmly on the side of Satan?"

Elena muttered under her breath, "Satan's a lot more likely to hang out with the bombers."

11

Sunday, May 19, 2:45 P.M.

"The Sacred Chamisa?" asked Connie Amparan as they entered the grounds of the convent. "What's that about?"

Elena happened to know. A nun injured downtown by a mugger had told the story from a hospital bed. "It's a French order. The Sacred Chamisa is the blouse the Virgin wore when she was giving birth."

"And they've got it *here?*"

Elena laughed. "Not likely. They've got a picture of it hanging on a coat hanger and surrounded by a bunch of candles. During the Middle Ages or something, a cathedral in France burned down, and the chamisa was all that was left, so they built another cathedral to celebrate the miracle."

"What's it made of? Asbestos?" Then Connie looked conscience-stricken, crossed himself, and said, "I didn't mean that." He studied the doors to the convent as if he expected the nuns to stampede out and attack him with rulers for his blasphemy.

However, once inside, they had better luck than they'd had at San Ysidro del Valle. Tall, sturdy Sister Gertrudis Gregory, whom Connie obviously found intimidating, led them into the convent parlor and, when asked, produced a membership list for Water Now.

With the papers in her hand, Elena remarked to the sister, "You're a lot more cooperative than Father Bratslowski."

"Father," said the nun grimly, "is a fine man and an admirable pastor, with his heart in the right place where the poor and underprivileged are concerned, but like all men, he suffers from an overly competitive nature. He should realize that other members of Water Now will want to stand up for this worthy cause, even go to jail for it if necessary, not that any of us are guilty of that bombing." She, too, began to throw facts and figures at them about health conditions in the *colonias*.

"Even the few shallow wells they have in the unincorporated barrios are contaminated by open cesspools."

Looking over the membership list, Elena was interested to see that it contained many Hispanic names and locations that signaled *colonia*. So far, the only Hispanics they'd interviewed had been Efren Maruffo and his wife Sylvia, not that she thought the *colonia* dwellers more likely to be the bombers. On the other hand, they did have more to be angry about.

"I suppose you were in Albuquerque at the water conservation meeting, too, Sister," said Connie Amparan, finally getting up enough nerve to talk to a woman who evidently reminded him of the disciplinarian nuns in his old school.

Sister Gertrudis Gregory scowled. "I'm not allowed to travel. I'm free on bond, my crime: protecting the lives of the unborn."

"So you were here in El Paso?" said Connie, eyes lighting up. "Friday night and Saturday?"

Much good it would do if she had been, thought Elena. Sister Gertrudis Gregory was definitely not the bomber. The nun stood six foot one and looked like a TV wrestler in drag.

"I was devoting two days to prayer and meditation Friday and Saturday," said the sister. "Reverend Mother will vouch for that."

She looked downright grumpy about her two days of devotions, but then, the few times Elena had seen her, the sister hadn't exactly shone out as a ray of meek Christianity. There was the time she disrupted a memorial service at H.H.U., setting off a prolife-proabortion free-for-all, and the time she attached chains to the H.H.U. Charleston Dancer and pulled it over with her jeep. Come to think of it, her fixation on H.H.U. made her a good candidate for some part in the sprinkler bombing, even if she hadn't actually planted the pyrodex. "Is there anyone in your organization who advocates violence?" asked Elena.

"Certainly not," said the nun. "And if they did, I wouldn't tell you."

Elena glanced through the list again. "I notice that there are two people named Reyes who've been marked out."

"Magdalena and Philomeno," said the sister promptly.

"Were they dropped for violent tendencies?"

"Hardly," snapped the nun. "I'm surprised they ever joined. Both are high school teachers, both too middle-class and complacent to devote themselves to public causes with any fervor. They claimed family responsibilities as their reason for resigning. I told them nothing should interfere with God's work, but they didn't listen."

"I see," said Elena. They didn't sound like very good bomb suspects, but on the other hand, they wouldn't have the Albuquerque alibi. She supposed she'd have to check them out, even if they hadn't shown Sister enough fervor.

"I'll just go have a word with Reverend Mother," Elena murmured to Connie and left the reluctant ATF agent in the clutches of Sister Gertrudis Gregory, who immediately began questioning him on his religious practices. Poor Connie. This was the second time today.

The Reverend Mother was a tiny, ancient lady all but lost in a voluminous, old-fashioned habit. In answer to a query, the abbess said, "Sister Gertrudis Gregory has just finished forty-eight hours of seclusion. She is a well-meaning woman but much too worldly. I thought a peaceful time of prayer and meditation would be beneficial to her troubled soul, especially as the poor woman faces a prison sentence for being somewhat overzealous in support of the Church's beliefs. Not that she seems to dread the prospect of going to jail." Reverend Mother shook her head sadly. "Be that as it may, she was here and was monitored periodically. So if you're thinking of arresting her for something that happened between Friday night and Sunday morning, you have the wrong person. She was in the chapel."

"The whole time?" asked Elena.

"Except for a few visits in attendance to personal needs," said the elderly nun primly. "At such times she was accompanied by a sister."

"How *often* was she monitored?"

"Every fifteen minutes," said Reverend Mother. "Sister Gertrudis Gregory has a rebellious spirit, and I was determined to bring calm to her soul by extended and uninterrupted conversation with God."

"I see," said Elena. Every fifteen minutes for forty-eight hours? That meant other sisters had had to get up in the middle of the night to be sure that Sister Gertrudis Gregory hadn't escaped from the chapel to pursue her career as a rabble-rouser in some other part of town. With that thought, she went back to rescue Connie, who looked pitifully grateful for the reprieve.

"I never want to see that woman again," he muttered as they left the convent. "She's a ball-breaker."

"Is that any way to talk about a nun?"

"I guess you didn't go to a Catholic school."

"I didn't, but I know what you mean. I've run into her before."

"How about dinner?" said the ATF agent. "My treat."

"You must make a lot more money than I do if you can afford to take someone out for three meals in one day." Connie had insisted on paying for lunch as well as breakfast.

"I like you," said Amparan.

Well, that was straightforward. "Thanks, I like you too, but my roommate's expecting me home."

"You're living with someone?" He looked disappointed.

"Dr. Sarah Tolland. She's a professor and chairman at H.H.U."

"You're not gay, are you?"

"I was married, remember? To a man. And I haven't changed

my sexual orientation since then." They headed back to Canutillo so that he could get his car.

"Maybe some other night," she suggested, realizing again that dating someone with whom she was working a case was a stupid idea. Still, she did like Connie Amparan. He was a good guy. "I was up late last night tracking down the Water Now names," she explained. "I'm really knocked out." Actually, her weariness was mostly due to another of those nightmares, which had awakened her in the middle of the night. She'd been unable to get back to sleep.

12

Homeowner Sues Builder
In Toilet Controversy

Home buyer George Pritkin is suing Coyote Creek Homes, Inc., for installing water-hungry, 5-gallon-per-flush toilets in his new house instead of low-flush (1.4 gallon) toilets. "They can either pay my water bills for the next thirty years or replace those toilets," said Pritkin.

Pritkin's lawyer has also reported the contractor to the city of Los Santos, which has legislated low-water-usage plumbing fixtures in new homes.

Coyote Creek could not be reached for comment, but a former employee, who asked to remain anonymous, says the builder gets the illegal toilets cheap and has "stiffed buyers before this."

Los Santos *Times,* Monday, May 20

Elena had expected to spend Monday morning with G. Washington combing the *colonias* for Water Now members. Instead, G. was investigating an aspirin bottle full of flash powder found in an elementary school, and Elena, after spending a half hour filling out a form and fifteen minutes reading about toilet fraud and other items of local interest while she waited, was closeted at headquarters with Lieutenant Felix Banuelos and his minions, trying to explain why she had discharged her weapon at the H.H.U. graduation.

Someone had ratted to her lieutenant, not that she hadn't meant to report the incident; she'd just been busy. The night before, a message on her answering machine from Beltran, the head of Crimes Against Persons, ordered her to report to the Shooting Review Team Monday morning at eight-thirty.

So here she was.

"Have I got this right?" asked Lieutenant Banuelos, studying her eight-page questionnaire. "You shot a hole in the ceiling of a plastic tent while everyone around you was panicking? Is that it?"

"That's it," said Elena jauntily, "but you'll notice that the tent was a lot bigger than me."

One section of the questionnaire sought to estimate the severity of the threat to the officer by a comparison of relative sizes. "Was the tent armed?" asked a smart-aleck officer from Juvenile Investigation.

"That's enough," snapped Banuelos. "This is serious business." He turned a somber face to Elena, who had been grinning. "Your actions strike me as ill-considered, Detective."

"Not given the circumstances!" she said defensively.

"Then why don't you explain the circumstances?"

"O.K. There'd been a bunch of explosions. Some of them in the tent. People were covered with mud and flower petals. They were trying to run in every direction with only my father and me to control the crowd. The Westside officers hadn't got there yet."

"Your *father*? You enlisted a civilian to help?"

"My father's the sheriff of Rio Arriba County, New Mexico."

"What was he doing at the H.H.U. graduation?"

"He came to see me get my honorary—uh—doctorate."

"Oh, right," said Banuelos sarcastically. "O.K., go on with your story. You and your father were trying to do what?"

"We were trying to get them to leave in a safe direction," said Elena. "And they weren't paying any attention. I figured if half the shrubbery on the quadrangle had blown up, maybe the other half was mined, and I was right." She pulled a report from her handbag. "With pyrodex, set off by some device that used water as a conductor."

She thought about those sprinklers. Why would the university start watering in the middle of a graduation ceremony? Obviously, the bomber had turned the system on. Which meant that he wanted not only to make a statement about water usage but to injure people. She'd need to find someone who had been around the sprinkler controls during the ceremony. To that end, she made a note on the back of the report.

"Detective, would you mind paying attention to the matter at hand?"

"You want to read the report?" Having finished her memo, she offered the FBI printout to the Shooting Review officer.

"No," said Banuelos. "We're interested in the discharge of your weapon, not the explosions."

"Yeah, well. As I said, who's to say the sprinklers on other side of the quadrangle weren't about to turn on and trigger more explosions? And if that crowd of uncooperative millionaires—"

"What millionaires?"

"The parents. They're all rich and don't want to take orders from anyone, especially me and my dad. I mean, I'm there wearing this graduation robe and high heels, in imminent danger of breaking my ankles in the grass, and my dad looks like some middle-aged Hispanic cowboy. So they weren't paying any attention to us. And then who turns up but Big Hank Spike."

Banuelos sighed. "And he is?"

"He's this Houston millionaire whose daughter is Melody Spike, a sex-crazed pseudofeminist."

"I thought *you* were a feminist, Jarvis," said Banuelos.

"Right, but not pseudo and not sex-crazed," said Elena. "And I'd run into Melody Spike before. She's one of the people responsible for the riot on campus before Christmas when they pulled down a statue, injuring three people, and then burned the statue and the shrubbery."

"Sounds like the shrubbery over there's taking a beating," said Bobby Moulton, a traffic officer who did double duty on the Shooting Review Team. His grin had become wider and wider on an acne-scarred, moon-pie face as Elena told her story.

Banuelos frowned at him. "So because you didn't like the daughter, you shot a hole in the ceiling when you met her father?"

"I shot a hole in the ceiling because I didn't want any more injuries. And it worked. They all headed in the right direction."

"Uh-huh," said Banuelos. "Given the fact that you had a panicky crowd on your hands, don't you consider discharging your weapon not only ill-considered but dangerous?"

"I don't know," said Elena. "If I hadn't shot the tent, we might have had forty injuries instead of eight."

"Would you say you've been under a lot of stress lately, Detective?"

"Of course. Wouldn't you be if a bunch of bombs had just gone off and you had several hundred—"

"I'm not talking about the incident at H.H.U. I'm saying in general, in the last couple of months, wouldn't you say that you've been under a lot of stress?"

"I'm functioning O.K.," Elena protested.

"You had a bad time back in March, didn't you? The mountain lion in your house—that must have been traumatic."

"That was two months ago," said Elena, but even as she said it, she thought of the mountain lion, snarling under her dining room table, of the bloody corpse in her bedroom, and she could see it all and hear it all as if she were there again.

"Are you O.K.?" asked Banuelos.

"Fine," said Elena. She did *not* want to be put on leave. If she had to sit around and think about what happened in March, she'd go completely crazy. "I'm fine," she repeated.

"So you consider your actions on the day of the bombing justified?"

"Well, it worked. They all stampeded in the right direction."

"Exactly," said the lieutenant, "and you were overheard saying, 'Git along little dogies,' to the stampeding millionaires."

Elena turned bright red and wondered who had overheard her—more important, who had reported it. Someone from H.H.U.? If they thought enough of her to award her an honorary degree, they ought to have kept their mouths shut about that little slip.

The other members of the Shooting Review Team were howling with laughter. Banuelos, although he tried to look grim and official, gave in to a smile twitching at the corners of his mouth.

"Well, Detective, did you actually say that?"

"Not very loudly, sir," said Elena.

13
..

When Elena returned to her desk from the Shooting Review session, there was a message from Perry Melon offering to go on interviews in the Herbert Hobart bombing case. She picked him up at the federal building and, glancing at him as she drove away, said, "You're going to be hot in that suit and tie."

"I always wear a suit and tie," he responded.

Elena shrugged and turned away from the heavy traffic on San Antonio Street. "Just be warned. People in the *colonias* don't have air-conditioning."

"That's O.K. Sure you don't want me to drive?"

"It's an LSPD car," she replied, irritated. "If it were an FBI car, you could drive." Men always thought they should drive. The years she'd served on patrol, every partner she'd had thought he should drive. "How do you like Los Santos?" she asked, trying to sound friendly. "I'm assuming you're not a native."

"I like all the hills. Reminds me of home—that's Pittsburgh— but we have more vegetation. And rain. I sure miss the rain. I don't like the heat, either. Are you from Los Santos?"

"Chimayo," she replied, then added, "New Mexico," when he looked blank. Entering the freeway on the Mesa ramp, she gave him one last clue. "It's between Santa Fe and Taos."

75

"Oh. That explains it."

"What?"

"Well." He looked embarrassed. "You're kind of—ah— exotic looking. Unusual. Beautiful, too."

The man was blushing. And *beautiful* was nice, but Elena wondered why he'd think that having grown up between Santa Fe and Taos explained her looks. Indian genes? Conquistador bloodlines? She certainly didn't think of herself as *exotic* looking. "Thanks," she said. "Anyway, we didn't have much rain in the Sangre de Cristos."

"The what?"

"Those are mountains in New Mexico. Means blood of Christ."

Melon looked taken aback.

"But I do miss a real winter," said Elena. "With snow."

Fifteen minutes later, Melon looked out the window and said, "This must be a *colonia*."

"That's right." Elena pulled onto an unpaved road, passing a woman and two children at a standpipe well. The woman was pumping water, ignoring the sign that said, *Aviso* with a large skull and crossbones between the Spanish word for *Warning* and the text beneath.

"What does that sign say?" Melon asked.

"Not to drink the water."

"Then why is she pumping it?"

"Maybe she can't read. Or she's so tired of trying to get water elsewhere that she doesn't care anymore. Or it's for baths or cleaning. Or she thinks boiling or Chlorox will make it drinkable." The dust plumed behind them as they drove into a neighborhood of small, bare lots, cinder block houses with tar paper roofs, and ramshackle trailers. The developer had evidently scraped the desert clean before subdividing and selling the unimproved land to people who couldn't afford anything else. There were no trees and only those bushes and wild grasses whose seeds might have blown in on the spring winds and taken root in unforgiving, unwatered soil. Little children, less than school age, played in the dirt, scantily clad, with sweat streaking the dust on dark skins.

In one yard, two little girls clad in pristine white dresses and ruffled anklets watched the other children wistfully. Perhaps they were going to a wedding or a christening and had been warned against getting dirty. Elena mused on how hard it must be for the mothers to keep their children's clothes that clean. The washing would have to be done by hand in water hauled to the houses in barrels.

"Hard to believe this is the U.S.," said Melon.

"Never been here?" Elena stopped in front of a rusty trailer with a canvas awning attached to one end and supported by two poles leaning crazily toward one another. A man in jeans and a faded tank top sat in a lawn chair under the sagging canvas, sipping a beer and ignoring their approach. "Mr. Rangel?" she asked.

He nodded, listened to her introduction, then waved toward two folded chairs that leaned against the trailer. Perry Melon opened one for Elena, then one for himself, looking distressed when he saw the ragged condition of the webbing. Elena suppressed a grin. His dignity, not to mention his neatly pressed suit pants, would suffer if the webbing gave up its fragile claim to support while he was sitting on it.

"I believe you're a member of Water Now," she said to Mr. Rangel, who looked rather gray under brown skin. She wondered if he was ill.

"Yeah." Rangel lit a cigarette. "Wanted to get water out here. Don't matter much now. I got laid off last week."

"The wire company?" she asked sympathetically.

"Bastards," he muttered. "Even if they put the pipes in now, I couldn't afford the hookup. Wife's still got work, but the garment manufacturers are goin' down one by one. S'pose hers will be next. Welfare ain't enough to feed the kids."

"There's a new plant opening on the Westside."

"Yeah, like I could get over there every day. My land's here, not that I'll be able to keep it if I don't make the payments. Screwed by NAFTA, that's what we been."

"Eventually NAFTA will be a boon to the local economy," said Melon.

"*Eventually* don't buy the *frijoles*. My father come across the river for work. Now the jobs are goin' back to Mexico."

Perry Melon cleared his throat. "We're inquiring of all Water Now members where they were on Friday and Saturday."

"How come? It's a crime to want water?"

"Could you just—"

"Lemme guess. You're not askin' the Anglo members, right?"

"We've already talked to most of them," said Elena. "We're investigating a bombing, Mr. Rangel, which seems to be connected to Water Now."

"Well, if someone from Water Now set off a bomb, it wasn't me, an' no one told me about it. I couldn't afford a bomb if I knew how to get one. You wanna know where I was Friday? I worked the four-to-midnight shift, picked up my paycheck, an' found out I was laid off. So I went out an' got drunk. My *compadres* hadda bring me home, I was that drunk. *Mi esposa* made me sleep on the floor."

Mr. Rangel's story checked out. From the car, Elena called the bar where the newest member of the unemployed had drowned his sorrows. Melon called the wire company where the personnel department verified that Rangel had worked Friday until midnight and had been laid off.

By the time they had visited four more *colonia* dwellers, Melon was grumbling about burrs in his socks and trouser cuffs, dust in his nose, and the possibility that he might contract some dread disease. When offered, he refused refreshments and thus insulted the ladies of the houses and trailers. Children who edged shyly in his direction were given no encouragement. He did not make a hit in Las Pampas or San Elizario or Agua Dulce.

Elena, on the other hand, chatted comfortably in Spanish and accepted coffee, because it had been boiled, bounced children on a knee that had known the weight of various nieces, nephews, and cousins in Chimayo, and gathered information from a "sanitation engineer," father of eight, who had been working a second job while the pyrodex was being planted at H.H.U.; an unemployed cafeteria worker who was taking care of a son and daughter with chicken pox at the time in question (the spotted children were brought out for inspection and confirmation); and a single mother who suspected that they were Human Services investigators pretending to be police and FBI so that they could purge her from the welfare roll.

By the time they reached their last stop in El Campestre, where they were looking for Celestina Ortiz, Perry had loosened his tie and taken off his suit jacket. They asked directions from a man selling recycled chemical barrels on a street corner. "Why would anyone want a chemical barrel?" Perry asked.

"To store water," said Elena.

He turned pale under his sunburn. "You've been drinking coffee made from water stored in barrels that may contain carcinogens or mutagens or—"

"—or parasites or fecal coliform colonies. Well, at least it was boiled," said Elena philosophically, "and I've been getting a lot more information than you have." She climbed out of the car.

He followed, saying "My Spanish isn't—" only to be interrupted by flying dirt from the broom of a two-hundred-fifty-pound woman sweeping her yard.

"Ms. Ortiz?" asked Elena. She was never sure she'd found the right house.

"Yeah, I'm Celestina Ortiz." The woman leaned on her broom, flattening the bristles in the dirt.

Elena produced her identification. Before she could introduce Melon as well, Celestina Ortiz grabbed Elena's arm and dragged her toward the house. Melon shouted a warning, but Ortiz was determined that Elena see the graffiti on her cinderblock walls. The woman was paying no attention to the FBI agent, who went for his gun. Elena shook her head at him.

"See that. *Los Fatherless*," said Ortiz, naming one of the largest gangs in Los Santos. "An' I know who done it, too. Either you haul him in, or I'm gonna wring his dirty little neck."

"You saw the tagging?" Elena asked.

"Yeah, an' I got the license on the low-rider. I've had it. I go down to the 7-Eleven an' call the cops an' it's two days before you show up."

"Actually, I don't handle graffiti," said Elena, "but why don't you call Crime Stoppers? That way, if he's convicted, you'll get fifty to seventy-five bucks for the tip, not to mention getting even."

"Yeah?"

"Yeah." Elena fished in her purse. "Here's the number." She passed over a Crime Stoppers card. "But I'm here about Water Now." She finally managed to introduce Melon, who had discreetly slipped his weapon back into its waist holster.

"FBI? Good. About time the feds did somethin' about the water. El Campestre is Phase Two." She took them into her small house, which showed the ravages of many children. "Know what that means? Means the water ain't gettin' here till the middle of the next century. If ever. Siddown." She gestured to a sagging couch.

"An' let's say we do get water. It costs to hook up. You gotta have the right plumbin', antisiphon valves an' like that. You know what an antisiphon valve is?" Elena didn't. "Keeps the toilet shit from gettin' into the drinkin' water." Melon looked horrified.

"Not that I'm a plumber. I'm a bricklayer. Unemployed. Rat-faced, bastard construction companies in this town don't hardly never hire a woman. So even if the water come in, I ain't got a job most of the time, so I couldn't get one a them low-cost loans so I could hook up."

"And that's why you joined Water Now?" asked Elena.

"Much good we done. Bringin' in Anglo guys with beards to tell us we're gettin' a raw deal an' we oughta take action."

"What action?" asked Melon.

"Militant action. Which is O.K. with me. I was in the army. It's about time we done something more than talk. City spends a fortune on a wastewater treatment plant, an' then they use the water to spray on some damn golf course, while I gotta haul water in my truck so my kids can get a drink. Oughta blow up the damn golf course."

"Did this person—the speaker—advocate bombing?" asked Melon.

"Why you wanna know?" Celestina Ortiz squinted at him suspiciously.

"What was his name?"

"Don't remember."

"But he advocated violence, and you agreed?"

"I never even talked to him. What are you doin' here, anyway?"

"Ma'am," said Melon somberly, "we're investigating the bombing at H.H.U."

"Someone take out them rich water hogs?"

"Both wells and sprinkler systems," said Elena.

"An' you think it was me?" Ortiz rolled to her feet. "Outa my house," she shouted. "I ain't sayin' another word. An' if I don't git my money from Crime Stoppers, I'll file a complaint against you. Got that?" She glared at Elena.

As Elena and Melon walked toward the car, Elena murmured, "Right sentiments, wrong body."

"She could have been part of it," said Melon. "She said she was in the military. I'll check her out, see what she did in the army. And construction. Construction crews use explosives. Just because she wasn't the man in the fake uniform doesn't mean she didn't—"

A vicious growl interrupted Perry Melon. Elena froze at the sound.

Melon turned and yelled, "Go away," at the one-eyed dog, who did, slinking off through the dust toward Celestina Ortiz's sway-backed porch. "I'll bet she sicced that mutt on us," said the FBI agent. Then glancing toward Elena, he asked, "Are you all right?"

Elena closed her eyes to shut out the flashback, the snarl of the mountain lion, the blood splashed over her wrecked—

"Elena?"

She clenched her fists, opened her eyes, and whispered hoarsely, "I'm fine."

"You look like you've seen a ghost. It was just a—" He looked down and exclaimed, "There's another burr!" By the time he'd rescued his sock and ankle, Elena had recovered.

"You've got a terrible sunburn," she said. "Shouldn't you wear a hat?"

"Not in the dress code," he mumbled and held the car door

for her. It was after five when they reached the federal building.
"Would you like a drink?" he asked. "I've found this a very
trying day." He looked at her beseechingly when she started to
shake her head. "We could go over to the Camino Real. It's
air-conditioned. And the water in a Scotch and water won't
come out of a chemical barrel."

Looking at the once neat, now dusty FBI agent with his new
crop of freckles and painfully red sunburn, Elena said, "Why
not? But let's have margaritas. Scotch tastes like liquid
mothballs." They parked in the police garage across from
Central Command and walked through crowds of office workers to the hotel, where they sat in comfortable leather chairs
under the Tiffany dome, enjoying the air-conditioning and the
bite of lime and tequila in icy, salt-edged glasses.

"I'm going to run Celestina Ortiz through the computer,"
said Melon. "Also, I'll find out who the guest speaker was. We
might have a case of domestic terrorism here, sponsored by one
of those national environmental groups. Eco-terrorists."

Elena grinned. "You just want to stay out of the *colonias* and
in your air-conditioned office."

"I resent that," said Perry Melon, grinning back. "I'm
actually delighted to get this case, even if it is hard on
fair-skinned agents with sensitive ankles. Anything's better
than another two-bit bank robbery." He pushed the bowl of nuts
across the table toward her. "Why don't we have dinner since
we're downtown and off duty?"

It didn't take Elena more than a second's thought to agree.
Anything was better than going home to another nagging session
from Sarah about getting psychiatric help. After her reaction to the
dog in Celestina Ortiz's yard, Elena didn't want to think about that
problem. She didn't even want to sleep anymore. "Why not?" she
said. Working with the feds wasn't nearly as bad as she'd
expected, not when they kept buying her meals.

14
..

Tuesday, May 21, 10:45 A.M.

Drip Irrigation Triggers
War Among Chili Growers

At a meeting last Friday of the Upper Valley Chili Growers Association, Rita Arredondo reported that the drip irrigation system she had installed last year in three of her chili fields has saved an estimated acre foot of water in one growing season.

Bolin Clark, her neighbor in the Canutillo area, said, "Water's cheap. It'll take you near about ten years to pay off that system. What if chili prices drop?"

Arredondo retorted that when drought emptied the dams, she'd still be able to grow chilies, while he wouldn't have a crop. She then hit Clark with her handbag. The president called for order, and Arredondo was asked to apologize. She refused and left the meeting under escort of the sergeant at arms.

Clark declined to press charges, saying, "Women is excitable."

Chili Growers president "Mano" Polloforo, interviewed after the meeting, said, "People are getting mean over water, and we're not even in trouble yet."

Los Santos *Times*, Tuesday, May 21

"I never expected the feds to be so cooperative," said Elena. She and Sergeant G. Washington were canvassing the last of the Water Now members.

"Local cops tend to feel they're in competition with the FBI an' the ATF," said Washington. "Sometimes they are."

He was the most careful driver Elena had ever seen, always traveling at the speed limit or below. She wondered if he drove like this when on his way to a bombing.

"It's different with explosives techs," he continued. "We're out to help each other, not compete. We meet at the trainin' sessions, an' we travel to bombin's away from our own jurisdictions." G. glanced into his mirror when the driver behind him honked because G. wouldn't turn left in front of an oncoming car.

"For instance, if I was goin' on vacation, say to California, I'd know bomb techs out there that I'd met before. So I'd just call someone, an' when I got out there, they'd show me an' my wife around. Bomb techs are like family. If one of us dies or gets hurt, we all mourn."

"Well, I can believe that of you and Melon and Amparan and your squad guys, but that Calzone from the army—"

"Yeah, he's a piece of work," Washington agreed. "Usually fellas in our profession are real sensible people."

Elena herself thought a person would have to have some sort of death wish to join a bomb squad, although it wouldn't be polite to say so.

"Maybe Calzone just needs to grow into the job." G. stopped at a stop sign for a long three-count, earning another loud blare from the horn of the same driver.

Turning off his motor, the sergeant got out of the car and walked back to confront the horn man, a bad move on G.'s part. Elena took her 9-millimeter from her handbag. You always parked *behind* someone you were stopping. Maybe she'd better get out. Did G. plan to arrest the guy for honking at a police officer? In the rearview mirror, she could see the motorist shouting, G. producing his badge, the motorist shutting up abruptly, G. giving him a short, calm lecture.

Elena took her hand off the door, for G. was coming back. He said as he climbed in, "Some people need to learn that patience is a virtue." He started the car and drove on, slowly enough so that even the potholes on Doniphan weren't too wrenching. "I take it you're gettin' lots of cooperation from Amparan and Melon," he said.

Elena had turned, watching the motorist, who was now following at a sedate pace. He hung a right at the first side street. "I'll say," Elena replied. "They volunteer. They want to pay for my lunch. They don't even make sexist remarks. Nicest bunch of guys I ever met. What are you grinning at?"

"Nothin'," said Washington, "but they never offer to buy my lunch." He turned off Doniphan onto a country highway and sped up marginally. "I don't see that we got anywhere with the last three folks we talked to. Maybe we'll have better luck with this Ollie Ray Ralph."

"I already know he can't say he was in Albuquerque. On the other hand, a neighbor described him as tall and skinny, so he wouldn't fit the description of the bomber."

However, when they arrived at Ralph's Upper Valley farm and insisted on extracting Ollie Ray from his cotton fields, they found that although he *was* skinny, as Sylvia Maruffo had said, he wasn't particularly tall. Elena and G. exchanged glances.

"Are you two the people who scared my workers Sunday?" Ralph asked.

"Actually Sergeant Washington wasn't here Sunday," Elena replied. "It was me and an ATF agent."

"Well, whoever. What I wanna say is, just because the men ran away don't mean they're illegal. I got papers on every single one of them. They all got legal with the amnesty."

"We're not here about your workers, Mr. Ralph," said G. politely. "We're here about the bombing at H.H.U."

"Maruffo mentioned you've been askin' about that."

Mrs. Ollie Ray Ralph had joined them in the yard, a lady with a weathered face and blond hair that came out of a bottle. "I told you the Maruffos are no friends of yours," she said. "Suggestin' that you—"

"Sylvia said that," Ralph interrupted. "Not Efren."

"That woman's a troublemaker. Always bragging about his Spanish colonial ancestors. They were probably a bunch of ragtag Indians."

"Norleen, why don't you go on in the house an' make some lemonade," said Ralph. "These folks are likely parched. We'll go set on the porch."

Mrs. Ralph flounced off angrily and in two minutes reappeared with a large pitcher. The contents had never seen a lemon; Elena was sure of that. There were little crystals sticking to the glass. Still, the mystery drink was cold and liquid, and the water probably safe.

As they sat on orange-and-pink flowered patio chairs, Mr. Ralph told them at great length what he had been doing Friday and Saturday: things like giving a 4-H lecture, visiting a cotton gin, hauling home fertilizer, talking to his broker, having a beer at a tavern down the road, taking his wife out to dinner, and on and on. Many of his claimed activities weren't anything he could prove.

Then he told them about "year 'round water," his reason for joining Water Now. "See, the city wants it," said Ollie Ray. "They're gettin' half their water from the river now, but only durin' irrigation season. Rest of the year—like five months— they gotta draw on the Hueco and Mesilla Bolsons, an' the Hueco's runnin' dry. So they want the year 'round water so they can save the bolson water. An' us farmers want it 'cause we can grow winter crops."

"Ollie Ray, these folks don't care about irrigation," said Mrs. Ollie Ray. She had risen from her chair to top off the lemonade glasses.

"Ever'body on the river cares about water, Norleen," said Ollie Ray. "Seen in the paper that the chili growers are punchin' each other out over irrigation methods. Don' know what the world's comin' to." He turned back to Elena and G. "Like I was sayin' about year 'round water, we need it 'cause of the soil, too. Fresh water from the dams don't build up the salt in our soil an' cut our yields."

"Your buddy Maruffo doesn't want winter water," said Norleen, her mouth curling snidely. "Probably too lazy to work year 'round. *Sylvia* probably thinks it wouldn't be traditional."

"Much you know, Norleen," snapped Ollie Ray. "You can bet Efren's grandfather grew winter crops—before the dams went in at Elephant Butte and Caballo." He turned back to Elena and G. "You ever look at farms in the Lower Valley where the salt content in the soil's worse?"

"Well—" Elena didn't pay much attention to the fields when she visited the Lower Valley. She was usually going after someone who had committed a crime.

"Course you have," said Ollie Ray. "An' you can't help but notice them fields with spindly little onion plants that ain't gonna get to market. That's salt. Cotton now—it tolerates the salt better. Vegetables don't. But if the soil salinity keeps risin', pretty soon we'll be in trouble here upriver. Then even the cotton'll . . ." He had a lot to say, and Elena listened. She figured she needed to know how people felt about water if she was going to solve a crime whose motive was evidently water.

Once they managed to escape and get on the road again, Elena said, "Ralph's a possibility. Medium height. So are Maruffo and Father Bratslowski, although they've both claimed to be in Albuquerque."

"Maybe," said G., stopping at a crossroad. "Perry's checking the Albuquerque alibis."

"For violence, Celestina Ortiz and Sister Gertrudis Gregory fit the bill better, but Sister's too tall and Ms. Ortiz is too fat," Elena mused. She glanced at her new partner. "How come you're first name's G period?"

"You plucked that one right out of the air, didn't you?" said Sergeant Washington.

Elena grinned. "Most people have a name. Or at least two initials."

"My name's supposed to been George, but since I weighed twelve pounds at birth, my mama was still pretty worn down when she filled out the form. She spelled George wrong an' never even noticed till we got the birth certificate back."

"Oh yeah? What'd she put down?"

"Gorge. G-O-R-G-E, but anyone who wants to be my friend doesn't go callin' me Gorge."

Elena wasn't about to argue. G. might be a slow driver and a slow talker, but he had a forceful way about him. "How did you get into explosives work?"

"Better ask why I joined the army. I wanted to be a preacher, but we didn't have the money for the education, so I joined the army an' ended up in an EOD. Sounded interestin', an' it's important work."

"But dangerous," said Elena.

G. disagreed. "You keep close to God, you got nothin' to worry about. That's why I always say a prayer before we start messin' with explosives."

"So how did you get from the army to the LSPD?"

"Met my wife Sharana when I was stationed here an' comin' up on twenty years. Both of us strong in the church. Reckon I fell in love the first time I heard her sing. Sharana's got a voice like an angel." He nodded for emphasis and turned onto Doniphan.

"So we got engaged, an' I didn't re-up once I hit twenty years. Course, I'd got to know lots of folks in the department here. Army's called out for bombs, just like the FBI an' the ATF. Sharana didn't want to leave Los Santos. She said—rightly—it's a good place for blacks, even if there wasn't very many. So I took my pension an' went to the Police Academy. Then they moved me up as fast as they could. They were lookin' to make me head of the bomb squad."

Elena and G. were on their way to talk to former Water Now members Philomeno and Magdalena Reyes and had called ahead to Pancho Villa High to inform the principal that they wanted an interview, only to be told that the brother and sister had taken compassionate leave and were probably at Thomason General Hospital where their brother was dying.

"I guess we know why they quit Water Now," said Elena, referring to the Reyeses. "Sister Gertrudis Gregory seemed to take it as a spurning of the public interest."

"Doesn't feel right—goin' to interview someone with a dyin' relative," said G. The brother and sister proved to be twins, a very handsome couple with glossy black hair and dark eyes, both slender and of medium height. Philomeno Reyes taught social studies; Magdalena, computer science. Both looked worn and sad as Elena and G. explained their business. Then the twins looked irritated.

"We don't even belong anymore," said Philomeno.

"We spend all our time here at the hospital," Magdalena added. "Our older brother's dying of liver cancer, and you want to know if we were out planting bombs?"

"Do we look like bombers?" demanded Philomeno.

"Do you think anyone in our situation would be interested in anything but their brother's welfare?" asked Magdalena softly. Tears were sliding down her cheeks.

Philomeno said, "My brother probably doesn't have more than a few days left. If we were rich or our insurance covered him, he could afford a liver transplant. He might not have to die. But he's unemployed, and Medicaid patients don't get liver transplants."

Elena didn't think patients with liver cancer got transplants, either, but she didn't want to argue with these unhappy siblings. "We'd like to know where you were Friday and Saturday night," she said, feeling like a louse for harassing the bereaved.

"Ask around here at the hospital. Ask the nurses," said the brother.

"I'm mighty sorry for your trouble," said Sergeant Washington. The twins had been turning away. "Maybe we could all bow our heads an' say a prayer for your brother."

The two looked at him in surprise but didn't object. Elena found herself in a small circle of people, two of whom were strangers, praying for a man she'd never met. Then the Reyes twins returned to the hospital room while Elena and G. pursued nurses up and down the halls getting assurances such as, "The Reyes twins are always here. Their brother's dying," and "Poor things. I don't think they ever get any sleep."

"He's the right size," said Elena as they left the hospital.

"They don't even belong to the group anymore," said G. reproachfully, "and this doesn't seem a likely time to be goin' out settin' off bombs."

"Besides that, they're teachers. Social science and computer science. Not a likely—"

"You're wrong there. The Internet's got information on how to make bombs," said G.

"You're kidding?"

"But *she's* the computer person. Jus' can't see her downloadin' bomb recipes from Jack the Ripper or any of the other guys who run explosives pages and dialogues."

"Suppose not," Elena murmured, still assimilating the idea that there were bomb-making classes on the Internet. "You know, I had a thought, G."

"Which you're about to share."

"Right. Those bombs, from what you tell me, wouldn't have exploded if the water hadn't been turned on, and it doesn't make sense that the university would turn on the sprinklers during graduation. I mean, all those parents in their designer clothes wouldn't be thrilled to get soaked while their kiddies were getting degrees. So I think what we want to do next is find out who turned on the water."

"Sounds sensible to me." Before they arrived at H.H.U., Perry Melon was patched through on their police radio.

"I found out who that guest speaker was," he said, sounding excited. "A man named Brazlitt. He has a thirty-year history of brushes with the law in the name of one cause or another. Brazlitt's never actually been convicted of a bombing, but he's certainly been a suspect. I'm even more convinced that this is a case of eco-terrorism with national implications."

"Sounds good, Perry," said G. Washington. "You just keep followin' that up. Have you got a picture an' stats on him?" After consulting Elena, he said, "Fax 'em over to the office of Dr. Sarah Tolland at H.H.U. We'll pick 'em up there." After he signed off, he said, "We still better find out who turned on that water. If it was Brazlitt, that's fine. If it was a local, we want to know that, too."

Brazlitt? Elena puzzled over the name. It tickled her memory, but she couldn't call anything up. Maybe the faxed photo would jog something loose.

15
..

Tuesday, May 21, 1:15 P.M.

When on the case with G. Washington, Elena had to buy her own lunch. She tried to tell him she knew places that sold spicier Mexican food than Taco Bell, but G. liked Taco Bell. He had a bacon and tomato burrito, which Elena pronounced "not authentic Tex-Mex." Then they went on to Herbert Hobart University, where they had to wrest the fax about Melon's bombing suspect, Lawrence Brazlitt, from the recalcitrant Virginia Pargetter, Sarah's secretary. The picture having arrived on Dr. Tolland's fax machine, sent to Dr. Tolland's fax number, Mrs. Pargetter felt that Dr. Tolland should see it before it was passed on to anyone, even the addressees.

"What's her problem?" asked G. as they left. "She doesn't like blacks?"

"She doesn't like me," said Elena. "I should have sent you in by yourself." Although the photo had come through, the stats hadn't. Staring at the picture of Lawrence Brazlitt, a slender, middle-aged, gray-bearded man with long hair and an earring, Elena was sure she'd never seen him before. So why did she feel that she should remember him?

They were welcomed more cordially by Hector Montes, although they had to listen to his litany of woe about the desiccated condition of the landscaping now that it could no

longer be watered. Elena tapped her foot. G. nodded sympathetically, asked when Montes expected to have the wells
repaired, discussed the problems of growing nondesert shrubbery in a desert region, and generally endeared himself to
Hector Montes, who had started out by asking if they'd caught
the bombers.

"Well, sir," said Washington, once Montes had had time to
air all his grievances, "in respect to that question you asked me
about the bomber, it occurred to Detective Jarvis here that you
wouldn't be turnin' on the sprinklers durin' graduation."

"Damn right," Montes agreed. "Why would I do that? I
overrode the system commands jus' so it wouldn't happen. The
whole shebang's computer operated, state of the art, sensors for
ground an' air moisture an' all that. It's a masterpiece of
engineering. An outdoor climate control system—that's what
they called it when they put it in. Not that I understand all the
ins an' outs. I just know how to work it, an', like you said, we
set it not to water on graduation day. Vice President Stanley
would have shit a brick if we'd a soaked the graduating class."

"Well, sir," said G., "someone turned those sprinklers on.
Otherwise, the bombs couldn't have exploded. Now, we've got
a few descriptions of the man who *planted* the bombs—"

"—so what we want to find out," Elena chimed in, "is who
turned on the sprinklers."

"We don't let just anyone in the control room," said Montes.
"They'd have to break in, but it hasn't happened. We'd a
noticed. An' the campus police check for break-ins."

"So either someone was careless about lockin' up, or the
person who turned on the water had a key. Maybe we ought to
look at the control area," said the sergeant.

Montes led them to another part of the building and proudly
showed them the computerized control panel, pointing out its
many features, all of which were useless now that the wells had
been destroyed.

"It seems to me," Elena said finally, "that in order to turn that
water on, you'd have to know all this stuff. *I* couldn't figure out
what to do just by looking at that board."

"It's complicated," said Montes smugly.

"Do you have any disgruntled employees who might be part of this plot against your sprinkler system?" she asked. "Or maybe employees with financial troubles who'd be amenable to a bribe?"

Montes shook his head. "Only two fellas have anything to do with this system."

"They in today?" asked G.

Montes summoned the men to his office. One, John Greetz, said he hadn't been on campus the Saturday of graduation day. The other, Jose Palacio, said he had been bossing a crew of three, who were replacing bits of turf thrown up by the high heels of proud mothers and female graduates. "High heels is worse'n horses," said Palacio, "'cept for the horseshit."

Elena was beginning to feel discouraged. "Does anyone else have keys to that room?" she asked.

"Nah, just us an' Hector," said Palacio.

"Hey, wait a minute," John Greetz objected. "There's the kid doin' the term paper on the system."

"Oh, sure, the engineerin' major." Palacio scratched his head. "Beau. Beauregard Pinter. We had a key made for him, but he give it back."

"Could he have had it duplicated?" G. asked.

"Don' see why not. But he's prob'ly gone home by now," said Greetz.

"Nope," said Palacio. "Him an' his fraternity—they're holdin' a whole week of parties an' stuff for the graduatin' seniors an' parents. He'd still be here."

"There might be a record in the computer," Elena suggested, "that is, if he changed the commands." Everyone in the room looked stumped. None of them knew enough about computers to agree or disagree. Elena considered calling Maggie Daguerre, the department's computer expert, who had helped her on a case in which they thought a computer scam might be connected to the murder of an H.H.U. coed.

However, Elena wanted information right now, so instead she called Electrical Engineering to convince Sarah to run the

computer search. When the E.E. chairman protested, Elena
said, laughing, "Come on, Sarah. If you help us solve this case,
maybe the police department will make you an honorary cop."

Sarah was not impressed, but she meet them in five minutes
to apply her expertise to the problem.

While Sarah worked at the keyboard, Elena pursued a train
of thought that anyone unfamiliar with the university would
have considered peculiar. She was pondering her last case here,
the hot regalia caper. Someone had kidnapped and held for
ransom all the gold and jewel-studded maces and necklaces the
university had bought to spruce up the big event, not to
mention the hand-embroidered satin banners of the colleges
and the specially ordered turquoise academic gowns and
mortarboards for the graduates. Instant panic in the halls of
academe! The university couldn't have graduation without the
proper accoutrements, not according to Vice President Harley
Stanley. Kidnapping, especially the kidnapping of *things,*
wasn't Elena's sort of case, but she'd been asked for, she and
the FBI.

The FBI had declined to take part, but whatever H.H.U.
demanded, they got from the city of Los Santos, the university
and its students being such an important source of revenue
locally. Cities on the border in Texas needed any money they
could get.

So Elena had run down the fraternity that stole the regalia,
the fraternity boys were duly forgiven by the H.H.U. administration, and Elena was rewarded with an honorary degree.

"Did he say what fraternity he belonged to?" she asked.

"I s'pose he did," said Greetz. "You remember, Jose?" Jose
didn't. Elena mentioned the fraternity that had kidnapped the
regalia. Neither man thought the name sounded right. She
sighed. Still, what if this was the same sort of operation,
another student prank meant to disrupt the ceremony? Of
course, planting explosives on the quadrangle and in the wells
was more than a prank. But what if—

By that time, Sarah finished and swung her chair around.
"What I found," she said, "is that the regular program was

overridden on the morning of the eighteenth at seven-thirty to keep the sprinklers off for the day."

"I did that," said Hector Montes.

"Then that command was overridden at nine-thirty and another put in to turn the sprinklers on for ten minutes at eleven-fifty, which would be right at the end of graduation. The person who executed the command took no trouble to hide it or have it erased once it had done its work, so it wasn't hard to find. Is that what you wanted to know?"

"Yes ma'am," said G. Washington. "We certainly do thank you for your assistance."

Sarah nodded graciously. Elena asked if she knew a student named Beau Pinter.

"Certainly," Sarah replied. "He's been in several of my classes. He's an engineering major."

"Could he have put the sprinkle-at-graduation command in?"

"Anyone could, given a minimum of computer knowledge. There was nothing complicated or surreptitious about it."

"Is he a graduating senior?" Elena asked.

"No, a junior," Sarah replied.

Elena nodded. The fraternity boys behind the regalia kidnapping had been sophomores and juniors, playing a trick on their graduating fraternity brothers. She turned to her partner and said, "We'd better visit this Beau Pinter."

"He caused the explosions?" asked Sarah, astonished. "I wouldn't have thought him violent or dangerous."

"Evidently he is," said Elena. "Dangerous, or really stupid. Could you find out what fraternity he belongs to?"

"I suppose," said Sarah. "All the information in this system is available to everyone, unfortunately."

16

Tuesday, May 21, 3:30 P.M.

Sarah had just found the name of Beau Pinter's fraternity when G.'s pager went off. He returned the page, saying, "Uh-huh . . . The one downtown? . . . You called the FBI? . . . Uh-huh . . . How many hostages? . . . Uh-huh . . . You called CIT and SWAT?"

Wow, thought Elena. *Hostages downtown with the Crisis Intervention Team and the FBI called in.* "What's up?" she asked eagerly. "Can I go along?" She'd love to get out of interviewing Beau Pinter and his fraternity brothers. Even if they had bombed graduation, they wouldn't be a danger to anyone else, any more than the regalia thieves were likely to turn their attention to the University of Texas at Los Santos or venture into New Mexico to hit other colleges.

G. patted her shoulder. "It's a bank robbery, missy. Some nut case with a bomb threatenin' to blow up everyone inside if he doesn't get to leave with the money."

Missy? That was as bad as *niña* or *babe.* She'd thought better of G. Washington. And Sarah, who was supposed to be her friend and a fellow crusader for women's dignity in the workplace, was all but laughing. Elena supposed that her own expression looked blatantly indignant, but G. didn't seem to notice; he was making another call.

"Don't you worry," he said to Elena. "I could tell you didn't like bombs when Calzone blew up the third well, but I'll get you someone to help with those fraternity boys. If all their mamas an' daddys are over there, likely they'll be as tough to talk sense to as they were when the shrubbery was blowin' up in their faces. . . . Connie, this is G. I gotta go downtown to a bank bomb situation. How you feel about meetin' Elena . . . I thought you would. Seems like a frat boy was responsible for turnin' on the water Saturday."

"I can talk to them on my own," Elena protested.

"What's that address, ma'am?" G. asked Sarah. More amused than ever, Sarah gave it to him, and he relayed the information to Connie Amparan. "Why don't you meet her there in fifteen minutes. Think you can . . ."

Elena had started to leave in a huff before he finished the arrangements, which she saw as another male end run around her competence to handle whatever came her way, even recalcitrant millionaires. If they gave her any trouble, she'd just put a shot in their—what?—trophy case? The fraternities and sororities competed in everything from sports to musicals. About the only thing for which they didn't seek trophies was academics. On the other hand, maybe she better not shoot up any fraternity treasures—even in the interest of encouraging cooperation. There'd been no word from the Shooting Review Team, and she didn't want to give them any ammunition against her. The department was very sensitive about lawsuits resulting from the discharge of firearms, justified or not.

"Wait for Connie. That's an order," had been G.'s last words. Since he was a sergeant, although not *her* sergeant, she supposed she had to obey. Accordingly, she sat drumming her nails on the steering wheel of her unmarked car and scowling at the object of her investigation. The sign in front said Siggies, with Greek letters underneath. The Siggies were evidently a droll group, for a smaller sign identified the architecture of their house as A Rip-off of Falling Water by Frank Lloyd

Wright. All H.H.U. buildings were identified by the original art deco structure from which they'd taken their inspiration.

The effect made by the Frank Lloyd Wright fraternity house was peculiar. The building was obviously designed to span a stream or river, but no water flowed in the concrete waterways. Deciduous trees—Falling Water was evidently not in Miami Beach—formed a thin line around the house and looked very strange because the miniforest was fronted by the palm trees and tropical bushes that decorated the rest of the campus, and because the Siggies' trees were responding to the sudden drought by weeping spring leaves.

However, the water disaster didn't seem to be causing any grief inside. Elena could hear the loud music, conversation, and laughter out here on the street. People holding drinks were also congregated, fanning themselves, on outdoor decks over concrete waterfalls.

A tap on her window pulled Elena from her uncharitable thoughts about the Siggies, and she unlocked the passenger-side door to let Connie Amparan in. Once she'd told him about Beauregard Pinter and his term paper on the sprinkler controls, Connie said, "Weird. Perry's sure that somebody named Brazlitt, an old-timey activist from the sixties, is behind the bombing. He was burning up the computer keyboard before some jerk threatened to bomb a bank downtown."

"Shouldn't you be there?" demanded Elena. "I may not be macho enough to get in on the big bombing cases, but I can certainly handle a few drunken fraternity boys."

Connie looked puzzled at the sharpness of her tone but said, "Hey, bank robbers are a dime a dozen. The bomb's probably a fake. But how often do I get to investigate a shrubbery attack with a detective who looks like Miss America, only smarter?"

If he hadn't added the smarter part, she might have taken his reassurances amiss, but *smarter* was O.K. She smiled at the ATF agent, and they headed up the "forest path" to the Siggies' house, having to let themselves in because no one heard the doorbell above the cacophony of the party in progress. Happy Hobart was the first person Elena saw—president of the junior class, nephew of the founder, the con artist who had been selling fake H.H.U. diplomas to rich nitwits last fall and managed to get himself forgiven by the administration. As a result of further financial shenanigans on his part, the administration had even declared him a "benefactor of the Hobart Foundation."

"Are you a Siggie?" she demanded, ready to arrest him on the spot for complicity in a bombing.

"Doctor Detective!" he exclaimed and tried to give her a hug.

She fended him off.

"Still mad at me?" he asked, looking forlorn, then answered his own question. "I guess you are. Well, I'm not a Siggie, just a guest."

"Fine," said Elena, disappointed. "This is ATF Agent Amparan."

"Oops," said Happy, and he started to laugh.

Elena eyed him suspiciously. "Can you point out someone named Beauregard Pinter?"

"Sure, but he likes to be called Beau. He won't even let his mama, who's the original Southern belle, call him Beauregard. Hey, Beau. Company." In response to Happy's summons, a languidly handsome fellow strolled over from a covey of pretty coeds.

He laughed with casual good humor when Elena and Connie were introduced. "Caught us, huh?" he said. "Well, you're three days too late, Detectives."

Elena stared at him. The idiot was admitting his guilt, laughing about it? Well, why not? No doubt, he thought he wouldn't be charged by the university, which tended to forgive anything its students did, that institutional magnanimity being a combination of the president's insistence on Christian charity and the vice president's pursuit of money for the Hobart Foundation. Maybe Beau's parents had already made a contribution meant to cover his peccadillo. Well, he'd miscalculated. People had been injured.

"Now, don't look at me that way, ma'am." Beau had a

Southern drawl thick enough to spread on pancakes. "Ah just turned on the water. That other stuff—Ah had nothin' to do with that. Why the university would put explosives in the sprinklers Ah wouldn't know. The only brother we got who took chemistry said maybe they had sodium stuck in there, but that don't make sense."

A middle-aged lady in a wide-brimmed garden-party hat said, "Beau Pinter, did you do somethin' to blow nasty leaves an' flahrs all ovah mah prettiest frock?"

"Who are these people, an' what's this you're tellin' them, boy?" asked a man in a white suit.

Beau grinned. "Well, you know how us Siggies won the trophy jus' now, Daddy? The bes' Graduation Mischief of the Year trophy? Which, it bein' the first graduation, makes it the most important trophy, don't ya know?"

"We'll win next year," said Bunky Fossbinder, a short, charming, rat-faced student Elena had met both before Christmas on the murder-by-statue case and just recently during the regalia caper. He had sidled up to eavesdrop when he saw Elena. "We might have won this year if Detective Dr. Jarvis hadn't caught us." He winked at her.

"The regalia business and the exploding shrubbery were part of a fraternity competition?" she asked.

"Sure 'nough," said Beau. "Bunky an' me, we're leaders of the finalist teams, an' Ah do thank you, ma'am, fo' stopping the enemy in their tracks."

"You're admitting responsibility for the bombing?" asked Connie cautiously.

"No, sir, not a bit of it," said Beau. "Ah jus' learned how to work the water computer an' programmed it to turn on durin' the prayer."

"You're under arrest for aggravated assault," said Elena. "You must have some federal charges as well, Agent Amparan," she added, glancing toward Connie.

"You can bet on that," Connie agreed.

"No way is waterin' folks on a hot day aggravated assault," said Beau. "Daddy, you got any lawyer friends around here?"

"My dad's a lawyer," said Bunky, "and just to show I've got no hard feelings about Happy awarding you the prize, even though I suspect you bribed him—"

"What does Happy have to do with this?" asked Elena.

"I was the judge," said Happy, "representing the playful spirit of my late uncle, Herbert Hobart."

"You think we should arrest him, too, Elena?" asked Connie. "This isn't my usual case."

Bunky had been holding a hurried conference with a wizened version of himself, whom he then introduced as his father, Reginald Fossbinder of Fossbinder, Fossbinder & Pratt, Washington, D.C.

"The young man is quite right," said the senior Fossbinder with ponderous confidence. "A light sprinkling does not constitute an assault. We're prepared to sue the police department for false arrest and the university for endangering public safety by putting those explosives around the sprinklers. If you have any doubt that these young men are innocent of malicious intent, consider the explosion of the wells, which I read about in your local papers. Why would the contestants do that? It would not impact the graduation ceremony or benefit them in the inter-fraternity contest. Some terrorist group is at work here."

"Then why are you suing the university?" asked Connie Amparan.

"Rule of thumb. Sue everyone you can find. Look for the deep pockets. The Hobart Foundation has deep pockets. I myself have contributed to their depth."

In the ensuing hours, Elena and Connie found themselves the focus of threats and arguments from all the parents of sophomore and junior Siggies, not to mention facetious remarks from the seniors, who had been the target of the sprinkler caper, and complaints from the newly initiated freshmen, who hadn't been allowed to participate.

The detectives finally had a private conference in the downstairs powder room and decided that they needed to investigate further before they arrested anyone. They'd have to prove that the fraternity boys had planted the pyrodex as well as arranging to turn on the sprinklers.

"Jesus," moaned Connie as they left the Rip-off of Falling Water, "talking to forty self-important parents, their lawyers, and their flaky sons makes Waco look like a stroll in the park."

"Therapy occurs in the strangest places," said Elena wryly. She'd just jumped a foot when, on the way to her car, someone had set off fireworks over the cement waterfall. "Can't you at least arrest them for illegal fireworks?"

He shook his head. "Somehow or other, the university got a permit."

A second rocket burst in the darkening sky, making Elena wish the interviews at Falling Water had been therapeutic for her as well. Her hands were trembling again.

17

Tuesday, May 21, 9:45 P.M.

Toothbrush Abuse Lands
Wife in Trouble

Last night during the Jay Leno show, Brian
O'Donnell of the 2300 block of Rio Bacco skipped a
commercial in order to brush his teeth. His suspicious wife Hannah, a stickler for water conservation,
snuck into the bathroom after him and caught him
with the faucet running.

Infuriated, O'Donnell attacked him with an electric toothbrush stand, loosening his upper front teeth.
Mrs. O'Donnell was arrested for assault and released
on a personal recognizance bond after spending the
night at the Los Santos County Detention Facility.

Los Santos *Herald-Post*, Tuesday, May 21

When Elena finally returned to Sarah's apartment Tuesday
night, she'd missed dinner and most of the evening, also the
time allotted for precooking her mother's *chili verde* recipe.
Concepcion Weizell was to join Sarah and Elena for dinner the
next evening, invited because her husband and Elena's usual
partner, Leo, was assigned to a border sting operation and hated

to leave his wife alone after dark when delivery of their brood was imminent.

"She won't go into labor in my apartment, will she?" Sarah had asked, alarmed, when Elena first suggested the invitation.

"If she does, you can bet it will be false labor number four," Elena had replied. "I wish she'd just let them do a cesarean and get it over with; that's what the doctors want."

Once Elena had assembled the ingredients for the dish, which required long cooking, she complained that she'd be up half the night monitoring it. In answer, Sarah unearthed a pressure cooker from a corner of the pantry. "You can stick the *chili verde* in here tomorrow night," she suggested, then passed Elena a clipping from the evening paper. "Does it seem to you that people are getting stranger and stranger here in Los Santos?" she asked.

Elena read the article about toothbrush abuse and shook her head. "First the lady who attacked the chili grower with her purse, now this." She grinned. "Maybe it's something in the water."

"That's not funny," said Sarah. "These things have started happening since our sprinklers were bombed during graduation."

Elena thought about that as she cubed a slab of round steak. Anarchy in the making? She shivered and, to get her mind off visions of Armageddon on the Rio Grande, fixed herself a snack and turned on the ten o'clock news. An excited local anchorman was reporting on the bank robbery downtown. The bomb had proved to be so eccentrically constructed that it would not have gone off. However, before that was discovered, the bank robber and two hostages were disabled by rubber bullets from the SWAT team after negotiations broke down and the robber, an escapee from the state mental hospital at Big Spring, threatened to detonate his bomb.

When Elena went to work Wednesday, the three explosives agents who had partnered her for the H.H.U. investigation were all unavailable. Connie was trying to determine where the bank explosives had come from, and Perry was trying to discover which Internet page had inspired the robber, who told them that computer communications were celestial messages ordering him to build the bomb. G. and his men were studying the device, which had been hauled off to a site outside of town. Calzone had not been called.

Elena had paged each man—except Calzone—then gone on to H.H.U. by herself, where she spent the day asking everyone she could find about sophomore and junior members of the sprinkler-caper fraternity. Did any of the Siggies have connections with Water Now? Did any have resentments against the university or their own graduating seniors? Could any of those witnesses who saw the "irrigation man" and the "water commission man" recognize pictures of fraternity members as the bomb planters? The entire exercise was slow going and unproductive.

Interrupting her efforts all day were lawyers hurriedly produced by indignant parents who did not want their offspring arrested for a prank gone wrong. Elena had never been crazy about lawyers, few cops were; but this bunch, being high-priced, were insufferable. Some were local criminal attorneys, bad-tempered because they wanted the money offered but were embarrassed by the triviality of defending fraternity pranksters. Some had been flown in overnight from other parts of the country, men and women under retainer by rich clients, but still resentful over lost sleep and hot weather. The temperature was ninety-eight degrees. Even Elena considered it unseasonably hot when she had to trudge around campus hauling a briefcase of fraternity photos. At least the sprinklers were still off, instead of spraying water and creating hateful humidity.

By the time she checked out at headquarters, again on overtime, and returned to the faculty apartment building, Concepcion had already arrived, dropped off by Leo before he headed for the border. She was describing pregnancy symptoms to an unnerved Sarah.

"Could you get her off that subject?" Sarah whispered in the kitchen, where Elena had retired to open a beer and put on the *chili verde*. "It's taken two scotches to fortify me through the conversation so far. I'll be drunk before you serve dinner. Then I'll eat more Mexican food than I should and get indigestion."

"Take one of those pills that prevent heartburn before you've even eaten anything," Elena advised. She had been puzzling over the pressure cooker, whose principle she understood, but whose rules of operation were beyond her ken. Sarah had not been able to find an instruction booklet and didn't have a crock pot; with a crock pot the *chili verde* could have cooked all day without supervision. "Do you know how to work this thing?" Elena asked, turning the heavy lid upside down.

"Of course, I don't," said Sarah. "I've never used it. I think it was a wedding present from the unmentionable person who killed that poet and framed me."

"Ah." Elena's first H.H.U. case. "Well, I guess I can figure it out." Sarah left to do hostess duty. Elena studied the pot, poured the *chile verde* in, fastened the lid, and turned on the gas. Then she whipped up a batch of guacamole, poured tostados into a silver bowl with a crystal dip cup at its edge and, carrying her version of hors d'oeuvres and her beer, went in to join the other two women.

"What's this?" Concepcion was asking as Elena entered. "Are you a Roman Catholic, Sarah?" The expectant mother leaned forward on Sarah's beige silk couch to pick up a paper on the teak coffee table, then discovered that her stomach wouldn't allow her to actually touch the item that had caught her attention.

"That's a photocopy of the threat the university received before the bombing," Elena replied. She put down the bowl, picked up the page with its message, "Turn off the water or we will," and passed it to Concepcion. Elena then dropped into a brown silk chair and leaned forward to scoop guacamole up with a tostado. Sarah was watching her vigilantly, no doubt afraid she'd cause a carpet disaster by dropping dip on the new, creamy Berber carpet, which looked to Elena as if it were made of rope. She always hesitated to walk barefoot on it.

"If I didn't know better, I'd say these words were cut from

headlines in *The Bishop's Newsletter* or the *Holy Name Gazette*," said Concepcion.

Straightening abruptly, Elena stared at her partner's wife. "You recognize the type?"

Concepcion shrugged. "I suppose other publications might use that medieval-looking typeface, and certainly the Church wouldn't be bombing universities." Suddenly she looked alarmed. "Elena, I hope you're not going to accuse the bishop of something. I want my children baptized in the Church. In fact, Leo and I hope you'll stand godmother to one of them."

"Why, Concepcion, that's lovely." Elena flushed with pleasure. The way her love life had gone since her divorce, the closest she'd come to motherhood was being an aunt and a godmother.

"It's not lovely if they won't allow you in a church," said Concepcion. "I can't choose someone who's been excommunicated."

"They'd excommunicate her for trying to solve a bombing?" asked Sarah. She wasn't eating the guacamole, although she passed it frequently to the immobilized-by-babies Concepcion.

"I don't think the bishop's involved," said Elena. "But Father Bratslowski and Sister Gertrudis Gregory might be." She tried to picture those two conspiring with the frolicsome Siggies and found it hard to imagine.

The doorbell rang just as Concepcion was pointing out that at least two of the babies had just kicked her, making bulges in the sky blue maternity tunic she wore. Sarah's eyes widened at the evidence, and she escaped to the front door, evidently glad of the interruption until she discovered who was in the hall—her ex-husband, Gus McGlenlevie. "What are you doing here?" she demanded.

"What's that wonderful smell?" he rejoined. "Nothing you're cooking, I'm sure. Ah, Detective Jarvis." He skirted his irritated ex-wife. "You must be the chef. Is that some exotic dish from your colonial Spanish heritage? Dear lady, let me introduce myself." He swept off a straw farmer's hat and bowed to Concepcion. "I am the renowned poet, Angus

McGlenlevie, author of *Erotica in Reeboks* and *Rapture on the Rapids*, ex-husband of this beautiful woman, who is happier to see me than she seems."

Concepcion stared at the red-bearded poet. He was wearing flowered shorts and an embroidered white shirt opened to the waist over a thatch of red chest hair intermingled with gray. Knowing Concepcion, Elena realized that Leo's wife was trying not to giggle.

"And what is your name, most radiant and expectant lady?"

"Concepcion Weizell," she replied.

"Most appropriate. I believe I know your husband. He once interrogated me. A stout-hearted policeman, grim and forceful. No doubt, your child—"

"Children," said Sarah, trying to scare him off. "Concepcion will be having five children—any minute now."

"Truly? Five? I am ecstatic to hear it, dear madam." He bowed to Concepcion again and placed his straw hat on the teak coffee table. "I want to be told all about it. Gracious Sarah, surely you'll invite me to dinner. No doubt Detective Jarvis has made a great plenty." He beamed at Elena. "I shall be happy to celebrate your expertise as a chef in my next book, and—" turning his charm on Concepcion "—your expectant motherhood, delightfully fecund madonna. What a wonderful subject for a cycle of poems—domesticity, food, babies—the passion and sensuality of the family experience. I feel the muse—"

"You are not invited, Gus," Sarah interrupted.

"Don't be so inhospitable, my love, former sharer of my bed and body, object of my youthful passion."

"Oh, shut up," snapped Sarah.

Concepcion was laughing so hard Elena worried that the hilarity might induce labor.

Gus sat down in another of the tobacco silk chairs and helped himself to guacamole. "So what's in the pot, Detective? It smells ambrosial."

"Chili verde," said Elena, grinning, "but I don't think you're going to be invited."

"If you get green slime on my carpet, Gus," said Sarah, "I'll—"

An explosion boomed in the kitchen.

"Tricked," cried Gus, turning pale as he jumped up and whirled on his ex-wife. "You're making snails, aren't you?" Gus had once accused her of trying to murder him at the dinner table with an exploding snail.

"I have never cooked another snail," said Sarah coldly, "for you or anyone else."

Shivering in the grip of a flashback, Elena managed to stagger toward the kitchen, where the pressure cooker, which she had evidently assembled improperly, had burst and splattered the room with *chili verde*. She turned off the gas and returned to the living room. "If we want to eat, we're going to have to lick the main course off the walls."

"And I was worried about the rug," muttered Sarah.

"My water's broken," Concepcion announced.

18
..

Antique Plumbing
Triggers Brawl

A Tuesday night anniversary party at the Kern Place home of Margaret and Oscar de la Hoya sparked police intervention, four arrests, and two hospitalizations when party guest Amos Wilkins, an assistant professor of psychology, smashed an antique toilet with a hammer.

Wilkins, described by a party guest as a "mean drunk," said from his hospital bed today, "The toilet used at least six gallons per flush. I was understandably incensed at such flagrant water wastage. Anyway, they should thank me. If I hadn't destroyed that toilet, the bomber might have targeted them."

Wilkins was arrested for malicious mischief and taken to Providence Memorial for treatment of injuries suffered when other guests intervened to keep him from destroying the De la Hoya bathtub. When a brawl erupted, neighbors called the police.

Margaret de la Hoya told the *Herald-Post* that her moss green plumbing fixtures were irreplaceable twenties antiques installed when the house was built.

El Paso *Herald-Post*, Wednesday, May 22

115

"It's not too late for a cesarean," said the obstetrician.

"No," gasped Concepcion when the contraction ended. Seconds earlier, her shriek had bounced off the walls of the delivery room, making two of the reluctant attendants, Sarah and Elena, wince, while Gus proclaimed, "The howl of anguish is the herald of new life."

"Who *is* that man?" demanded the obstetrician.

"I am the birth poet, sir," said Gus as he scribbled down the new line for his poem.

"Where's Leo?" Concepcion gasped.

"I called him," Elena assured her for the twentieth time. Without any training and in the absence of Leo, Elena had become Concepcion's labor coach. However, Elena longed to drag her hand away from Concepcion's grip and run for her life, or at least flex her fingers to see if they were broken. Instead, she mopped Concepcion's face and said, "He'll be here. I called from Sarah's apartment. Remember?" What she hadn't told Leo's wife was that the operator at headquarters refused to call Leo because he was on stakeout down on Paisano.

"We don't want to break radio silence for what's probably another false labor," said the dispatcher and hung up. Afraid to wait any longer, Elena had driven Concepcion to the hospital herself, with Sarah and Gus along for moral support and because they had to take Sarah's car.

Once there, Concepcion had again insisted on natural childbirth, causing the doctor to declare that he would not be responsible for the consequences. Somehow or other, in the confusion that followed, the obstetrical nurses had gowned them all and escorted them into the delivery room, although Sarah and Elena would have backed off if they could. Gus, on the other hand, had insisted on attending the birth and had been mistaken for the father.

"Now, dear," said the nurse when Concepcion refused Gus's coaching, "just because you're in pain, don't take it out on hubby. It takes two to make a baby."

"He's—not the father," Concepcion had groaned. The nurse

gasped, evidently under the impression that the husband had just learned he was to be presented with another man's children.

"This is madness," muttered the obstetrician. "I told you months ago you shouldn't have natural childbirth. Now——"

Concepcion let out another shriek and mangled Elena's hand. Elena said, "Breathe, breathe, breathe, breathe, breathe," hoping she was saying the right thing, patting Concepcion's forehead with a cool, wet cloth, wondering in desperation why Leo hadn't arrived yet. She'd called a second time from the hospital to tell the operator it was the real thing and to get him over here, for God's sake.

"Wherefore falls the agony upon the woman, the wife?" said Gus. "You notice I'm going for rhyme in this poem. Life, wife."

"Oh, shut up," said Sarah, who looked distinctly green. McGlenlevie seemed to be enjoying every minute, although he was a peculiar sight, his red beard encased by the nurse in a plastic thing that looked like a shower cap but tied on the top of his head.

"Don't bear down yet, Concepcion," said the obstetrician. "You're not completely dilated. I can't even tell what position the babies are in."

"'S O.K.," she gasped. "I'm not——"

"For all I know, they're all tangled up in there, which is why——"

"No cesarean," she interrupted. "No deliveries till Leo gets here."

"As if you could control that," snapped the doctor. "When they decide to start appearing, your body——"

Concepcion interrupted him with a groan that escalated to a wail. Elena was again treated to a bone-crunching hand-lock. She felt like groaning herself. Concepcion's face was pale and dripping with sweat.

"How about a local anesthetic?" said the O.B. who was assisting.

Her doctor nodded. "Take it or leave it, little mother," he said to Concepcion. "If you won't allow a cesarean, at least let us relieve the pain."

Elena mopped Concepcion's face. "Take the shots," she advised. "My sister Josie did, and she said delivery was a breeze."

"Your sister wasn't delivering quintuplets, I presume," said the doctor.

"Might hurt the babies," Concepcion gasped. Another contraction was starting.

"No way," Elena assured her. "My niece is brilliant, talented, best kid you ever met."

Concepcion screamed as the contraction wrung her with pain. "O.K.," she agreed when she could speak again. The doctors sprang into action, ordering the nurses around, ducking under the draperies at the end of the table.

"What about Dr. Fong?" Concepcion asked. Then another contraction started, and she shrieked lustily.

When the noise died away, Elena thought that surely her hand was broken. "Who's Dr. Fong?" she asked weakly.

"We don't have any Dr. Fong," said the obstetrician. "She may be hallucinating."

"I am not!" snapped Concepcion, getting testier by the minute. "Millard Fillmore Fong, the psychologist from the university. He wanted to be here."

Lord, thought Elena, *is he the drunken psychology prof who attacked a toilet last night?* Elena had read the evening paper in the waiting room while Concepcion was being prepped.

"I don't think we need any more people in this room," said the obstetrician. "I've never heard of an expectant mother insisting on attendance by a poet and a psychologist."

"The poet wasn't my idea," said Concepcion, "and the university is paying your bill, so you'd better let Dr. Fong in. It's part of the deal."

"I'll call him," said Sarah and scuttled out.

"Millard Fillmore Fong?" Elena stifled hysterical laughter. *What self-respecting mother names her son after a nothing president like Millard Fillmore? No wonder the psychologist drinks.*

And why are the lights so bright in here? Babies are supposed to be born in restful, quiet, dim places. Elena felt as if she were getting a sunburn from the delivery-room overheads. And the room was so crowded. Pediatricians, neonatologists, and nurses awaiting the babies, two obstetricians and their nurses, not to mention Gus, Sarah, and herself. They shouldn't be in the delivery room, especially Gus. She'd heard of birth mothers but never birth *poets.*

"I think I'm having another contraction," said Concepcion. Elena prepared to have her hand broken again, although, for good or ill, she could hardly feel it anymore. Maybe all the nerves had died.

"After the first one's born, I'll probably have to drag the others out by whatever extremity I can get hold of," said the obstetrician gloomily.

That didn't sound good to Elena. She hoped Concepcion hadn't heard him. Or maybe she should; then she'd agree to a cesarean.

"I know it's a contraction, but I can't feel a thing." Concepcion beamed at Elena.

19

Wednesday, May 22, 11:50 P.M.

"You oversexed bastard. You did this to me," Concepcion shrieked at Elena. The painkiller had worn off.

Taken aback, Elena protested, "Hey, I'm not Leo."

"Woe is the father who attends the birth of his own son," said Gus.

"I am *not* the father," Elena protested. "I'm just his partner."

"Let's try the gas," one obstetrician murmured to another.

As the contraction strengthened, Concepcion wailed, then let the sound die away with the pain and gasped, "So where is the s.o.b.?"

"On his way," Elena assured her once again, although she knew no such thing.

Another person crowded into the delivery room before Concepcion could voice her disbelief. "I am Dr. Millard Fillmore Fong," he announced.

"Never heard of you," said the preoccupied obstetrician from his stool at the end of the table. "What are you doing in my delivery room?"

"I told you about him hours ago," said Concepcion. "And how come I'm hurting again?" She craned her neck to glare at the doctor.

"We're taking care of that," the obstetrician replied.

"Well, I should hope so."

The assisting O.B. clasped Concepcion's hand around a breathing apparatus. "When you feel the pain coming, just inhale," he told her.

"Why?"

"Because it will help."

"Don't argue," advised Elena, whose hand mirrored Concepcion's labor pains.

Concepcion took one sniff, then another. "That's more like it," she said, sounding much more vigorous. She rolled her head to see the newly arrived psychologist. "You're just in time, Dr. Fong."

"Stop talking and bear down," said the obstetrician.

Concepcion obeyed.

"Millard Fong," the man said and shook Elena's free hand.

Even in loose scrubs, he seemed very slender, but his face, light brown and rather squared off, looked eerily like that of a full-blooded Indian with whom Elena had gone to school. Except for the little round glasses; her friend wouldn't have been caught dead in little round glasses. "Are you the professor who attacked a toilet last night?" she whispered. She wasn't letting some nut attend the birth of Leo's kids. If Fong went in for smashing plumbing fixtures with hammers, Sarah would have to arrange for some other H.H.U. psychologist to do the Weizell research project.

"Certainly not," said Fong. "That man is with the *other* university. Millard F. Fong, Ph.D.," he said to Gus.

"Gus McGlenlevie, birth poet," Gus replied. "The first child is imminent."

"Bear down," said the obstetrician. Concepcion let out an exaggerated grunt, ending in a giggle. "It's a boy," said the doctor. Elena patted Concepcion's forehead with the washcloth and mumbled, "Hang in there."

"No problema," said Concepcion and took another sniff. "Let's call baby number one Leo, Jr. You did say it's a boy?"

"Right, a boy," said the neonatologist who had just been handed the baby.

"And the s.o.b. isn't even here to see him. Mother told me not to marry a cop."

"My gosh, he's pretty big for a multiple birth," said the baby doctor.

"This is where it gets tough," said the obstetrician.

"Don't I get to see the baby?" Concepcion was somewhat breathless with the effort of having produced her first child, but otherwise seemed remarkably cheerful.

"There you go, dear," said a nurse, holding up the howling baby.

"He doesn't look very big to me," Concepcion protested. "In fact—" She giggled. "He's itsy bitsy."

"There are four more coming, dear." The nurse carried the infant away.

"Back to work, little mother," said the obstetrician.

"Little mother?" It was the first time Sarah had spoken since she had returned, escorting Dr. Fong. "I consider that a condescending, patriarchal remark."

"Damn," muttered the doctor. "That's a foot."

Elena clung to Concepcion's hand, saying, "Breathe, breathe," and thinking "a foot" didn't sound good. She'd heard about breech births.

"Shame, shame," Concepcion caroled, waving her inhaler, from which she had just taken a hit. "Wrong instruction, sweetie."

Dr. Fong patted Elena's arm consolingly and said, "I've heard that fathers tend to forget everything they learned in the birthing classes."

"I'm *not* the father," Elena objected. "I'm female, for Pete's sake."

"Oh, pardon me," said Fong. "No one mentioned that this was to be a nontraditional family. How fascinating! My research should certainly break new ground. Am I to understand that the child was conceived by artificial insemination, and you're the mother's sexual partner?"

"All right, bear down, Concepcion," said the obstetrician.

"I'm the *father's partner,*" snapped Elena.

"Good heavens," said the psychologist. He had produced a microcassette recorder and turned it on.

"Umph-ph," said Concepcion.

"It's a girl," said the obstetrician. "Wipe my forehead, Nurse."

Elena glanced at him. The poor man was sweating like a chili picker and looked decidedly stressed. "Wow!" said Concepcion. "This is hard work." She looked better than the doctor. "Gabriella," she announced. "After my mother."

"Are you O.K.?" It didn't seem normal to Elena for a woman to deliver two babies, giggling.

"Wonderful," said Concepcion. "This is great stuff." She took another sniff. "Want to try it?"

Elena shook her head and flexed her fingers. Even with painkiller and laughing gas, Concepcion was still mangling her hand when she actually pushed a baby out. The fingers no longer had any feeling, not even pain.

"The second one was harder than the first," Concepcion remarked. "Oops. Dropped the gas."

"Of course it was," snapped the doctor. "It was breech. We're lucky it went that easily. God knows in what positions the rest are."

"Would someone pick up that inhaler for me?" said Concepcion.

Elena glared at the doctor, resentful that he wasn't being more reassuring, not that Concepcion seemed to have noticed.

"Look at that baby girl," said Gus. "Isn't she beautiful?"

"For God's sake, Gus," said Sarah. "Are you coming on to a newborn?"

"I am overwhelmed by the miracle of birth," said Gus huffily.

"Well, it looks pretty ugly to me," Sarah muttered under her breath.

"Let's see Gabriella," said Concepcion. "How come everyone gets to look but me?"

"Here I am," called a voice from the doorway, and Leo, delivery smock flapping off his long, lean frame, mask tied haphazardly across his face, pushed his way through the crowd.

Concepcion turned her head. "It's about time."

"Listen, sweetheart, I had to disable two Mexican bandits to get to you."

"Who are you?" demanded the obstetrician.

"I'm the father."

"Oops, sorry, Detective. Didn't recognize you."

"Millard Fillmore Fong," said the psychologist and pumped Leo's hand. "You're the father of two so far."

"I missed two of them?" Leo looked crestfallen.

"Most unusual for a sperm donor to attend the birth, I should think," said Dr. Fong. "After the deliveries I'd like to interview you about your sexual relationship with your partner. Did it come about because your wife is a lesbian?"

"My wife's *what?*"

"What sexual partner?" Concepcion asked, then giggled.

Leo looked astounded and stammered, "I—I don't—what are you talking about?"

"He means me," said Elena, "but he's confused."

"Listen, honey," Leo said to his wife, "Elena and I aren't—"

"Of course, you aren't, Leo, sweetie. Elena's my best buddy," Concepcion replied, although she was usually a very jealous woman. "Show him the babies, someone."

"Oh God," cried the obstetrician. "A shoulder. Don't bear down, Concepcion. I've got to get it turned."

"I haven't even seen Gabriella," Concepcion complained.

"You named one of them after your mother?" Leo asked.

"Of course, but I named the first one after you."

"Girl or boy?" asked Leo suspiciously. He took his place beside Concepcion, murmuring thanks to Elena.

"You owe me," Elena whispered back.

"Want a whiff?" Concepcion sat up and pushed the inhaler under his nose.

"Stop that," yelled the doctor.

Leo backed up so abruptly that Elena had to grasp him by the waist to keep him from falling on her. Concepcion was giggling again.

"Got it turned," said the obstetrician. "Bear down, Concepcion. Nurses, hold up those other two babies. Are they still in the room?"

"Over here, sir," called a nurse.

"Another girl," said the obstetrician.

"Elena," Concepcion gasped.

"What is it?" Elena asked.

"No, I'm naming her after you. I'd probably have delivered at home by myself if you hadn't invited me to dinner. Then I wouldn't have got to breathe this lovely—this really lovely—"

"Is that stuff addictive?" Leo asked.

"Believe me, you wouldn't have delivered more than one at home," said the doctor. "And it would have been an even bigger disaster than this is."

"What disaster?" Concepcion asked. "Is little Elena all right?"

"*She's* fine; *I'm* having a nervous breakdown," mumbled the doctor.

"Is Sarah still here?"

"I'm here, Concepcion," said Sarah in a weak voice.

"Here's your baby, little mother." The obstetrician held up the newest girl.

"Beautiful," said Concepcion, but with a little less enthusiasm than she'd manifested for the first two. "I'm sorry about your couch, Sarah."

"Think nothing of it," said Sarah.

"You weren't that gracious when I knocked the guacamole over on it before we left," Gus complained.

"You were an uninvited guest," Sarah replied.

"If the next one's a boy, dear lady, maybe you'd like to name it after me," said Gus, "since I'm the birth poet."

"You're weird," said Concepcion. "Can I take a nap now? I feel kind of tired."

"Isn't this exciting," said Dr. Millard Fillmore Fong. "I think I'll write a preliminary article for the *Journal of Psychological Education.*"

"It'll be a miracle if this whole theater isn't contaminated with all these people in here," muttered the obstetrician. "Oh damn, the womb's closing. Quick, forceps. Don't bear down, Mother."

"She's not your mother," snapped Sarah.

Concepcion yawned.

"I think they're tangled up in there," said the obstetrician. "Mr. Weizell, I must ask you again to let me do a cesarean."

"No, this is fine," said Concepcion. "I'll just have another sniff."

"She's already had three," Leo protested. "Why—"

"Look, Doctor," cried the nurse beside him. "A foot."

The doctor groaned. "It's a good thing you're a big woman, Concepcion." Two doctors and a nurse congregated at the bottom of the table, murmuring among themselves while Concepcion grasped Leo's hand and strained, mumbling to herself. "A boy," said the doctor finally. "Wipe my forehead, Nurse."

The nurse mopped him up.

"Angel," whispered Concepcion, hoarse and exhausted. "After my father."

"Honey," Leo protested, "how can you saddle a boy with a name like that?"

"So we'll name him Angel Jose and call him Joey. We have to name him after my father."

"How many is that?" asked the doctor, his voice faint.

"Four, Doctor," called one of the pediatric nurses.

"Almost done, Fred," said the assisting obstetrician.

"I don't know about you doctors," said Concepcion, "but I'm all worn out. I think I'd like to wait till tomorrow for the next one." Her voice was notably weaker.

"I'm afraid it doesn't work that way," said the O.B.

"This is fascinating," said M. F. Fong. "Perhaps I should write an article on the psychology of naming."

"The young Casanova bursts passionately from his mother's womb," said McGlenlevie, scribbling in his notebook.

"What's that supposed to mean?" demanded Leo. "And what are you doing here? I recognize your voice."

"He helped us get her to the hospital," said Elena, "but I swear I never invited him to the delivery."

"You're that dirty poet," said Leo.

"I, Detective, am the birth poet for your children. And look at that boy. Small as he is, he has impressive genitalia." A nurse held up the howling baby.

Leo stared at his newest son. "You're right," he agreed. "Chip off the old block."

"That's disgusting," said Sarah. Elena was trying not to giggle.

"The name of an angel, the cock of a stud," said Gus dreamily. "What rhymes with stud? Maybe I shouldn't have elected to use rhyme; it interferes with the creative spontaneity of the event." He beamed at Concepcion. "You should have named him after me."

"No one ever said your equipment was impressive," murmured Sarah.

"You were perfectly happy with it," Gus retorted.

"I'll have to use the forceps this time," said the obstetrician.

"This is it, sweetheart," said Leo. "Number five. It's almost over."

"Oh, all right," grumbled Concepcion, "but frankly, I don't know why I ever wanted to have children." She took a long hit from the inhaler, then gritted her teeth.

"As the last babe greets the world, the mother retreats in postpartum regret," said Gus, scribbling busily in his notebook. "Notice the internal rhyme in that verse."

"Sir," called M. F. Fong, "would you be willing to give me a copy of that poem for my article?" He was putting a new tape in his hand-held microcassette recorder.

"Delighted," said Gus. "I've never been published in a psychological journal."

"Except as a case study," murmured Sarah.

"North American serial rights only," called Gus.

"Done," said Fong.

"Another girl," the pediatrician announced from the end of the table.

"You choose a name," said an exhausted Concepcion to her husband.

"Sarah," he said. "We couldn't have afforded these babies if Sarah hadn't got us the money."

"I'm touched," said Sarah, "but I'm not Catholic. I can't be a godmother."

"My stomach is flat," said Concepcion, laying a hand on the area in question.

"I should think so," said the obstetrician, who was leaning, exhausted, against the nurse. "You had five reasonably good-sized babies. There's not a one under three pounds, unless I miss my guess."

"I hope there aren't any more in there," said Concepcion, "because I absolutely refuse to—"

"It would be a surprise to me if there are," her doctor interrupted. "Just the afterbirth, and you're through."

"How touching is the miracle of birth," said Gus. "I find that I, too, long to be a father. Sarah?" He turned to his ex-wife, the shower cap that covered his beard quivering. "My dear and only spouse, we must remarry."

"In your dreams," said Sarah.

"We must have children of our own."

"A suggestion like that's enough to leapfrog a woman right into menopause," said Sarah and marched out of the room.

Elena stared with consternation at little Sarah, whose head showed the marks of the forceps. Concepcion had dozed off. "I couldn't even get the operator to call you at first," Elena said to Leo. Had he noticed those indentations on the temples of his youngest daughter? "And then it took you forever to get here. I think your wife broke my hand having the first two."

Leo said, "Well, they called me right when the tires blew and the bandits jumped out of the brush."

"Did you arrest any?"

"Damn right," said Leo. "Got all four. I personally dropped two."

"Wow! That's impressive. Usually they get away."

"Put an expectant father on the sting, and the job gets done. Pure desperation."

A parade of babies was being wheeled to the nursery when Elena's pager went off.

"Here comes the afterbirth," said the obstetrician.

Concepcion woke up and mumbled, "I told you I could do it without a cesarean."

"But would you want to try it again?" the doctor retorted. "I sure as hell wouldn't."

"I need to get to a phone," said Elena.

20

Thursday, May 23, 1:45 A.M.

When Elena went out into the waiting room, removing her mask and gown, Concepcion's whole family had gathered on the plastic chairs. Gabriella Forti, Concepcion's mother, grasped Elena's arm and said, "What's happening?"

Elena hugged her. "You've got five healthy grandchildren: Leo, Jr., Gabriella, Elena, Angel Jose, and Sarah."

"Thanks be to the Virgin," cried Gabriella. "She has answered my prayers."

"Are you the happy grandmother, madam?" asked Gus. He, too, was divesting himself of his mask, shower caps, and gown, a nurse following on his heels to snatch the hospital's property from him, then Elena. "Let me be the first to congratulate you," said Gus. "Perhaps you would like to hear the poem I have written for the occasion. It is as yet in rough draft, but—"

"Who are you?" the grandmother demanded, staring at his red beard and flowered shorts.

"Angus McGlenlevie, madam, the birth poet." He whipped his notebook from a pocket and began to read.

Elena hurried to the telephone, staring at the pager number. Once she had called and identified herself, G. Washington said, "You'd better get over here. Looks like the bomber hit again."

"Where?"

131

"Pan-American Stonewashing."

Her heart sank. She'd hoped the bombing at H.H.U. was the end of it, that it was only the university the bomber resented. If he planned to keep attacking large water users, the city had a disaster in progress.

"Melon and Amparan are on their way. Can you—"

"Fifteen minutes," said Elena. She hung up and looked around the waiting room, spotting Sarah, toward whom she hurried. "I've been called out on another bombing. Can I borrow your car? My truck's at your place."

"By all means, do," said McGlenlevie, interrupting his reading. "I shall be delighted to call a cab for Sarah and myself." Gus beamed at his ex-wife. "A man has to look out for the future mother of his children."

"I wouldn't board a train with you if you were sitting twenty cars away and it was the only means to escape nuclear holocaust," said Sarah, handing her car keys to Elena.

"So passionate. So intelligent. So imaginative. Our children will be geniuses," cried Gus.

"I'll get my own cab." Sarah stamped away.

"I do not consider poems about the genitals of my grandson to be acceptable subject matter," said Gabriella Forti. "Especially when read in front of my innocent daughters." She gestured to the four young women in the room, two of whom Elena knew to be married.

Elena decided to escape before the confrontation escalated. As she was leaving, she saw Gabriella jostle her sleeping husband and say, "Angel! Angel, get up and hit this disgusting man, who has insulted the Forti family."

Within the promised fifteen minutes, Elena arrived at Pan-American Stonewashing, a vast, three-story concrete structure whose walls appeared and disappeared in the darkness under cones of security light. In front of the building, the company's water tower had toppled and crashed; that scene—jagged chunks of concrete, twisted steel supports, still pools of dark water—was illuminated by the flashing lights of police cars.

She had to drive into a foot of spillage to park, then wade out to find G, in all probability ruining a good pair of shoes. "How did it happen?" she asked.

"We're not sure," he replied. "One of the watchmen heard the explosion, ran over, and found this. Someone evidently blew one of the legs, so the tower fell and broke. It killed the other night watchman."

"Crushed him?" Elena asked, shifting uncomfortably as the water squished between her toes.

"He may have drowned."

Connie Amparan came up and said, "My guess is the bomber wrapped the tower leg in detonating cord, attached a long fuse, set it, and took off." He noticed Elena and added, "Detonating cord looks like wrapped clothesline. The explosives are in the center."

"How could the night watchmen not notice if the bomber had to climb that leg?" G. asked.

"They don't come on till midnight, and the rounds of the watchman who was killed didn't take him out here until one o'clock."

"Talk about bad luck," said Elena.

"Unless the bomber planned it that way," suggested Perry Melon, joining the group. "I haven't been able to locate Brazlitt. Maybe he's here in town."

"You still think it was an outsider?" asked Connie.

"He could have had local help," Perry admitted.

"Sergeant," said Otis Blevins, "we've found footprints and tire tracks out at the end of the fuse."

"Good man," said G. "Get the crime scene people to make casts and take photos."

"Will do." Blevins jogged off.

Pete Amador returned and told them that patrolmen were canvassing the area to find anyone who had seen or heard anything.

"Was there a warning?" Elena asked.

"There was," said G. grimly. "Same one. Turn off the water or we will."

"Same kind of letters?" Concepcion had said they looked like typefaces from Catholic publications.

"Yes," said Perry Melon. "That same fancy type."

"I've got a line on it," said Elena. "A friend saw the note and said it looked like type from *The Bishop's Newsletter* and the *Holy Name Gazette*."

"You're kidding? Catholic publications?" The ATF agent looked shocked.

She shrugged. "There are Catholics in Water Now."

"Nothing in the computer to show that Brazlitt's Catholic," said Perry Melon. "Or even religious at all."

"If the watchman drowned, it must have been in six inches of water," said G. morosely.

"Will this put the plant out of business?" Elena asked.

"For a while."

She shook her head. "More jobs lost. The way things are going, everyone in the city will end up unemployed."

"First a university, then a stonewashing plant. Peculiar combination," said Connie.

"Brazlitt's peculiar," Perry remarked.

"So are some of the people from Water Now," said Elena, remembering Gladys Furbow, who thought the Second Coming might have occurred at Waco because of the approaching millennium; of Sister Gertrudis Gregory, who couldn't wait to go to jail; of Celestina Ortiz, who didn't hesitate to advocate bombing. "I wonder how many other people got notes they ignored," she murmured.

"Pretty soon we're going to have public hysteria on our hands," said G. glumly.

21
··

Swimming Pool Bandits
Caught in Chaparral Park

Dr. and Mrs. Edgar Bustamante returned from a performance of the Verdi Requiem at the Civic Center to find an entire family bathing and washing clothes in their swimming pool.

The Tarrangos, Mateo, Rosa, and their four children, who live in a waterless *colonia* on the border between Texas and New Mexico, were arrested for trespass and damage to private property. Rosa Tarrango told Officer Brent Love of the Westside Regional Command that she got tired of taking baths from a dishpan and washing clothes in a barrel. "I'll be an old woman before the water gets to us, and I wanted a real bath before then," she said in Spanish.

Los Santos *Times*, Thursday, May 23

"You get any sleep before I called?" G. asked. They were sitting in an all-night diner, sharing the previous evening's *Herald-Post*, since the *Times* wasn't yet on the newspaper racks.

"None," said Elena, but she didn't mind. Sleep meant nightmares, which she'd just as soon skip. The white tile and bright lights of the diner reminded her of the delivery room. "Leo's wife had her five babies last night. I acted as her labor coach until he arrived. Then, by the time they were all born, you called."

"A joyous event," said G. "They must feel blessed by God. Are the little ones all healthy?"

"Seem to be," said Elena.

"Still, perhaps we should say a prayer. Dear Lord . . ." He bowed his head over his eggs, bacon, sausage, waffles, orange juice, and hash browns. A waitress who had been approaching with the coffeepot veered off. *Another prayer*, thought Elena and bowed her own head, but she was looking longingly toward her hot flour tortillas, eggs, and chorizo. She hadn't had anything to eat since the guacamole last night at Sarah's, and the only people she knew who ate during prayers were H.H.U. faculty. "Amen," said G.

"Amen," echoed Elena and dug in. She did love chorizo. Having lost when they flipped a coin to see who got the front page, Elena began to glance through the local news. "Oh, wow!" she exclaimed. "This guy says there won't be any more hookups for the *colonias* until the year 2010, no matter what the water district claims. You think the bomber read that last night and went out with the idea of freeing up some more water?"

"If you're gonna use detonating cord, you have to plan ahead," said G. "It isn't an item you can buy at the 7-Eleven while you're filling up your gas tank."

He had finished his eggs and started on his bacon. *How strange,* Elena thought. *He eats one thing at a time.*

"I suppose you noticed we've got two different M.O.s here," said G. "So we could have two different bombers, even if the notes were the same. Could be all of 'em were different people—the note writer an' the bombers."

The waitress made a second try with the coffeepot and also brought along the early edition of the Los Santos *Times,* for which they thanked her. The *Times* had coverage of the stonewashing debacle. Interviewed on the telephone, the owner said, "Sure, I know who bombed my plant. Water Now. They picketed me last month. I told them I provide jobs in Los Santos, and if they give me more trouble, I'll move my plant to Juarez and get the water out of the same bolson and river."

Elena whistled thoughtfully. "That quote must have gone down well with everyone—like Water Now, and the people who work at Pan-American Stonewashing, and the Chamber of Commerce. It's no wonder the plant got bombed. Did anyone interview the owner?"

"He never even showed up. Said he'd be in this morning at seven-thirty when the plant opened."

"Can they open without water?" Elena wondered. "I don't see how."

"Well, the workers will have to come in to see, so we can question them. The company vice president got the note for us last night. Did you look at it?"

Elena nodded, rolled up a flour tortilla, and took a bite. "Looked like the same typefaces to me."

"And you think they were clipped from some Catholic publication?"

"Possible."

The two of them took their time over breakfast since they had to return to the plant at seven-thirty, which didn't give them leeway to return home for short naps and clean clothes. Elena felt decidedly grubby after slogging through the flooded area around the water tower.

"I'll get hold of the publications my friend mentioned," she offered before returning to the newspaper.

"Look at this," she said five minutes later. "*Colonia* people got arrested for a taking a bath in a backyard swimming pool."

"Next someone will be bombing swimming pools," predicted G. gloomily. He turned a page, and Elena picked up the feature section, where she read the recipe column, which she expected to provide respite from bomb topics. It didn't.

Tips for Cooks:

Casserole dishes require less washing water than pans and serving dishes. Your dishwasher uses twenty-eight gallons per load.

When washing your hands before preparing meals, wet, turn off the faucet, soap, then rinse. You'll save six gallons of water.

Potatoes Au Gratin with Chilies

Peel four Idaho potatoes. Do not leave the faucet on while peeling. The water bomber may have his eye on you. . . .

Elena quickly turned the page and read Ann Landers, but her concentration was interrupted at seven by the sound of her beeper. She used the pay phone in the diner to put in a return call to a number she recognized as Lieutenant Beltran's.

"Where are you?" he demanded.

"I'm having breakfast with G. Washington, the leader of the bomb squad. Someone blew the leg off a water tower last night at—"

"Saw it in the paper," Beltran interrupted. "You've got an eight o'clock appointment at the Police Academy."

"What for?"

"Banuelos decided that you should get tested on the FATS machine. Means Firearms Training System, a new gadget that trains rookies to shoot or not shoot at the right time. They want to see how you react."

"Listen, I'm on a case. I don't have time—"

"Get over there."

"But—"

"That's an order." Beltran hung up.

Scowling, Elena returned to the table to tell G. that she couldn't accompany him to the stonewashing plant.

G. squinted at her thoughtfully when she explained where she was going at the behest of Lieutenant Banuelos of SRT.

"Why are they so worried about you? Shooting a hole in a tent's no big deal. Weird, but no big deal."

"I had a bad case in March," Elena admitted. "They all think I'm stressed out."

"Are you?" asked Washington.

"You got complaints about me, too?"

He shrugged. "You seem all right to me. So get over to Pan-American as soon as you can." He summoned the waitress and paid his own bill while Elena paid hers. Then she returned to the phone to inform Sarah that if she wanted to drive that day, she'd have to use the truck. "There's an extra set of keys in the top dresser drawer in my room," said Elena.

"I've never driven a truck," Sarah protested.

"Well, I guess I could ignore the lieutenant, miss the appointment, and bring your car back."

"I suppose it won't hurt me to go without my car for a day," Sarah admitted grudgingly, "but I told you to get psychiatric help. I saw you go into shock when the *chili verde* blew up last night. Did you have a hallucination?"

"None of your business," said Elena grumpily. "I'll see you at dinner tonight if I get loose."

"You haven't had any sleep. That's not going to improve your condition."

"O.K., Mama, maybe I can catch a catnap between interviews over at Pan-American."

"Maybe M. F. Fong could help you."

"Listen, I'm not telling my problems to a man whose mother named him after Millard Fillmore. Besides, he's still trying to figure out whose lover I am—Concepcion's or Leo's. He probably wouldn't want to talk about flashbacks."

Elena drove from the diner to Scenic Drive, a road that snaked upward, clinging precariously to the eastern slopes of the Franklin Mountains. Partway up, she turned right through stone pillars that supported the entrance arch to the Los Santos Police Academy. Fifty years earlier, the enclave had been a limestone quarry, after that a firing range, and finally the training area for the local police. Cut stone walls towered on all sides; temporary structures and stone buildings with an overlay of stucco were scattered over the floor of the quarry, while a large field was devoted to two shooting ranges. Elena reminded herself that she should make an appointment for her quarterly requalification. What if she missed all the subjects projected by the FATS machine? Would they take her off duty for stress and lousy shooting?

Well, what the hell, she thought, and walked into the academy, where she was taken to a small room with a screen at one end, a few chairs on the side wall, a large console, and a uniformed officer, staring at her mud-spattered clothing. "What happened to you?" he asked.

"A flood," Elena replied sharply.

"In Los Santos? It hasn't rained in months."

She glowered at him.

"O.K.," he said, "here's what you do. Take this gun—it's a regulation 9-millimeter, but it's been fixed up to use a laser. You stand on this black line and watch the screen. As the scenario unfolds, you react. You know, shoot the suspect, if that's the thing to do. Don't, if it isn't. Then FATS will tell you whether you should have shot or not; whether you missed or not; if you did shoot, how long it took and whether the shot was lethal."

"O.K.," said Elena, toeing the black line with the weapon in both hands. "Roll your film. I oughta do just great since I haven't slept in thirty-six hours."

The officer cocked an eyebrow and said, "Tell it to the people who are judging your performance. Ready?"

Elena tightened her hands around the gun. A voice explained that she and her partner were going to arrest two suspects in a bar. They entered and spotted the man and woman on stools, drinking. The partner said, "I'll take the woman; you take the guy." The male suspect evidently pushed Elena aside and ran for the door. The camera panned as if she were chasing him. Outside the bar, he dashed behind a slender tree, paused, and raised a gun. Elena shot him.

"A hit. It was a shooting situation." The officer glanced at the printout and exclaimed, "Wow! You're fast."

She took a deep breath.

"So here's the next one."

Before she was through, she'd shot a guy who'd shot her partner. She'd shot an unarmed suspect who'd got loose while she was handcuffing him. And she'd shot a man who tried to take a picture of an ambassador she was guarding. The photographer was armed only with a camera. She hit them all, killed two, and did it very rapidly. "Quick on the trigger, aren't you?" said the officer running the FATS machine. "I'll send these results in to Banuelos at SRT."

Great, thought Elena; *I shot everyone in sight*. She was surprised she hadn't shot the ambassador or one of her scenario partners or turned the laser on the FATS officer. After taking Sarah's car to headquarters, she picked up a police vehicle. If any more bombs went off, she didn't want Sarah's Mercedes damaged by falling debris. The carpet was already damp from the flood at the stonewashing plant.

22
##

As soon as Elena left the diner, G. Washington began making calls. It took him twenty minutes to find out about the mountain lion attack and death at Elena's house in March. A few more calls, and he knew that her superiors were concerned about her psychological state, although no decision had been made to put her on desk duty or leave. With that information, he drove to Pan-American to meet his federal counterparts. "Is the FBI going to take over as the primary investigator on this one?" G. asked Melon.

"Probably," the agent replied. "Because of the notes, it looks like we've got a serial bomber here."

"So—" Washington tented his fingers and looked from one man to the other. "We may also have a problem with Elena."

"What problem?" Connie demanded. "She's put in twice as many hours on this case as any of us."

Washington told them her story. "When you got bombs involved, you can't afford to be makin' mistakes."

"God, that's awful," said Melon. "A corpse in her bedroom, and a mountain lion waiting for her under the table? No wonder she's stressed." He thought a minute, then added, "Which is not to say I think she should be edged out. She's a good detective, good interrogator, and she knows the case."

143

"Yeah," said Amparan. "We can't afford to lose her."

"She does have a reputation for solving some tough ones," Washington admitted. "Still, can we afford to keep her? She could end up gettin' herself killed—or us."

"We'll look out for her," said Melon. "I'm willing."

"Me, too," said Amparan. "We dump her, we'll screw up her career."

"O.K.," said Washington. "So we're agreed?"

"Agreed. Let's get to work. When will she be here?" Melon asked.

"Whenever she gets through with the FATS machine."

"Video games for cops," said Amparan disgustedly. "And she hasn't had any sleep. Let's hope she doesn't blow it so bad we don't have any say about whether she stays or goes."

Teen Car Washer Attacked

Late Tuesday afternoon Cecilia Bermudez observed the teenage son of a neighbor washing his red Blazer. Water was running from the driveway into the street. Offended by this blatant disregard for the water ordinances, Bermudez snatched the hose from the surprised youth's hand, unscrewed his gas cap, and forced the nozzle in.

When Charlie Sosofaltes realized what was being done to his car, he tried to remove the hose from Bermudez's hand. She then stuffed the nozzle into the pocket of his trousers, returned to her house, and called the water police.

Sosofaltes received a $200 fine. The family threatens to sue Bermudez for damage to the Blazer.

Los Santos *Herald-Post*, Thursday, May 23

Elena and the explosives men talked to employees of the stonewashing plant first, a very unhappy group; they were being sent home. One told Elena in Spanish, "What good's bombing our water tower and putting me out of work? These people want water for the *colonias?* I live in one. Now I won't be able to afford hookup and plumbing if the sewer and water lines ever get to my neighborhood."

"It's a bummer," Elena agreed. "Have you seen any strangers lurking around the plant?" She showed him composites of the two men who'd evidently planted the bombs at H.H.U. She even produced photos of the fraternity boys, but neither he nor any of the workers or executives at the plant recognized anyone or remembered any suspicious lurkers. Even the surviving guard had seen no one.

All day long, as she and the bomb techs were pursuing their futile investigation, they got calls and reports of calls from all over town. When the story of the bombing hit the morning paper, other industrial water users who had received threats, which they had previously ignored, telephoned the department demanding protection. The high-priced lawyers for the fraternity pranksters were calling to demand that their clients be exonerated. Reporters from the local papers and TV stations kept stopping the investigators to ask if they expected more bombings. At the end of the afternoon, when Elena had interviewed her last subject, Perry Melon ducked out of the storeroom he was using and said, "Why don't we have dinner tonight? I want to talk to you about this Brazlitt. See what you think."

She was groggy with fatigue but accepted. She could eat with and talk to Perry Melon and not think about how her quick trigger finger that morning might affect her career. She could delay deciding what to do about the dreams and hallucinations—if anything could be done. Vietnam vets were still suffering flashbacks years after the war. She remembered one diving into a grave during a twenty-one gun salute at the Fort Bliss National Cemetery. Poor guy. She knew just how he felt. An exploding pressure cooker in Sarah's kitchen had set her off. It was ironic that she was working a bomb case during a period in her life when every loud noise catapulted her back in time.

"Sure," she agreed. She took the police car back to head-quarters, checked herself out, drove Sarah's car to campus, and walked into the apartment as Sarah was eating a TV dinner and watching the evening news.

"The whole city's in a panic," said Sarah. "Businesses that have received notes are threatening to close. Their workers are raising Cain about the wages they stand to lose. Home owners are calling to ask if it's safe to water their lawns. I hope you have a lead on who's doing this."

"Not really," said Elena, "but it's certainly brought the water problem to public attention. Up to now, nobody, including me, has done much but grouse about rationing. Anyway, I've got a date. I need to take a shower and get dressed."

"You need sleep."

"Uh-huh," Elena agreed.

"And you're afraid of the nightmares, aren't you?"

"You've got it," Elena replied and headed for the bathroom.

23
..

Golfers Suffer for Their Greens

A coordinated attack was made on golfers at the Ascarate and Painted Dunes courses today by groups carrying signs that said, Water for the Colonias. The sprinkler systems of both public courses are supplied with water from a Los Santos waste water treatment plant.

Evidently under the impression that this water is potable, groups of *colonia* dwellers harassed golfers verbally, by stealing balls and golf carts from the fairways and, in some cases, actually driving golfers off the courses.

Among those arrested for creating a public disturbance and misdemeanor theft was Celestina Ortiz, a member of advocacy group Water Now. Ortiz claimed that Water Now was not behind the golf attack, but police are questioning officers of the organization, which is also suspect in the bombings at Herbert Hobart University and Pan-American Stonewashing.

Los Santos *Herald-Post*, Thursday, May 23.

Melon took Elena to a Westside Italian restaurant, rushing to open doors for her, holding her elbow and her chair as if she were an elderly lady. The worst of it was that she found his courtesy soothing to her frazzled nerves. "Maybe no one's mentioned it," she said defensively, "but I'm a feminist. I can open doors for myself."

"O.K.," said Melon cheerfully. "Are you comfortable? Perhaps you'd rather have a table by the window."

"This is fine," said Elena, glad to have her back to the wall. *Getting paranoid, lady,* she said to herself and opened her menu. The prices made her gasp. "Can you afford this?" she asked. "I didn't know the FBI paid so well."

"I have outside income," said Perry modestly.

Lucky you, she thought, her own fragile finances coming to mind. Among other expenses, she was paying the mortgage on a house she was afraid to live in and a weekly stipend to a boy who watered a yard she wasn't enjoying.

"Order anything you want," said Perry.

"O.K.," said Elena. Light-headed from sleep deprivation, she accepted his generous offer and ordered the most expensive thing on the menu, Tuscan rack of lamb.

Melon didn't blink. He ordered the same thing, plus a bottle of wine. Once he'd handed the wine list back, he said, "I'm really convinced that Lawrence Brazlitt is mixed up in this. The man's been in our files since the sixties." The FBI agent reached down to remove a sheaf of computer printouts from his briefcase. "Offenses, indictments, misdemeanor convictions, aliases. He's always managed to worm out of the felonies, but—"

"Celestina Ortiz just got arrested for harassing golfers," Elena remarked.

"That's hardly the same as bombing something," said Perry, looking a bit offended.

"Does Brazlitt have any connection to the fraternity boys?" she asked, popping a piece of *bruchetta* into her mouth. It tasted great. She decided she could get to like Italian food as much as she did Mexican.

"I think the frat boys were just a fluke." Melon was eating antipasto. "The bomber sent the turn-off-the-water message to the university and then planted the bombs. The frat boys turned on the water, and the bomber got what he wanted without risking another visit to the campus." He gestured with a round of pepperoni on his fork. "Look at it this way. Water Now has been demonstrating and proselytizing for some time, but nothing violent happened until Brazlitt showed up and addressed one of their meetings. He was in Albuquerque on Sunday, the last speaker at the conference, but he wasn't there Friday and Saturday, the pivotal days in the H.H.U. bombing. He left immediately after his speech, saying he was going to Phoenix, but he's disappeared. We can't locate him, and another bomb went off last night. I think he's here in Los Santos."

"Boy, that salad looks terrific," said Elena. "So what's he done in the past?" she asked, trying an endive leaf.

"You name it; he's done it." Perry picked up the printout and let it fold open to the floor. "Last year, he was called the Garbage Can Bandit," said the FBI man, glancing at the last page as he draped Lawrence Brazlitt's FBI file over the empty chair to Elena's left.

"You mean he was blowing up garbage cans?"

"No, he and some locals were stealing containers from people who wouldn't participate in a recycling program in Pennsylvania."

"Wow. Scary stuff," said Elena, and forked up a marinated salad mushroom.

"Before that"—Melon glanced at his printout—"someone was going around sticking potatoes in the exhaust pipes of automotive execs in Detroit, men accused of faking tailpipe exhaust results. Several people were arrested, but there was a shadowy figure called Spud Man that we never caught. We think it was Brazlitt."

Elena sampled the wine and, liking it, took a second swallow. It went to her head immediately, and she giggled.

"I suppose that doesn't sound serious, but he belongs to the Bunyan Society."

"I had a suspect with a bunion," said Elena. "She had a whole closet full of handmade shoes."

Perry gave her a quizzical look.

"I never realized they had a society for people with bunions." She took another sip from her wineglass. "You think the pain makes him dangerous?"

"What are you talking about?"

"Bunions." Elena stuck her foot out and pointed to the joint in question. A waiter, trying to avoid tripping over her foot, staggered and dropped salad on a woman at the next table.

"Paul Bunyan," said Perry. "It's an ecological group."

"Oh." Elena leaned across the aisle to brush wet radicchio off the woman's dress. "Want my napkin?" she asked. "I've got some water if you want to wipe out the stain." She reached for her water glass.

"Don't touch me," the woman snapped.

"Some people are so grouchy." Elena plopped the generously offered water and napkin down on the table and held her goblet out for a refill. "So what's the big deal about the Bunyan Society?"

"Tree spiking," said Perry.

The waiter, having finished his apologies to the woman with salad stains, hurried to relieve Perry of the wine bottle and pour for Elena.

"It's very dangerous business." Perry's voice was solemn. "Two years ago in the Northwest, he was registered in a motel as Paul Bunyan. The society was trying to stop a lumber company from clear-cutting an old-growth forest. Two months later, when the environmentalists' injunction failed and the loggers went in, the injuries started. Their saws ran into spikes."

"Uh-huh." Feeling sorry for the endangered lumberjacks, Elena sampled her lamb. Delicious.

"And there was the power plant in the Midwest," said Melon, consulting his list again. "They were accused of killing fish by dumping hot water into a river. One Harry Trout, whom we think was Brazlitt, registered at a local motel. The next night, three skunks were released into the plant. It took the company a week to catch the skunks and get back on-line. Workers were vomiting because of the stench."

"None of this has anything to do with bombing," she said.

"Oh, we're sure he's been connected with bombings— bombings of draft boards and army recruiting offices in the sixties and seventies, bombing of California growers who were using dubious insecticides on their broccoli. There was an incident right here in Texas where an animal rights group he belonged to let loose a pack of rabid dogs."

"You're kidding," said Elena. She knew about that one. "You think Brazlitt was in on that?"

"We do. He comes to town; there's trouble. The Japanese Consulate in L.A. received a package bomb, which we managed to defuse before it did any damage. The newspapers got a call saying the bomb was a protest against Japanese whaling activities. And a chicken plant selling salmonella-infected poultry blew up in South Carolina."

"I'll bet the feathers flew there," said Elena, savoring a mouthful of crispy vegetables. She had thought they were raw; Perry corrected her, calling them *al dente*.

He gave her a look that said he disapproved of her cavalier attitude toward chicken slaughter. "They killed a hundred thousand chickens—no people, fortunately. The man's record goes all the way back to Berkeley."

"Ah, Berkeley," said Elena. She'd just scooped up the last of her potato puree, having finished the lamb. "What happened at Berkeley?"

"He was known as Lightbulb Larry. He went around unscrewing lightbulbs in university offices and—"

"—sticking chewed gum in the sockets so they couldn't be used again. I knew that name rang a bell," said Elena, putting down her fork just as the waiter arrived to remove their dinner plates and serve thin pieces of dark chocolate torte in pools of raspberry sauce. "I'll tell you about him as soon as I finish my dessert."

"Come on," said Elena when Melon had paid the bill. "I don't know if Lawrence Brazlitt is our bomber, but I do know someone who knows him."

"Who?" asked Perry, following her out to the car.

"My mom. I'll call her from the apartment."

"Your *mother?*"

"Oh yeah. My mother was a big activist at Berkeley for about a year. Then it got too violent, and she moved to a commune in New Mexico where she met my pop, got married, and turned into a New Age weaver."

"New Age?" echoed Perry as he started the car.

"Right. She sees auras. Believes in the power of crystals. She even wants to hire a witch to clear the evil spirits out of my house." *Which might not be a bad idea,* Elena thought. *Even better if the witch can clear the spirits out of my head.*

"I see." Perry looked nonplussed.

Perry and Sarah sat on the tobacco silk chairs since the beige sofa was gone after its brush with incipient childbirth. Sarah had sent it off to an upholstery specialist the next morning. Paul Zifkovitz, Sarah's lover, was stretched out on the Berber carpet, thinking about his next masterpiece, a twelve-by-six-foot canvas to be painted with enamels. Elena was in the kitchen calling her mother.

"I'm so glad you phoned," said Harmony before Elena could get to her subject. "Johnny and Bets are turning into soulless money grubbers."

"I didn't know the tourist-kitsch business was that lucrative," said Elena. "What are they producing now?"

"They're taking advantage of our tragic controversy with the Mexican spotted owl fanatics. Bets is designing little clay spotted owls weeping beside trees and giant papier-mâché spotted owls with huge wingspreads and little Hispanic figures in their claws. And Johnny is selling them. I can't believe they'd do anything so crass."

"I'll bet the tourists love it," said Elena.

"Indeed. But our people will freeze next winter if we don't keep our wood-gathering privileges. Do you realize that the Forest Service spent eight years and one point five million dollars trying to *find* spotted owls? They could have used that money to help the poor in the Sangre de Cristos."

"Mom, I can't help but think that if you hadn't married Pop, you might be on the side of the spotted owls."

"I would not!"

"Which brings me to the reason I called. Do you remember a guy at Berkeley named Lightbulb Larry?"

"Of course."

"Do you keep in touch with him?"

"As a matter of fact, we burned him in effigy last November. He belongs to one of the forest conservation groups."

"So I guess you don't think much of him."

"I didn't say that. He just happens to be on the wrong side of the controversy in this case."

"Well, let me ask you this: Was he into bombing when you knew him?"

"Certainly not. Larry was actually a very sweet graduate student in Anglo-Saxon literature. He recited pages and pages of *Beowulf* one night when we were camped out in a dean's office. In the original Anglo-Saxon. No one understood a word. The poor man might bore you to death, but he was an innovative protester, and he never caused injury to anyone."

"Are you sure, Mom? Maybe he's changed over the years. After all, depriving poor people of heat in the winter—"

"He never thought of it that way until we had coffee after the burning, and he does believe that animals have the same rights to the planet that people do. Actually, his position has its merits, but—"

"O.K., Mom. Thanks for the information."

"You will get hold of your brother and tell him to stop producing those disgusting owls?"

"Sure, Mom, I'll give him a call as soon as I'm through with this case."

"And get hold of that *curandera* , Elena. You'll never be able to live in your house until it's cleansed."

Back in the living room, Elena told Melon that her mother vouched for the nonviolent nature of Lightbulb Larry.

"Your mother's naive," said Perry. "This Brazlitt is dangerous."

"Could you give me a call the next time there's a bombing?" asked Zifkovitz. "I'd like to do a painting called *Explosion*."

"Explosions aren't particularly geometric," said Sarah, replenishing their brandy snifters.

"No," Elena agreed. She remembered the flash of fire, the shredded greenery, the jagged pieces of the water tower. Where would the bomber strike next?

24
..

Friday, May 24, 9:45 A.M.

Security Businesses Flourish

Since the bombing of Pan-American Stonewashing, security consciousness among high water usage businesses in Los Santos is snowballing. The local smelter has hired ten new guards. Smelter President Grant Astoreth said, "A bombing here would be a disaster, not only in financial losses but in lives."

Refineries on the east side of the mountain are following suit, as are garment washing facilities. "Can you imagine what a bomb would do in a refinery?" asked petroleum engineer Vance Brim. Fire Department Captain Lorca-Mendez agreed. "We'd never get the damn thing put out."

Security companies, far from being dismayed by the danger, are hiring and training new guards as demand increases. "This looks like our most profitable year yet," said Corben Mitzer, president of Border-Best Security. "And believe me, the bomber won't be getting to any of our customers. We're high-tech and tough as nails."

Los Santos *Times*, May 24

Elena struggled out of the nightmare, sick with fear, the cat's eyes still blazing in the dark, the feral odor, the screaming snarl, the kick of the gun in her hand, and worse, what hadn't been part of the real event, the terrified expectation of discovering the gnawed, bloody corpse in the bedroom. With the knell of that horrible death ringing in her ears, Elena forced herself up on one elbow and drank in the belated realization that she was lying in the guest bed at Sarah's.

She was not at home. And the ringing wasn't the call of a dead man but the summons of a telephone. She stumbled out of bed to the computer desk, realizing that she'd slept all night after Perry left, no dreams that she could remember until just now. Maybe she was getting better.

"Jarvis," she said into the receiver.

"It's G. Sorry to wake you."

"'S O.K.," she mumbled.

"I know you need the sleep, but we've heard from the bomber."

Elena rubbed her eyes. "What'd he say?"

"He's planted a big one in the water utilities offices. Says he'll blow up the building unless they reverse their decision to delay laying pipes to outlying *colonias*."

Elena shook her head, trying to clear out the cobwebs. "So what do we do now?"

"He promised to call again in an hour for an answer, but there's nothing the utility can do unless they lie to him. They don't have the money to continue since the federal government's been cutting back on the grants. There's a bond issue coming up in June that will help some. The state will kick in fifty-two million if the Lower Valley Water District puts up fourteen, but the bond issue's got to pass. In the meantime *we've* got an hour. We're clearing the building; we're evacuating everything around the office, including the mall."

"Oh, God, that's right. The office is on Hawkins."

"We've called for a dog."

"A dog?"

"An explosives sniffer."

"Oh, right. Where do you want me?"

"The command post. It's across the street from the utility building—in an insurance office. Doesn't have as many windows as most of the places around here. If you're up to it—"

"What does that mean?"

"I just thought you're probably pretty tired."

"Aren't you?"

"Yeah," said Washington.

"I'll come straight over. Half an hour, tops," she said, and hung up.

As she drove to the crisis scene, Elena heard on the radio that industrial water users were hiring guards. She shook her head. Private citizens were getting crazy; business executives were panicking. And she couldn't blame them.

The freeway was crowded with streams of traffic escaping on I-10 West from the mall and other buildings in the area. The incoming lanes carried emergency vehicles. When Elena walked into the command post, having taken a parking place behind the protecting bulk of the insurance building, she found a mob of law enforcement officers and public officials, and one ecstatically happy police dog, rolling around on the floor, slobbering over a ball. "That's not the bomb, is it?" she asked, only half joking.

"Nah," said the trainer. "That's Ralph's reward for finding the bomb."

Ralph? Wasn't that a pretty prosaic name for a dog who spent his time sniffing around for explosives? "That's all he gets?" Elena asked. "A ball?"

"Hey, it's the only time we let him play," said the officer, scratching behind the ears of the happy dog. The ball squirted out of Ralph's mouth and hit the toe of Elena's right boot. Ralph bounded after it, jostling her in his eagerness. She jostled back.

"Careful," warned the trainer. "Ralph's worth about sixteen

thousand. The department would rather lose me or you than him. He can sniff out eleven kinds of explosives."

Ralph snapped at the ball, and Elena jerked away, then found herself hugged by Connie Amparan. "Welcome to the party," he said. "These guys are about to take the bomb out of the water utilities office."

"Isn't that dangerous?" she asked G.

He gave her a wry look. "It would be more dangerous to leave it until the hour's up, when we gotta tell the bomber he's not gonna get what he wants. O.K., men," he said to Pete Amador, Otis Blevins, and another bomb tech she hadn't met, "let's have a quick prayer here and get on with it." They all bowed their heads. "Oh Lord, if it be thy will, make it a dud," said G. "Amen." Then the four of them walked across the street, Elena watching. Beside her, Ralph, who was sensitive to heat, was noisily lapping up Blue Light, a canine version of Gatorade.

"What are the chances the bomb will blow?" she asked Connie, who still had a friendly arm on her shoulder. To her surprise, Perry Melon came over and squeezed her hand. And neither agent was coming on to her. G. had been right. Once you were in with the explosives guys, they all treated you like family.

"Well, it's a pipe bomb, but we're not sure what's inside. And unless the bomber's lying, it's not going off before"— Connie glanced at his watch—"at least twenty minutes. He promised to call back then. Since he says he can blow it without being here, it's either radio triggered, in which case, he may not be able to get near enough to set it off, or it's on a timer, in which case maybe we can get it to a disposal site and blow it ourselves. City Council had a conference call meeting and said absolutely no blowing it in place. They don't want to lose the building."

"But they don't mind losing a few policemen?" Elena asked.

"That's not going to happen," said Perry. "G. will know more when he's had a chance to X-ray it."

"Unfortunately," said Connie, "he won't be able to tell us because we're not using radios."

"You mean we could set it off with police radios?" asked Elena anxiously.

"Yeah, we don't know what channel the bomber's using, if that's what he's done. Even some trucker could set it off, but we're doing what we can to prevent any accidents," Melon assured her.

"Once we get it in the unit"—He waved toward the large, cone-shaped vessel on the bomb squad trailer—"we'll have it contained." He paused, then added, "Unless it's bigger than we think. But the bomber hasn't concocted anything that big yet."

"I wonder how mad he is at the water utility," she murmured. "And why. They're at least trying to solve the problem instead of adding to it. Maybe it isn't even a real bomb. Or maybe he screwed up. Not all of them went off on campus."

"All the ones the water got to did," said Perry, sounding gloomy.

Connie frowned at him. "Let's not take that attitude, man," he said.

"You're right," Melon agreed. "We couldn't have a better tech than G. on this. He's had years of experience with explosives."

Elena stared at the vessel across the street, which was supposed to protect G. and his men from injury while transporting the bomb. "That thing's open on top."

"Right. Top and bottom," said Connie. "It directs the force up and down—in other words, away from people."

"They're coming out," said Melon. The four LSPD bomb techs were carrying something. Very carefully. However, G. took the trouble to give a thumbs-up sign with his free arm.

Elena watched as they transferred the pipe into the container. "There's a net in there," Connie explained. "And the roads from here to the site are pretty good, so it ought to go O.K." Two members of the squad climbed into the cab of the truck and drove slowly out of the parking lot. Once they turned onto Hawkins, a fire engine and EMS vehicles trailing them at a distance, the truck and trailer headed east behind a car that held G. and Otis.

"So far, so good," said Perry.

"Are we set up to trace the call from the bomber?" Elena asked.

"Oh, yeah. And we've got a tape of his first call and the number of the phone in the mall he used," Connie told her.

"It must be awful riding in the cab of that truck," said Elena as she watched the slow progress of the bomb squad vehicle. "If it were me, I think I'd want to drive as fast as I could."

"No, you wouldn't. Some bombs can be set off by jostling," Connie explained.

Perry remarked optimistically, "When we catch him, the tape of his voice will help us convict. And since we've cleared the area and we're not allowing the media in, he'll have no way to know we've found the bomb."

"How far do they have to go?" Elena asked.

"Three miles on back roads," said Perry. "It'll all be over in an hour."

Even as he spoke, the cracking sound of an explosion stunned them all. Because Connie's reflexes were even faster than her startle response, he pulled her to the floor, but not before she saw flame erupting from the top and bottom of the bomb container. When they scrambled up, shaking glass from their clothing, and peered through the shattered window of the insurance company/command post, they saw that the trailer, pulled by the bomb squad truck, had reached the I-10 underpass. As if in slow motion, the elevated west lane of the interstate sagged, dropping chunks of concrete onto the roadway. Crooked steel support bars sprouted like spider legs from the jagged edges of the overpass. Elena gasped, and Connie tightened his grip on her arm.

"If the truck was out from under the overpass," said Melon, "they'll be O.K."

"You want to go with us?" Connie asked Elena.

"Yes," she replied, and the three of them left their shelter and piled into Perry's FBI car. Once the last piece of the interstate had fallen, only the sound of sirens broke the ominous stillness of the evacuated area.

"It may end up costing more to repair the interstate than if we'd blown it in the water utilities office," said Connie angrily.

Elena and the feds had to drive to the airport exit and circle back to get to the men on the other side of the Hawkins exit. There they found that the bomb squad truck was safe. As the eastbound lanes remained standing, the two men in the truck had escaped injury, while the emergency vehicles following were far enough back to sustain only minor damage from falling debris. However, there was a deep crater in the road and the prospect of a long repair period before the Hawkins section of the highway could reopen.

"Black powder," guessed Connie Amparan.

"Right," said G., who had returned immediately to check on the well-being of his men. "Friction caused the explosion." Then he added bitterly, "If the city had come up with the hundred thou for a total containment unit, they'd still have the Hawkins overpass."

"The question is: How did the s.o.b. deliver it without blowing his own head off?" Connie wondered.

"An even bigger question," said Melon. "What are we dealing with here? We've had three bombings using four different explosives, different triggering devices, different targets."

"Makes you wonder if we've got some amateur who's working his way through the *Anarchist Cookbook*," said G.

"Or a Web page," said Connie. "Maybe we'd better check what's been posted the last few weeks. See if he got the recipes there."

"More likely it's Brazlitt, playing games with us," said Melon.

Elena was listening to the speculation and watching the crews arrive when her pager went off. She used Perry's cell phone to return the call. "It's Manny," said her sergeant. "We've had another bomb."

"I know. I'm here."

"In Las Pampas?"

"At the Hawkins exit."

"Wrong bomb. Someone's house in the *colonias* just exploded. Deputies on the scene say the people there think it's retaliation for the other bombings."

"Why would—"

"There were letters in the paper this morning, people saying *colonia* residents knew there was no water when they bought those lots, so they shouldn't be making trouble. We've got a war of the haves and have-nots heating up."

Elena groaned. "It's pretty scary here, too. Half the overpass is gone."

"That bad? Well, unless you can rebuild it, you better go find out what happened out there near San Eli."

After a quick conference among the bomb techs, Connie went with her and determined, with the help of fire marshals, that the explosion in Las Pampas had been caused by a propane leak, not a bomb. The neighbors, however, as they filtered back from jobs and job hunting, cried cover-up, said they were being targeted by the power structure, who wanted to scare them into giving up their right to sanitary living conditions.

Celestina Ortiz had heard and come over from El Campestre, fresh from her triumph on the golf courses. If the jail weren't full, she might have been incarcerated for her golf course activities, but misdemeanor offenders were bonding out on personal recognizance. As it was, the bricklayer-cum-water activist was among those who, in Elena's opinion, were setting themselves up for charges of inciting to riot.

25

Loan Applicant Accuses Banker
of Retaliation

Harold Carney, owner of Harold's Tejano Ice Cream Parlor on Alameda, reports that he has filed a complaint with the Federal Reserve alleging that Rio Bravo National Bank loan officer Mel Obregon denied him a home improvement loan because Carney turned him in for watering his backyard on a Saturday. Obregon has an odd-numbered address, which only allows him to water on Wednesday, Friday and Sunday. He received a $50 fine.

In a telephone interview, Obregon said, "I didn't even know who turned me in until I heard him on TV."

Carney told the *Herald-Post* that if Obregon got bombed for his water sins, Carney's house, which is next door, could be damaged as well. "I got a family to think of," said Carney.

Los Santos *Herald-Post*, Friday, May 24

Sarah flicked off the news. "I can't believe this is happening. Terrorists in Los Santos?"

"Out in the real world people are unhappy, scared, and crazy," said Elena, thinking about the ice cream guy and the loan officer, about whom she'd read in the evening paper. She was sitting in one of the silk chairs, wearing the pueblo print pajamas her medical school sister had sent as a birthday present, and dreading the thought of going to bed, even though she could hardly keep her eyes open. "This afternoon in Las Pampas—that's near San Elizario—there was a propane explosion. All the residents assumed it was a bomb, retaliation because they'd been demanding water service."

"I never understood why anyone would use propane. It's so dangerous."

"They don't have natural gas out there," said Elena dryly. "You H.H.U. people don't know what's going on in the rest of the city. How many of your fellow professors have asked why anyone would want to bomb the campus?"

"A lot," Sarah admitted. "It was quite a shock to the faculty."

"It was no surprise to me, Sarah. The first time I ever came here, I thought how unfair it was that you should have all that shrubbery and water anytime you wanted, and I had to get up at sunrise if I wanted to keep my trees alive." Her beeper went off.

"You wear that with your pajamas?" Sarah asked.

Nodding, Elena looked at the tiny screen and punched in the number on Sarah's living room telephone.

"It's G.," the bomb squad leader said when she identified herself. "I just saw Brazlitt. You know? Perry's favorite suspect? He was going down the airport escalator with some old lady who uses a cane."

"Gladys Furbow," Elena guessed. "Did you stop him?"

"Couldn't," said G. "I'm confiscating a piece of luggage with a hand grenade in it, but I did call airport security. The girl at the parking lot ticket booth spotted them. She gave us a description of their car. A metallic green late-model Buick, license plate 815-YVV. She overheard the old lady saying she'd take him to La Hacienda for dinner. Patrol cars are heading in that direction. You better get over there."

"What about you?"

"I'll come when I can."

"Surely, you're not going out again?" Sarah asked as Elena hung up.

Elena shrugged. "It's better than nightmares."

"Do you wear that beard because you have a weak chin?" Gladys Furbow asked Lawrence Brazlitt. They were hurtling around a curve on Paisano Drive in her green Buick.

"I do not," he replied resentfully. "I've been told by any number of people that the beard complements my character."

"You shouldn't have come back to Los Santos." She turned her lights down when a car came toward her in the opposite lane.

"I wouldn't have missed this visit for the world," said Brazlitt. "Do you know who's setting off the bombs?"

"The authorities consider Water Now their best suspects. We'll probably end up in jail, you among us." Mrs. Furbow turned her high beams back on. "Of course, they didn't try to arrest anyone for the eight injuries at the university or the death at the stonewashing plant," she said sardonically, "but knocking down a part of the freeway—the city's going to take a dim view of that. The federal government, too, since they paid for it."

"Someone's doing good work," said Brazlitt cheerfully.

"Oh? Was it you?" she asked. Before he could reply, her front left tire hit a rock, and the car slewed wildly.

"Steer into the skid," shouted Brazlitt. The car came to a rough stop in the brush at the side of the road and was surrounded immediately by ragged men, rising up like ghosts in the night.

"Bandits," said Mrs. Furbow in disgust.

"*What?*" exclaimed Brazlitt.

Mrs. Furbow's door was wrenched open, but she had already reached into the backseat for her cane. The bandit grinned at her and said, "Gimme *su dinero, abuela.*"

"I'll grandmother you," she snapped and shoved the cane into his stomach.

Brazlitt was dragged out of the car on the other side, crying, "*Compadres, compadres,* I am a champion of the underprivileged."

"*Que dice?*" one bandit asked the other.

"*No se,*" said his colleague and ripped Brazlitt's pocket while taking his wallet.

"Keys, keys," shouted a thickset, bearded fellow who hauled his fallen comrade aside and addressed Gladys.

"In your dreams," the old lady replied. She hurled the keys into the brush and set off the auto-theft siren, then whacked the surprised leader on the ear.

"*Bruja!*" he screamed.

"Police! Hands in back of your heads. Hit the dirt, or I'll shoot." Elena jumped out of her truck, shouting in Spanish, carrying the shotgun she kept in the rack. The bandit who had just relieved Brazlitt of a gold necklace whirled on her with his knife in hand. Elena dropped him with the shotgun barrel, mindful that the FATS test had shown her to be trigger-happy. Gladys Furbow took the opportunity to slam her door in the face of the leader, who looked over his shoulder toward Mexico, but Elena had circled the car. He put his hands up as two patrol cars pulled in ahead of the Buick and cut off any retreat.

"This is a disgraceful way to treat visitors," said Brazlitt. "What's the border patrol for if not to keep such things from happening?"

"Lawrence Brazlitt?" Elena asked.

He nodded.

"We want to talk to you at headquarters."

"I told you we were all going to be arrested for that I-10 bombing," said Mrs. Furbow. "Highways are sacred in Texas."

26
..

G. met them at headquarters. "Sorry, I didn't make it to Paisano," he said to Elena as they watched the parade of prisoners being led to interrogation rooms.

"No problema," she replied exuberantly. "How'd the grenade caper go?"

"We arrested the couple carrying it, hauled the suitcase off, and blew it up. They're claiming it was a pineapple sculpture they bought in Hawaii. And they're threatening to sue."

Elena laughed. "Well, we caught five Mexican carjackers, Gladys Furbow, and Lawrence Brazlitt. Boy, am I wired."

"Did you shoot anyone?" he asked, frowning.

"No," said Elena, "and since you mention it, I've got a call to make." She whirled and dashed toward her cubicle. "Back in a minute."

"Where's she going?" asked Connie, who had just come in.

"No idea," said G. "I asked if she'd shot any of the seven prisoners she took, she said no, and disappeared."

"Oh, boy, I wonder what happened," said the ATF agent, looking worried.

Elena was using the telephone in her cubicle, oblivious to time and discretion. "Lieutenant Banuelos, this is Elena Jarvis. Remember? Your team thinks I'm too quick on the trigger?

167

Well, I took seven prisoners tonight, five of them armed with knives, and I didn't shoot anyone."

"And you called me at midnight on a Friday to tell me that?" rumbled Banuelos.

"Absolutely. I didn't want you to put too much faith in my FATS score. I hadn't had any sleep."

"Have you had any since then?" the head of the Shooting Review Team asked dryly.

Elena ignored the question. Her sleeping habits were none of his business. If she wanted to stay up for weeks on end, she damn well would. "Just so you won't think I'm misleading you, I did hit one of them with the barrel of my shotgun, but I didn't shoot him. The other injured guy got it in the belly with Gladys Furbow's cane. You want to hear about—"

"I'll wait for the written report," he interrupted. "Consider yourself lucky the chief hasn't instituted reviews of nightsticking, choke holds, and punching yet. A shotgun barrel might fall in that category." Elena stared at the phone, dumbfounded. "Thanks for calling, Detective," he was saying when she put the receiver to her ear again. Then he hung up. No goodbye. And after she'd taken the trouble to call. Elena shrugged and sprinted toward the interrogation rooms, only to discover that the others had decided she should question the border bandits.

"Who cares about them," she complained. "Let the border patrol handle it."

"They assaulted Brazlitt," said Perry Melon reasonably, "and they don't speak English."

"I'll bet Connie speaks Spanish, don't you?" She glared at Connie. "I know what this is. Sexual discrimination. You guys are trying to dump me off the serial bomber case. You think it's Brazlitt, so it's a big national deal, so a local detective who doesn't know beans about bombs—"

"I'll join you on the carjacking interrogation," said Perry. "It's federal."

"You're the principal investigating agency on the bombings," G. objected.

"Hey, isn't anyone going to talk to us?" asked Brazlitt,

sticking his head out of an interrogation room. "I'm going to lose my reservation at the Camino Real if I don't claim it by midnight."

"The county's got a bed with your name on it," said Perry.

"Young man, I don't suppose you're going to arrest an old lady who's just been victimized by foreign ruffians," said Gladys Furbow, coming into the hall as well. "I'd like to give my statement, sign my complaint, and go home. I retire at midnight and rise at eight, and I don't believe in erratic sleeping hours."

"You're here about the bombings, ma'am," said G. politely, "you and Mr. Brazlitt."

"What about those men with knives? What about my tires? Those are almost new Michelins, and—"

"Would you two just step back inside the interrogation rooms? Otherwise, we'll have to cuff you."

"This is an outrage," said Gladys Furbow.

"Those of us who have made it our mission to protect the world from the robbers of resources and polluters of paradise have to expect persecution from a corrupt, money-grubbing power structure," said Brazlitt, looking pleased with himself.

"Money-grubbing!" exclaimed Elena. "On what I make, I'm lucky to afford a new tree now and then."

"In a desert ecology, trees are a selfish indulgence," said Brazlitt.

"Idiot," snarled Elena. Perry grabbed her arm and pulled her down the hall. "I'm telling my mother what a stupe you've turned into," she yelled at Brazlitt. "In fact, she already knows. She burned you in effigy last fall, you heartless exploiter of poor Hispanics."

"I don't know what you're talking about," Brazlitt shouted back, but by that time Perry had yanked Elena into the room where the Mexican bandits were being kept. "Are you O.K.?" he asked, a worried frown running his forehead freckles together.

"Why wouldn't I be? All right, you scumbags," she said to the bandits, who cowered away when they saw that the shotgun-wielding *gringa* was in their midst. "First, we want your names," she snarled in Spanish.

The leader insisted that they had simply been crossing the road, hoping to get to the hiring area for migrant workers, when an old lady stopped her car and attacked one of them with her cane, after which the *policia gringa* had disabled one of their number with a large gun.

"What garbage!" said Elena and translated for Perry, whose Spanish was good enough to pass an FBI test but not good enough for communication with those whose Spanish caused disdain among Spanish-speakers all over the world.

"You always carry knives when you're looking for illegal jobs? You usually throw rocks in the road to stop cars so you can get across?" she asked curtly.

The leader insisted that they hadn't put any rocks on the road and that the knives were for peeling fruit and paring fingernails. Then he said he wouldn't speak to anyone except a sane INS officer, no more *mujeres locas*.

"He won't talk," Elena told Perry. "Let's get back to the bombers." Since Perry's Spanish was inadequate to further interaction without her cooperation, he gave up. Elena arranged to have the prisoners transported to the county jail.

When she and Perry checked the interrogation rooms where the Water Now people were supposed to be, Gladys Furbow had gone home, her lawyer having arrived and whisked her away with a 'charge her or let her go' instruction. Mrs. Furbow had refused to say a word about her whereabouts before and after the bombings. Brazlitt, on the other hand, wouldn't shut up, Connie complained as he pulled out a chair for Elena at the table where he and G. were sitting with the suspect.

"I can get her chair," snapped Melon.

Connie glanced at him, surprised.

"I can get my own chair," said Elena. "Well, the bandits are headed for jail. They claim they were innocently on their way to solicit farm work—at midnight— when an old lady stopped her car and attacked them."

"That's a lie," cried Brazlitt. "We were on our way to dinner on the patio at La Hacienda, an innocent enough destination I would have thought. By the way, I haven't had dinner. The dinner hour on airlines lasts about fifteen minutes these days, and no airplanes fly then." They all stared at him. "Don't you feed your prisoners?" he demanded. "I'll have to contact Amnesty International, of which I am a member, to file a complaint about the Los Santos PD."

"Gosh," said Elena sarcastically, "we can't have that." She fished in her purse and tossed him a baggie of beef jerky she kept for emergencies.

"What is it?" he asked.

"Dried tidbits of Mexican spotted owl," Elena replied.

She grinned because both Lightbulb Larry and Perry Melon obviously believed her. Larry drew back in horror and exclaimed, "That's disgusting!"

"No respect for Native American customs," she replied. "The pueblo Indians of New Mexico and Arizona have been eating spotted owl for centuries. It's called sacred wise meat. That's why there are so few owls left. It doesn't have anything to do with wood gathering in the national forest by poor Hispanics."

Brazlitt began to look worried. "Who's your mother?" he asked suspiciously.

"Harmony Waite Portillo," said Elena. "Remember her? She said if you didn't quit hassling the locals in the Sangre de Cristos, she'd have a witch put a curse on you."

"I don't believe in curses," said Brazlitt uneasily. "Is that true about the Indians eating owl meat? That's against the law. The Mexican spotted owl is endangered."

"You can't mess with tribal religion," said Elena jauntily. This was really fun. She felt downright giddy.

"The Indians *are* preservers of the land," Brazlitt admitted.

"Right. Especially the Apaches, who want to put a nuclear waste dump on the Mescalero Reservation."

"They've been poisoned by the greed of white capitalism," said Brazlitt defensively.

"Could we get back to the bombings?" G. suggested.

"I had nothing to do with them," said Brazlitt.

"So where were you?" Connie asked, evidently not for the first time. "And don't give us any more speeches."

"I don't have to tell you a thing," said Brazlitt. "I'm not guilty of anything, and my movements are my own business. I know you feds. Anyone with a cause has been suspect since the days of J. Edgar Hoover."

"If you don't want the owl jerky, I'll eat it," said Elena. "I'm hungry, but I want it noted that we offered you sustenance."

"Isn't that a federal crime?" he asked Perry.

"Bombing sure is," said the FBI agent. "As for the jerky, I wouldn't think there'd be that much meat on an owl."

"Spoilsport," said Elena, tearing off a piece of the leathery treat with her front teeth. "Let's take a picture of him and show it to everyone who saw the original bombers. And—lemme think—we should check the tires on Mrs. Furbow's car to see if they match the tracks at the water tower." She then ducked under the table and popped back up, saying, "Look at the bottoms of his sneakers. Right size, right pattern. I'll bet he's a match for the footprints."

"Good thinking for someone who looks as if she hasn't slept in weeks," said G.

"I protest," Brazlitt cried. "And I refuse to let my picture be taken or my shoes examined without a lawyer." He had turned pale as soon as Elena mentioned his shoes.

"I think Elena looks wonderful," said Connie, smiling at her.

"I think she's—exotic," said Perry.

"What's this exotic business?" she demanded. "You've said that twice now. Is it because I'm descended from savage Spanish Conquistadors and gentle pueblo potters, not to mention one Anglo hippie?"

"It was a compliment," said Perry defensively.

"Well, what I am is sleepy," said Elena. "Maybe someone else could get the warrant for his shoes and whatnot. Do we need a warrant?" She stifled an enormous yawn.

"Hello? Is anyone listening? I want a lawyer," said Brazlitt.

27

Teen Car-Washer Charged
with Malicious Mischief

Carlos "Charlie" Sosofaltes, 18, was charged last night with malicious mischief after allegedly tagging the house of Cecilia Bermudez on the 200 block of Paloma Way. The word *Snitch* was written twenty times across walls and windows.

Sosofaltes said, "She turned me in to the water cops. And she ruined my car. I spent two weeks painting racing stripes on it, and now it won't run." Other teens, not apprehended as yet, are believed to have participated in the tagging of the Bermudez house.

Los Santos *Herald-Post*, Friday, May 24

Elena sat at Sarah's dining room table reading last night's *Herald-Post* and feeling wan. By the time she'd got home from the fruitless interview with Lawrence Brazlitt, she'd been so tired she'd fallen into bed without giving a thought to the nightmares that awaited her. And they did. The mountain lion awakened her at 3:35, she in a cold sweat, Sarah at the foot of her bed, saying, "Have you been to a doctor yet?" Elena hadn't and put the pillow over her face to avoid any friendly nagging while she was still shaking with horror and fright.

"Croissant?" said Sarah, pulling her back to the present. "Fresh out of the microwave."

Sarah bought supplies of tasty pastries from Vie de France, a local bakery and deli, froze them, and then ruined them in the microwave. Elena took a chocolate croissant, poured a cup of coffee, and picked up the front page of the *Times*, which said:

Spotted Owl Discovered in Sangre de Cristos

She read the story as she drank coffee and ate her soggy croissant. It was amazing that Sarah, who was such a persnickety gourmet in a restaurant, didn't care what she ate at home. The story was bad news for Elena's mother. Forest conservationists had triumphantly announced the discovery of several Mexican spotted owls in the Carson and Santa Fe National Forests. The conservationists had claimed that fallen wood, which was collected by locals, sheltered the rodents that fed the owls; Harmony, Elena's mother, said residents of the Sangre de Cristos couldn't destroy the habitat of an owl who wasn't there. Now, suddenly, the wretched owls had appeared.

Then Elena remembered her owl jerky spoof. Brazlitt would probably have her charged with eating an endangered species. Had she finished the jerky? Let's hope not. She might need some to prove that it hadn't come from an owl, just a deceased cow.

"Are you listening?" Sarah asked.

"What?" Elena looked up from her newspaper and her thoughts.

"The baptism is today. As one of the godmothers, you have to be there."

"The babies aren't out of the hospital," Elena protested. She had to get back to her case.

"It's being held in the hospital chapel, the Weizells' parish priest officiating. Wear that dress I chose for you; it can't be ruined if little Elena spits up on you, something that Concepcion assured me does happen."

Elena nodded and moved on to the local news.

Stonewashed Jeans Boycotted

Following the bombing of Pan-American Stonewashing, the *Times* published an article on the amount of water used by stonewashing plants. As a result, public-spirited students at Pancho Villa High School have organized a boycott against prewashed and stonewashed jeans.

Pancho Villa was the high school where the Reyes twins, former members of Water Now, taught. Had they organized the boycott? Probably not; because their brother was dying, they wouldn't have time. Anyway, it wasn't illegal to organize a boycott. She read the second paragraph of the article.

"I'll never wear them again," vowed Virgie Melendez, a sophomore who thinks citizens of Los Santos have an obligation to eschew water wastage. "Nobody knows where the bomber will strike next. It could be at people wearing stonewashed jeans."

You had to admire a teenager who was keeping up with current events, Elena decided.

"I almost forgot," said Sarah. "Some FBI person wants you to meet him at the county detention facility at nine or as soon thereafter as you can make it."

Still in her bathrobe, Elena looked at her watch, didn't find it on her wrist, and went into a panic when Sarah told her the time.

"So you'll be late," said Sarah, calmly picking up another droopy croissant.

"Why didn't you wake me up when he called?"

"Because you needed the sleep," said Sarah. "Do you want to drive to the baptism with me?"

"I may have to go straight from the jail," said Elena.

"You're late," said G. "Are you O.K.?"

Why did people keep asking her that? Elena wondered. She'd looked at herself as she threw her clothes on and decided she looked pretty good, especially since she was dressed for godmotherhood. "Sarah didn't wake me up."

"You look gorgeous," said Connie admiringly. Elena was wearing a teal silk dress that clung from below her breasts to her calves with a back pleat so she could walk. The bodice was round-necked, flowered, and the dress was fitted with drifting handkerchief sleeves. Sarah had dragged her to a sale, picked the dress out, and insisted that Elena buy it in anticipation of the baptismal ceremony. Since the material wasn't real silk, it was washable. Baby Elena could throw up all she wanted without causing a wardrobe crisis.

"Indeed," said Perry. "Stunning."

"Aren't you a little dressed up to grill a suspect?" G. asked.

"My partner's babies are being baptized at one," said Elena, "so let's get busy. Anything new on the environmentalists?"

G. grinned. "Tire tracks on Mrs. Furbow. We've hauled her back in. Footprints on Brazlitt. You were right about his sneakers."

"They're new, though," said Connie, "so we don't have any wear marks for comparison. His lawyer will argue that anyone with that shoe and shoe size could have made the print."

"That Billy Roy," said Perry. "He's identified Brazlitt as the bearded man who planted the well bombs. He must have used one of those temporary beard dyes."

"Mrs. Furbow was in Albuquerque for the H.H.U. bombings," said Elena.

"But she has no alibi for the stonewashing plant, and Brazlitt hasn't talked to us since last night," said Perry. "If we can break him, maybe he'll implicate her, which would be a break. Although the tires match, they're new, too, no wear patterns.

And maybe we can find someone at the mall who saw one of them making the phone calls about the water utilities bomb."

"Then let's get at it," said Elena. "I haven't got all day, and I need to sit down. These heels are killing me."

When Brazlitt heard the evidence against him, he went pale. "You're accusing me of murder?" he cried.

"In the commission of a felony," Elena agreed.

"I was up in New Mexico," he said, obviously shaken.

"You told people you were going to Phoenix after that water conservation conference," Melon reminded him.

"I lied."

"So where were you before and after the conference?" Melon demanded.

"In the forest," Brazlitt mumbled.

"What forest?"

"Carson. Santa Fe."

"Doing what? Meditating?" Connie asked sarcastically. "All by yourself?"

"With colleagues."

"Who?"

"You're asking me to snitch."

"You're saying you were in the forest doing something illegal?" asked Elena.

"It wasn't illegal."

"Mr. Brazlitt doesn't have to answer your questions," said Fred Block, Gladys Furbow's lawyer, who had just raced in. "You shouldn't be questioning my client without his lawyer present."

"Fine," said Perry. "You'll want to explain all the charges to him."

"It wasn't illegal," cried Brazlitt.

"If he actually has an alibi and it isn't anything illegal and there were people with him—in the forest—" Elena grinned. "—then he'd be dying to tell us about it. Right? I mean capital murder—that's the big one." The bomb men nodded solemnly and started to rise.

"We were salting the forest with owls," Brazlitt cried.

The group turned and stared at him. Even his lawyer looked incredulous.

Remembering the story in the morning paper about the astounding discovery of owls in forests where they hadn't been sighted in over a hundred years, Elena said indignantly, "Wait till I tell my mother about this!"

"I can't believe Harmony's turned into such a yuppie type," Brazlitt grumbled.

"My mother? A yuppie?" Elena began to laugh. "She's a weaver in Chimayo. She gathers firewood herself. So do all my dad's relatives. You want to let them all freeze for some bird that doesn't exist?"

"It does now," said Brazlitt smugly.

"So you're saying you smuggled in the birds? From where?" asked Perry, who obviously didn't believe Brazlitt's lame excuse.

"I'd rather not say."

"You and who brought them in?" asked Connie, scowling. "This is bullshit. Let's get him indicted and—"

"I'll give you the names," Brazlitt cried. "I didn't kill anyone. I didn't set off any bombs. If Water Now was behind it, they didn't tell me."

"Has Brazlitt seen a paper?" Elena asked. If he'd seen the article, he could have devised the owl-salting story to fabricate an alibi.

The others looked at her oddly.

"We need to find out," said Elena.

"I haven't seen a paper. Why do you want to know? Is there something about me in it?" Brazlitt's voice was rising with anxiety.

"We can't take his word for it," said Elena. "We need to know what news, if any, he's seen or heard since last night."

"Conference," said G., and the three men followed Elena out of the interview room.

"I didn't bomb anything," Brazlitt called after them. "I'll give you names."

"Any of you read the *Times* this morning?" Elena asked. "Unlikely as it sounds, the s.o.b. could be telling the truth."

28

They had worked all morning checking the alibis of Gladys
Furbow and Lawrence Brazlitt. Mrs. Furbow had been in
Albuquerque for the H.H.U. bombing and on a prayer vigil at
her church for the Pan-American Stonewashing explosion.
That alibi was not airtight because the male church member
who stayed in the sanctuary while female members were on
vigil had admitted to sleeping most of the night when Gladys
was there. Nor could he say whether or not her Buick had been
in the church parking lot during the critical hours.

None of the investigation team, which had now been
designated the Water Bomb Task Force, actually believed that
Gladys Furbow had climbed the leg of the water tower to wrap
detonating cord around it, but they did believe she could have
provided transportation and assisted in other less mobile
activities.

Mrs. Furbow said that she'd bought those Michelins at a
Discount Tire sale, having been influenced by their ads about
the little old lady throwing a tire through a window.

"Have you always wanted to throw a tire through the
window of a tire store, Mrs. Furbow?" Perry Melon had asked.

"Don't be silly, young man," she snapped. "But I did enjoy
seeing someone else do it."

179

"A violence voyeur," he murmured to Elena. "Makes her a perfect accomplice."

However, Furbow's lawyer properly said they didn't have enough to hold her. Brazlitt was another matter. His alibi for the period of the last two bombings could not be substantiated. He had indeed provided them with a list of names, but not one person on his list would admit to having joined Brazlitt in salting the forests of New Mexico with Mexican spotted owls. Brazlitt remained in jail.

With only a few minutes to spare, Elena arrived at the hospital chapel and found it crammed with people. The crowd bulged out into the hall, jamming the chapel doors open and admitting hospital noises: announcements over the loud speaker, the rattle of carts, the whole less-than-soothing cacophony of medical care in action. Elena had to force her way through the crowd, saying, "Excuse me, excuse me. I'm one of the godmothers."

Concepcion's numerous relatives were all in attendance. Gabriella Forti enveloped Elena in a motherly embrace and said, "We were afraid you wouldn't make it, dear. Has there been another bombing?"

"No, ma'am," Elena replied.

Both tall and lean, Leo's grandmother and mother were in the front row. His father evidently hadn't been able to tear himself away from his latest ballroom dancing tour. The elder Mr. Weizell, since retirement, had been traveling the country entering ballroom dancing competitions with the lady next door. Leo's mother, the ultimate homebody, refused to travel for any reason other than family visits.

Everyone in Crimes Against Persons who wasn't on duty attended the baptism, including Lieutenant Beltran. When Detective Beto Sanchez, who was to join Elena in godparent-hood, caught sight of her in her new dress, he said, "Wow! Nobody'd ever know you're a cop."

Beltran said, "Aren't you sleeping? You've got circles under your eyes." Then he clapped her heartily on the shoulder, which made her jump and him frown. "Are you all right?" he asked suspiciously.

"Great," she replied.

"Well, for now, I'll have to take your word. Oh, there you are, Leo. I want you to know that a commendation for bravery has gone into your jacket."

Leo flushed with pleasure.

"Did he tell you what he did out on Paisano Drive?" Beltran asked Elena. "The night these babies were born."

Elena grinned. "Here I did the same thing a couple of nights later, and Leo gets the commendation." From behind their superior's back, Leo thumbed his nose at Elena, who broke down and giggled.

"Sure you're all right?" asked Beltran suspiciously. "You're being considered for commendation, too."

"I'm great," said Elena and noticed that Gus McGlenlevie had situated himself behind the pulpit and cleared his throat loudly.

"Friends," he said, "on this touching occasion, I would like to read a poem I've written in honor—"

Gabriella Forti, the grandmother, shouted at her husband, "Angel, make that man go away. I don't want him reading any of his disgusting poetry at the baptismal sacrament of my grandchildren."

Sarah, who had been sitting beside Zifkovitz, stood up and strode to the pulpit in her conservatively festive suit, grasped the arm of her ex-husband, and dragged him down toward the pews, hissing, "Don't you dare make a scene, Angus McGlenlevie."

"Dear Sarah," he replied, hand on heart, "anything for you."

Zifkovitz glared at him.

Relieved that one crisis had evaporated, Elena scuttled over to Concepcion and asked, "Which baby's mine?"

Concepcion replied, "You don't get to keep her, you know. She's just on loan for the ceremony, except for your religious responsibility."

Elena felt somewhat nervous about that, knowing she wasn't all that good a Catholic. Leo came up holding Leo, Jr. "Take off that booty, will you, Concepcion? I want to show Elena his feet."

"Oh, for heaven's sake," said his wife, "you can't tell from a baby's feet whether he's going to be a tap dancer."

Elena started to laugh. "Leo, are you going to give all your kids dancing lessons, or just the boys?" she asked.

"Would I practice sexual discrimination?" Leo protested.

"Absolutely," said Elena. "You're always harassing me."

"What's that?" demanded Concepcion, a woman of jealous temperament.

"He called me *babe* not two weeks ago," Elena hastened to explain before she became the only woman to be dumped as godmother minutes before the ceremony. "A couple of months ago, he even asked if I was suffering from PMS."

"That's one thing about pregnancy," said Concepcion. "You don't have trouble with PMS." Then she turned to talk to one of her sisters, and Elena moved toward Sarah and Zifkovitz. She spotted Dr. Millard Fillmore Fong interviewing the attendees, tape recorder in hand and—good Lord!—the president and vice president of Herbert Hobart University had come.

Dr. Harley Stanley, a motorcycle enthusiast, was talking to a C.A.P. detective named Mosconi about the fleet of all-terrain vehicles used by H.H.U.'s Desert Adventure Club. University President Sunnydale had cornered the priest, Father Hornado Melendez, and was describing to him H.H.U.'s Wednesday-afternoon prayer and cocktail parties.

"In my parish," said Father Hornado, "we couldn't afford to provide cocktails to the congregation. They have to make do with communion wine."

"What wine do you use?" asked President Sunnydale. "California, I hope. Cabernet Sauvignon? Pinot Noir?"

The priest gave him a pained look and edged away toward the large crowd of parents, godparents, attending pediatric nurses, and babies at the front of the chapel. He clapped his

hands for silence, and the ceremony began. Elena held Baby
Elena, a tiny creature swathed in a waterfall of ruffles and
embroidery, a little ruffled cap on her head, the gown trailing
over Elena's arms. Looking down at her goddaughter-to-be, she
admired the baby, who was snoozing peacefully, her tiny face
peeking out of its ruffle and snuggled against the teal silk on
Elena's breast. Elena sighed; the baby had drooled on her.
Thank God the dress was washable. But when the ceremony
ended, it was going to be embarrassing to talk to people while
her left breast sported a big wet spot.

The drone of Father Hornado's voice was soothing and
almost drowned out the clanking and squawking of the hospital
outside the open chapel door and the shiftings of the audience,
many of whom were standing. The baby felt so precious and
comfortable in Elena's arms that she thought wistfully how
nice it would be to have one of her own. Not, of course, under
present circumstances, since she wasn't married, except in the
eyes of the church, which didn't recognize her divorce from
Frank the Narc. There'd be no church baptism if she were to
remarry and have a baby. Besides that, motherhood and
homicide detecting would make for a difficult balancing act.
She smiled down at Baby Elena, whose eyelids had fluttered
briefly.

Elena would have to make do with the pleasures of being a
godmother, she decided. The priest was now baptizing Gabriella, so little Elena was next. Feeling more peaceful than she
had in several months, Elena paid closer attention to the
ceremony. Father Hornado was intoning, "I baptize thee in the
name of the Father, the Son—"

His words were interrupted by a terrible crash, cries of
dismay, breaking glass. The noise catapulted Elena out of her
happy reverie and into action. The rest of the audience turned
to stare at the door. She and Baby Elena somehow landed on
the floor behind the pulpit, the baby still cradled safely in her
arms but now howling indignantly. Elena felt like weeping
herself. She had hit the floor on elbow and hip, and they hurt
enough to take her breath away, but not enough to blot out the

realization that the priest was gaping down at her in astonishment, and Concepcion, a tigress protecting her cub, was striding toward them, shouting, "What do you think you're doing with my child?"

29

Saturday, May 25, 2:05 P.M.

Scrambling to her knees, rocking the baby and whispering, "Sh-sh, sh-sh," Elena glanced around to see how many people had seen her making a fool of herself and endangering her godchild. Then she tottered to her feet, still clutching the baby, and stammered an embarrassed, "She's okay." Sergeant Manny Escobedo steadied her, his first service as a godfather, although he was godfather to Angel Jose. At that moment, Baby Elena stopped howling, opened her tiny mouth in a dainty yawn, snuggled back into Elena's arms, and dozed off.

"She's unconscious," cried Concepcion. The baby's eyelids fluttered. She gave her mother that blind infant gaze and dozed off once more. Since a pediatrician had been attending the ceremony because the children were so small, he performed an immediate examination of Baby Elena, who woke up again and produced a few sleepy yowls. However, he pronounced her "fit as a fiddle," reassuring the distraught mother and embarrassed godmother. Then the ceremony proceeded until, last and smallest, little Sarah Maria was put under God's protection and the protection of Concepcion's sister Maria and her husband.

When the service concluded, Sarah hurried to Elena's side and asked, "Are you all right?" She stared at her friend. "I don't know why I bother to ask. You've *got* to get some sleep. If you won't see a psychologist, at least get your doctor to prescribe sleeping pills."

"I'm fine," said Elena. "Didn't you hear that noise in the hall? It sounded like shots."

"It sounded to me like two hospital carts colliding."

Before Sarah could go on, Gus put his arm around her and said, "This is a time of rejoicing, my dear, both for the blessings of the present and those of the future." He turned to the milling crowd, and his voice boomed over the chatter, "Ladies and gentlemen, I hope you'll all attend when Sarah and I have our first baby."

"What's that supposed to mean?" demanded Zifkovitz.

"It means," said Sarah, "that Angus McGlenlevie is completely insane if he thinks he'll ever get his hands on me again, much less talk me into having a baby, and, Gus, if you embarrass me in public one more time, just one more time, I'm going to get a restraining order."

"Methinks the lady doth protest too much," said McGlenlevie cheerfully.

"Methinks the lady is about at the end of her rope," muttered Sarah, "and I may just knot it around your neck."

Before the argument could proceed further, Beltran pushed his way through the crowd of well-wishers and fastened a broad hand on Elena's arm. She whirled to find herself looking into the gimlet eyes of her lieutenant. "Jarvis," he said very softly, "you get help or you're going behind a desk, maybe even on leave."

"But Lieutenant—"

"Ever heard of the doctrine of vicarious liability? You screw up and everyone in the chain of command, including me, is responsible. So no arguments. Get help." He turned and stamped away, leaving Elena with visions of her career self-destructing.

"Beloved of God," boomed a voice from the pulpit. The group milling around in the chapel turned to find President Sunnydale addressing them. "On behalf of Herbert Hobart University, sponsor of these charming babies, I would like to offer a prayer for them and their parents and godparents, friends and family. Let us all bow our heads."

Various members of Concepcion's family, not to mention their priest, Father Hornado, looked indignant. The police contingent and the H.H.U. spectators shifted uneasily. Elena wondered whether the professors would insist on cocktails being served since the president seemed intent on praying.

The pediatrician, who had been going from baby to baby to make sure they were enduring the excitement without problems, said, "These children need to return to the nursery."

"Dear Lord," boomed President Sunnydale, "you who have seen fit to bless this family with the care of five young souls, we pray that thy blessings do not prove too much for them."

"Amen to that," muttered Leo.

Concepcion elbowed him in the ribs. Elena stifled another giggle.

"We pray that Herbert Hobart University, in its own small way, will be able to lift some of that burden from these fine young parents. We pray that not only thy divine guidance but the guidance of Dr. Millard Fillmore Fing—"

"Fong," Elena wanted to yell at him.

"—who is the principal investigator in this family-living project, will be able to assist Leon and Concertina Wiggins—"

He doesn't even know the parents' names, thought Elena.

"—in guiding their children's psychological and intellectual development."

Dr. Fong beamed and chucked Angel Jose under the chin. Or maybe it was Gabriella; they all looked pretty much alike to Elena, except for Baby Elena, who was a very distinctive child. At any rate, the tickled baby woke up and howled.

"Tickling my baby was not part of the agreement," Concepcion snarled at Dr. Fong, who jerked his hand back in alarm.

"And if you're planning on taking pictures of them with that camera," she said, "don't even think of it. I'm not having flashbulbs going off in my babies' faces."

"But Concepcion," Gabriella protested, "your father and I wanted to take pictures."

"And madam," said Dr. Fong, "we need to record—"

President Sunnydale cleared his throat loudly. "We pray, Lord, that such heavy responsibilities do not cause dissension among the caretakers of these sweet babies, these children of God, these—"

Harley Stanley edged up beside the president and whispered in his ear.

"And last but not least, Lord, we pray that all those who have so gladly attended the baptism will join us in a joyous cocktail party at the university, given in honor of this festive occasion. Amen."

"What cocktail party?" Elena murmured to Concepcion.

"It was their idea," the mother of five whispered back. "I said O.K. because, otherwise, my mother and sisters would have had to do it. I don't really think I'm up to entertaining this many people yet. Anyway, we've got cribs all over the house."

Leo, Jr., woke up and whimpered. His mother snatched him out of the bassinet and cuddled him. "Isn't he beautiful?" she said.

"They're all beautiful," Elena replied, but she heard Sarah murmur to Zifkovitz, "Do you think they really believe that?"

"If you truly take a look at those babies, Sarah," said Gus, sidling up to her, "you'd certainly want one of your own."

"I certainly wouldn't," snapped Sarah, "and if I did, it wouldn't be yours. And Paul, if *you're* getting any ideas—"

Zifkovitz held up his hands as if warding off evil. "I don't even want to get married," he said, "much less have babies."

"That's what I like about you," said Sarah. "For an artist, you're a sensible man."

"But he doesn't respect you, Sarah. He hasn't offered marriage," said Gus. "Whereas I—"

"Oh, shut up, Gus."

The crowd was beginning to drift out of the chapel. Elena managed to work her way to the far side of the room, which wasn't very far, but still it put six or seven people between her and Lieutenant Beltran. She'd finally admitted to herself that she had to get help, but she hated having the decision forced on her by Beltran or even by Sarah.

As the crowd spilled out of the hospital, they were met by a rain of leaflets. Elena looked up and spotted the papers spewing out of a small plane, crop-duster variety, flying low over the city. She caught one and read, "Water for the Colonias or Bombs for the Water Wasters." And the typeface, all curlicues and double lines, was reminiscent of other words snipped from headlines in publications she had yet to track down.

Elena sighed. She wouldn't be going to the post-baptism party at H.H.U. Instead, she'd be chasing church bulletins and pilots. At least she had comfortable shoes in the truck. They wouldn't complement her teal silk dress, but they'd make her feet happy. She glanced down and noted with relief that little Elena's drool was drying in the ovenlike heat of Los Santos. Benefits of living in the desert.

30

With the leaflet from the crop-dusting plane in her hand, Elena called G. and read the text to him, "Water for the Colonias or Bombs for the Water Wasters."

"O.K.," said G. "I'm at the airport. I'll find out who the pilot is and where he's landing. Call you back when I have the information."

"Good. I'll try to track down these typefaces. It looks like the threatening notes that the bombing victims received." Elena decided that to get a copy of the *Bishop's Newsletter,* she might as well go to the source. Starting her truck, she set off for the offices of the diocese of Los Santos, where she found one lone lady typing.

"Hi," said Elena cheerily. The woman looked up, her bifocals flashing in the overhead light.

"What a pretty dress," she said.

"Thanks," said Elena. "I just stood godmother to a friend's child."

"That's a great honor. I hope you intend to take your duties seriously."

"I do," said Elena, thinking of the tiny, cuddly baby she'd held—and almost injured because loud noises sent her into

191

shock. "With my responsibilities in mind, I wonder if I could get a copy of *The Bishop's Newsletter?*"

"Certainly."

"And maybe you'd have a copy of the *Holy Name Gazette*."

"You'd have to go to the convent for that."

"The Convent of the Sacred Chamisa?"

"Yes, dear. Do you need directions? I gather that you're godmother to a Catholic child."

Elena nodded.

"Well, in that case, perhaps you'd like a subscription to *The Bishop's Newsletter*."

Oh geez, thought Elena. If she hadn't mentioned being a godmother, she wouldn't feel any obligation to get a subscription. "How much does it cost?" she asked warily, thinking of her tottering budget, which hadn't been helped by the dress she was wearing.

"Well, my dear, if you don't have enough money, we'll give it to you free." But the woman was eyeing her dress.

"I bought it on sale," said Elena defensively. "Just tell me how much the subscription costs."

"Twelve dollars a year."

"O.K." It could be worse, she decided and pulled the billfold from her handbag. Twelve dollars. That left her with twenty-three and plastic till payday. Reluctantly, she forked over the money, gave her name and address, and received her first copy of the newsletter.

"You're a professor at the university?"

"No, I'm just living there with a friend because my house—" She stammered to a halt. What could she say about her house? "—gives me the creeps lately."

"Really? Have you ever considered that the devil may have inhabited your house?"

Elena thought of her mother's demand that she get a *curandera* to cleanse the place. "My mother thinks so."

"Mothers know best. Perhaps you should consider an exorcism. Father Bratslowski—"

"I know just who you mean," said Elena hastily. "I'll

certainly consider getting in touch with him." For thirty seconds. Conrad Bratslowski was the last person she wanted messing around with her head or her house.

"Good luck, dear," called the lady as Elena scampered through the door and headed for her truck, where she studied the type in the newsletter, page by page, comparing it to the leaflet and the photocopies she kept in her purse. Some of the words matched, but not all. She'd have to get a copy of the *Holy Name Gazette* from the convent since she certainly wouldn't put sending those notes past Sister Gertrudis Gregory, even if the nun hadn't had bombs in mind when she devised the warnings. But then there were the airplane leaflets. Those actually mentioned bombs.

Still, Elena didn't want to go to the convent, didn't want to see Sister Gertrudis. She stared at her pager, willing G. to call and tell her they needed to get out to the airport, or to some crop duster's house. Not a peep from the damn thing. Reluctantly, she started the motor, shifted, and set out for the convent.

The sister who let her in insisted on taking her straight to Reverend Mother, who said, "Ah, you're still investigating Sister Gertrudis Gregory."

"Well, sort of," said Elena. "Actually, all I wanted was to get a copy of the *Holy Name Gazette*."

Reverend Mother brightened and buzzed for her secretary. "Were you thinking of taking a subscription?"

"Maybe," said Elena cautiously. "To tell you the truth, no matter what it costs, I don't have enough money this month, but I would like to have a copy. To look it over, you know."

"By all means," said the old lady, eyes twinkling in the midst of many wrinkles and an elaborate wimple.

Elena accepted the copy and got out of there with Reverend Mother's voice ringing in her ears. "Do call us if you want to subscribe." Worse than that, the nun who saw her to the door and said, "You look rather haggard, Detective. Perhaps you're in need of a retreat. We provide cells for retreat, meditation, and prayer for Roman Catholics in need."

That shook Elena up, but she had to wonder as she left whether a retreat might not help. Would religious meditation overcome post-traumatic stress? Actually, it sounded pretty good to her—after she was through with this case, of course. The department couldn't fault her for taking a religious retreat, but she doubted that Lieutenant Beltran would accept a few days in a convent cell as therapy.

Back in the truck, she started the motor, turned the air-conditioning on, and made a comparison between the *Holy Name Gazette*, the photocopies, and the leaflet. There, that typeface looked just like one in the gazette. She compared the *W* in *Water* to the *W* in the headline "Palermo Nuns Witness Virgin's Tears." "Sister Gertrudis," Elena said aloud, "you're in big trouble if you're behind these bombings."

She laid the gazette on the seat beside her, shifted, and drove toward headquarters, where she'd get someone from I.D. & R. to confirm her identification of the typefaces. Half a mile away from her destination, her pager at last beeped. She pulled into a 7-Eleven and used their outside phone to dial. As G. was saying "hello," Elena was saying, "Damn it to hell!"

"That your usual phone greetin'?" asked G.

"It is when some scumbag sticks chewing gum in the earpiece of the telephone and I get it in my hair."

"The pilot's waitin' for us at that airport in Sunland Park."

Elena was holding the sticky phone away from her ear with one hand while she fished in her purse for a mirror. "Look at that," she said. "Pink chewing gum. How am I going to get it out of my hair?"

"Don't mess with it," said G. "Freeze it when you get home. Now, are you gonna meet me at the airport, or are you gonna stand around worryin' about your hair?"

"Meet you at the airport," Elena muttered and hung up. She did take the time to enter the convenience store, point to the pink blob in her hair, and snarl, "Look at that!" The clerk behind the counter snickered. Elena said, "I ought to arrest you for interfering with a policewoman in the performance of her duties."

The clerk turned pale. "I didn't put the gum in your hair," he protested.

"But you probably sold it to whoever put it in your telephone receiver outside."

"Oh, shit! Someone did that again? Happens all the time."

"Then why don't you keep an eye on the phone and clean it off instead of letting your customers—"

"You're not a customer. You haven't bought nothin'."

Elena rolled her eyes. "Well, if a robber comes in here with a big gun and holds you up, don't call me." She slammed out of the store and back into the truck, heading for her meeting with G. at a small private airport in New Mexico.

31

Sonny Zachariason chewed tobacco. The fact that he spat into an empty Hellmann's Low-Fat Mayonnaise jar, instead of on the ground, made his habit only marginally less offensive to Elena. Otherwise, he was a good-looking young man with cheery blue eyes, enviable black lashes, and tightly curled hair that burst endearingly from the opening of the baseball cap he wore backward. Draped in a greasy coverall, he continued to tinker with the innards of his small airplane while she and G. questioned him outside a hangar at the small private airport that was his base of operations.

"What's your connection to the water conservation movement?" G. demanded sternly.

"What movement?" asked Sonny, clanging a wrench inside the engine. Elena wondered how the poor little plane managed to survive his muscular ministrations.

"You just plastered Los Santos with flyers that say Water for the Colonias or Bombs for the Water Wasters."

Sonny looked up at G. with surprise. "The hell you say?"

"I do," snapped G, "an' don't try to tell us you don't know what you were distributin'."

"Sure I know. Flyers that said Support the Free Clinics. Which I do. Not that I didn't charge for the flight. I'm in

197

business; I ain't no charity. But hell, I think the country needs socialized medicine. Us that work for ourselves ain't got health insurance. What happens to me if I crash?"

"Who paid your bill?" asked Elena. She had changed her high heels for old sneakers she kept in the truck, but she was sweating in her new baptismal dress, and the cleaners had said they weren't sure they could get the mud out of her graduation suit. This case was hell on her wardrobe. "The bill for distributing the leaflets. Who paid the tab?" she prodded.

"Dunno." Sonny dived back into his engine.

G. gave him half a minute, then pounded on the cowling, bringing the pilot out in a hurry. "Hey," he cried reproachfully. "You never heard of hearin' damage? Watch the ears."

"Answer the question." G., who seemed uncharacteristically short-tempered, took the wrench away from the young pilot and fixed him with a hard eye. After that, Sonny Zachariason became more cooperative. He also spat tobacco juice more often. They learned that he had a machine that fed flyers through an opening in the plane's belly, that he had been contacted about this distribution Thursday and had received the flyers and a money order by overnight UPS just that morning. The one package with a flyer pasted on the outside had borne the message, Support the Free Clinics, which he did. He used the Tillman Clinic in downtown Los Santos when his toenail fungus became troublesome. Would he do that if he was into illegal activities? The clinic was right by the Central Police Command, for God's sake. So why hassle him?

"You distributed hundreds of flyers that said Water for the Colonias or—"

"What's wrong with that? I know folks who don't got water. It's a big pain in the ass. Whole families with the trots."

"Water for the Colonias or Bombs for the Water Wasters," Elena finished.

"Bombs?" Sonny spat disgustedly into his mayonnaise jar. "Well, I don't know nothin' about bombs."

"You got the wrapping the flyers came in? The UPS box? Whatever?" Elena asked.

"It come here." Sonny waved vaguely toward a small cinder block freight terminal. "Could look in the trash."

"So do it," snapped Washington.

"Me?" Sonny's eyes opened wide in blue astonishment. "Hey, man, I'm runnin' a business here. I got a kid comin' in for lessons in—" He looked at a large, greasy watch. "Little pisser's late."

"Did you have a license to drop those flyers?" Elena asked.

"What license?"

"We've got him for littering if nothing else," she told G.

"I can't believe this," wailed Sonny. "The whole damned town's blowin' up, an' you're gonna arrest me for litterin'. You think that's gonna stop a bomber?"

"It's a start," said G. grimly. "There'll be more charges later, I shouldn't be surprised."

"What charges? I got offered a job. I done it. I got paid. Not my business what the flyers said. Even if I'd a known. Which I didn't. Top one said Support the Free Clinics. I din pay no attention to the rest. I just loaded 'em an' took off."

"So next time look before you leaf," said Elena, and giggled.

G. frowned at her.

"Leap, leaflet. Get it?" Elena grinned at him.

"I got it," muttered G.

They wrote Sonny Zachariason a citation, told him not to leave town, and departed to interview employees of a Postal Annex on the Eastside from which the leaflets had been sent. There a clerk remembered the person who mailed the flyers. He'd brought the boxes in on an old dolly that had ragged, loosened wrappings around the handles. No one had seen the customer's vehicle, but the customer was described as five-ten, light brown beard, otherwise unexceptional.

"Sounds like the water resource man at the wells," said Elena, "but Billy Roy identified Brazlitt as that guy, and Brazlitt's in jail. She fished in her bag for the computer composite, and the Postal Annex employee agreed that the customer looked something like that. Was Brazlitt innocent and the beard a fake? Elena wondered. If so, the bomber obviously didn't have a wide wardrobe of disguises. If real, had he shaved if off already? "Are we getting anywhere?" she asked G. as they turned to leave.

"Darned if I know," said the bomb squad sergeant, "but I gotta get home to dinner. Sharana's expecting me to cook out tonight."

"Lucky you," said Elena. "I'm rooming with someone who either wants to eat at a restaurant too expensive for my budget or stay home and eat TV dinners. It's a temporary arrangement until I move back into my own house." They were standing in the parking lot between her truck and his car.

"The mountain lion still buggin' you?"

Elena frowned at him. "How did you know about that?"

"I heard."

She sighed. "I guess everyone knows. You probably want to dump me off the case. I guess—"

"—I guess we better answer our pagers," said G.

Both had beeped, which gave Elena an uneasy feeling. "It has to be another bomb," she said, heading back to Postal Annex.

"Won't know till we call in." G. used the phone first, listened, and said to Elena, "Some doctor's greenhouse in the country club area."

"Oh, God," said Elena. "Now he's hitting private users?"

"You better call, too. Just in case we've got two situations. An' I'd just as soon you didn't use the Lord's name in vain. Won't help us solve the case if we offend Him."

Elena flushed. He sounded like Grandmother Portillo, who didn't allow blasphemy in her house. Elena's message was the same. Dr. Bates Morrison, ob-gyn, had activated his garage door opener after returning from a delivery at Providence Memorial Hospital. While the door trundled up, his greenhouse exploded.

Given the situation, G. called his wife to postpone the cookout. Elena wondered whether she was ever going to get home and change out of her baptism finery.

32
∵

Saturday, May 25, 5:47 P.M.

Rio Grande Water
Destroys Mexican Crops

Mexican farmers in the Juarez Valley took their concerns yesterday to the state government in Chihuahua City. They claim that crop yields are falling yearly because of fecal coliform from sewage, not to mention heavy metals and other pollutants dumped into the river by maquiladora plants in Juarez.

KLMN Radio, Los Santos, Saturday, May 25

Elena heard the news story on the radio as she recrossed the mountain to the home of doctor/victim Bates Morrison. She wished everyone would just stop talking about water, writing about it, obsessing about it. They kept the wackos all stirred up. Next thing you knew the Juarez Valley farmers would be blocking the international bridges again. Threatening to blow them up with bombs made from fertilizer and gasoline.

The thought of gasoline reminded her of her budgetary problems. She was putting work miles on her own truck, running the gas down to nothing. She could see herself having to borrow from Sarah at the end of the month in order to put gas in the tank.

They were all at the doctor's house when she arrived: G., Connie Amparan, Perry, three or four other FBI agents whose names she forgot immediately. The estate had a lush green lawn in front, flowers blooming in neatly tended beds, huge weeping willows trailing ferny branches onto the grass, a pebbled circular drive with an offshoot that led to a three-car garage in front of which a Mercedes was parked. The house featured white stucco and ornate grillwork balconies. It was so beautiful. And so undesert. To the side the velvety lawn surrounded heaped broken glass glittering in the westering sunlight, blackened shriveled plants fallen from burned tables, and the twisted iron skeleton of the greenhouse that was no more.

Dr. Morrison stood in his driveway, hand on the polished fender of his midnight blue Mercedes, a tall, ascetic looking man of middle age. When Elena was introduced by Perry, the doctor had been talking about orchids, thousands of dollars worth of lovely orchids that had died in the explosion.

"Detective Jarvis will interview you, sir," said Perry, "while we investigate the wreckage."

The doctor didn't invite her in. He seemed unable to let the remains of his greenhouse out of his sight—as if keeping watch might lead to some miraculous reconstitution of the structure. "It was my refuge," he said. "Some people run; some play bridge, golf, musical instruments. I grew orchids."

"What's your monthly water bill?" Elena asked.

He looked surprised. "Summer or winter?"

"Let's start with summer."

"Six hundred I suppose. You'd have to ask my wife."

"O.K., let's do that."

"She's in Maine, opening a cottage that belongs to her family."

Elena sighed, speculating on what the temperature in Maine might be. Not in the middle nineties with zero humidity and no rain in sight. "So six hundred would be a ballpark figure for summer?" Imagine paying that every month for water. Her monthly house payment wasn't that much.

"I don't see the relevance, Detective. This is about abortion. Investigate the Antiabortion Brigade and you'll find the bombers. They've picketed my house and my office, although abortion isn't any large portion of my practice. I don't suppose I do more than five or six a year. But if an abortion's called for, I perform it. And I won't be intimidated by a group of self-righteous bullies." Then he looked sadly at the glittering shards of his greenhouse. "By God, I hope you catch them. Because I'm going to sue. By the time, my lawyer gets through, neither the organization nor any of its members will have a penny left."

"When was the last time you were threatened or harassed by prolifers?"

"Prolifers? A misnomer. Orchids are alive. And beautiful. They're—"

"Doctor," she prodded.

"Two or three months. My secretary could tell you."

"The antiabortionists have been relatively quiet lately, but you must have seen in the papers that bombs have been exploding over water usage."

"Well, yes, but—" The doctor looked nonplussed. "Those were protests against—ah—public usage, industrial usage, not—"

"Have you received any threats about water?"

"Not that I know of. You'd have to ask my wife. I rarely look at the mail."

"I think we'd better do that," said Elena. "Can we reach her by telephone?"

The doctor nodded, but before they could enter the house, Paul Resendez, a reporter from the *Times,* who had done Elena a number of favors in recent years, as she had him, approached and asked what the police had learned. Was this another water bombing?

"We don't know yet, Paul." Had she actually had information, she couldn't have told him, not now that the FBI was the primary investigating agency.

"Doctor, you've been targeted by the prolifers as recently as eight weeks ago. Do you think this bombing is their doing?" the reporter asked.

"I just told the detective I thought so," said the doctor grimly.

"Do you plan to stop performing abortions?"

The doctor's fine-lined face went cold. "The last abortion I performed was the result of a positive amniocenteses for Tay-Sachs disease. Had that fetus been allowed to reach term, the baby would have lived only long enough to break its parents' hearts. The abortion I performed previous to that, which, incidentally, was some six months ago, saved the life of the mother. Do you think I should allow myself to be intimidated?"

Resendez looked embarrassed. "Can I quote you, doctor?"

"Yes."

"Sorry about your greenhouse," said the newsman. "I remember the feature we did on your orchids."

The doctor nodded and led Elena into the house, where they called his wife, Carole, in Maine. Morrison gave a brief description of the destruction, which evidently horrified his wife. He told her not to come home, suggesting that he might take an early vacation and join her. Then he handed the phone to Elena, who asked if Mrs. Morrison had received a note that said, "Turn off the water or we will."

"Why, yes," said the high, clear voice at the other end. "I did get a note, but I couldn't imagine what it meant. I thought maybe my next door neighbor was still irritated because our sprinkler system undermined his rock wall. But we paid for rebuilding the wall. I pointed that out to him. Of course, he denied sending me an anonymous note, but—"

"It was addressed to you?" Elena interrupted. "Just you."

"Well, Bates and me. Are you saying someone blew up our greenhouse because they think we use too much water? We do use a lot, but we pay exorbitant water bills. Good heavens, we must finance water for all the poor people in the county."

Elena doubted that. A lot of those poor people didn't have water. "Did you keep the note?"

"Of course not. I threw it away."

"Was it one of those pasted-up deals. Words cut out of—"

"I know what you mean. Like kidnap notes in movies. It was. I remember thinking, how melodramatic! I was amazed that Harold—that's our neighbor—would go to so much—"

"Do you remember what the typefaces looked like?"

"Ornate. Sort of Old English."

Bingo! Having ascertained that the doctor had not had any work done on his greenhouse that week, nor any yard work, Elena set out to canvass the neighborhood. When she found a maid, just leaving for some Saturday-night festivity, who had seen a panel truck parked in the Morrison driveway sometime in the last several days—she couldn't remember, even when prodded, which day—Elena thought she'd caught another peek at the bomber.

According to the maid, the panel truck said something about a gardening service, again the maid wasn't sure what; she was, after all, very busy, the only help in a very large house, and you'd think with all that space for themselves, they could provide a bigger maid's room and a bath with a tub; she had only a shower stall with no detachable spray. How did they think she could keep her hair clean when—Elena managed to interrupt this stream of complaint by asking for a description of the man in the panel truck.

"Ponytail, medium height, wearing a coverall. White but smudged."

"The man?" asked Elena.

"No, the coverall," the maid responded, "although the gardener was cute." She grinned.

Bonnie Murillo's sprinkler man, Elena thought. Remembering the ex-circus lady's comments, Elena asked, "What about his buns?"

"Buns?" The maid looked confused, then evidently stopped thinking in terms of bakery goods and chuckled. "Very nice," she said. "Tight. I waved to him when he left the greenhouse, but he didn't notice me."

It was dark, after nine, by the time Elena finished talking to the neighbors and the mob of explosives men from three different government entities finished sifting through the wreckage, collecting evidence, suggesting hypotheses. Perry Melon was disappointed. The bomber couldn't have been his favorite suspect because Brazlitt was still in custody. The explosive was different, not black powder, pyrodex, dynamite, or explosive cord. This time the experts thought the bomber had used plastique, radio detonated by the signal on Dr. Morrison's garage door opener.

"Maybe we should find out when he last put his car in the garage," Elena suggested.

"And how do we explain the phone?" asked Connie. They had found a radio fuse in the base of a melted telephone in the greenhouse, suggesting that the plastique was supposed to blow when the phone rang.

"Guess the garage door frequency just happened to be the same," suggested G., frowning.

Elena knocked on Morrison's door, spoke briefly to the doctor, and returned to tell her colleagues that he hadn't bothered to garage his car in four or five days, and had only done so that day because his knee was aching, which sometimes signaled rain.

"Rain?" said one of the FBI techs. "That'll be the day. I don't think it's rained since last fall."

"February," said G. "Didn't we have about a tenth of an inch in—"

"Hey," said Elena. "we've got a case here. My information means either the bomber didn't know the doctor's habits if he figured to blow the greenhouse with the garage door opener, or he meant to telephone and blow up the greenhouse that way, but the garage door did it first."

"Which may mean he hoped to blow the doctor up with the greenhouse," said Connie. "Didn't you say the doctor works on his orchids in his spare time?"

"Yeah," Elena agreed. "The bomber could cruise by, look for lights in the greenhouse, call from a car phone, and boom! Goodbye abortions. Or goodbye water-waster. Whatever the motive is. Water probably. The wife received and ignored the usual note."

"But to kill a doctor because he waters his flowers?" Perry shook his head. "This bomber's a psychopath."

"The doctor's a strange choice," said Elena. "Especially if the bombings are about water for the *colonias*. Morrison volunteers in the free clinics. He *helps* in the *colonias*. Why choose Morrison to make an example of a private user?"

"Because the bomber's nuts," said Connie.

"We'd better get in touch with other citizens who have big water bills," said G. "See if they've been threatened. Warn them if they didn't take the note seriously."

"Seems to me that the water utility could do that," said Perry. "I'll contact them. Anyone think of anything else we can do tonight?"

No one could, so Elena started toward her truck, still in her godmother dress and sneakers.

"Hold up!"

She turned to see Connie hurrying after her.

"There's a country music club on the Eastside having line dancing and fifty-cent beer tonight. Wanna go?"

"Do they serve food?" Elena asked. "I'm starving."

"We'll stop for barbecue."

She looked down at her dress. "Not exactly line dancing clothes."

"You'll bowl them over," Connie assured her, and he was right. Various urban and rural cowboys made heroic attempts to get her attention, but Connie fended them off. At one in the morning, she and Connie were still laughing, drinking beer, and dancing to the country-western band.

33

Drought Destroys Ranchers

Ranchers in the Juarez Valley are selling off their herds at bargain-basement prices. With less than an inch of rainfall since the first of the year, there is not enough grass or water to maintain the cattle.

In West Texas, ranchers face the same problem, which will only be exacerbated because drought is destroying the wheat and grain crops and driving up the price of feed. The encroaching agricultural disaster is being compared to the Dust Bowl years of the thirties.

Farmers in the Rio Grande Valley have not been affected by this drought because their crops are irrigated from the river. The first water allotments from Elephant Butte and Caballo Dams will be released before June.

Los Santos *Times*, Sunday, May 26

When Elena staggered out to the breakfast table, Sarah had finished the local paper and started on the New York *Times*. Elena dropped into a seat, poured coffee, and glanced at the lead stories: the Morrison bombing and drought in Mexico and West Texas, although not Los Santos, not yet. She didn't want to read about drought—or water. Sarah shook out the "Week in Review" section and eyed Elena over narrow reading glasses. "The paper mentioned another bombing yesterday."

Elena nodded and poured orange juice from a crystal pitcher. She knew, however, that the juice came from a cardboard carton that labeled it *reconstituted*.

"You can't have had more than five hours sleep. Is that where you were so late?"

"There and line dancing with Connie Amparan," said Elena, helping herself to more of the instant coffee available in Sarah's silver coffeepot. "I'm going back out on the case in about three-quarters of an hour."

"Fine," said Sarah. "Work yourself into physical and psychological collapse. Just be sure you're here at seven for my dinner party."

Elena groaned. "Why are you giving a dinner party, Sarah? You hate to cook. The last time you made anything elaborate, it blew up."

"You're hardly in a position to criticize me for exploding foodstuffs," said Sarah. "Not after you catapulted Concepcion into labor with your *chili verde* and, incidentally, exposed me to the horrors of childbirth and renewed attentions from my detestable ex-husband."

Elena grinned. "Gus been courting you again?"

"He had four dozen jonquils delivered last night. Paul was not amused. Nor was I." Sarah cut a piece of Danish pastry, gesturing to the plate on the table. "Have one."

"Most people eat Danish with their fingers. Of course, they don't microwave it into rubber first. Now about this dinner—"

"Catered. Thirty dollars a person. If you don't show up, I shall charge you for your plate."

Given the state of her finances, Elena couldn't afford to miss the dinner. She'd spent four dollars of her last twenty-three on her share of the pizza the investigation team had sent out for during the Morrison investigation. "Who's going to be there?"

"You, Paul, myself, and three members of the faculty."

"Which members of the faculty?" Elena asked suspiciously.

"*Interesting* members of the faculty. Is that Mr. Amparan honking for you?"

Elena went to look out the window.

"My mother always insisted that my escorts come in and introduce themselves," said Sarah disapprovingly.

"My escorts, when I was living in Chimayo, if they were lucky enough to have wheels, could be heard coming from the next valley. Muffler problems usually. Often their horns didn't work, so they *had* to come in. Unless they stood outside on the patio and shouted."

"I never know whether to believe these peculiar reminiscences of yours, Elena," said Sarah, forking up another piece of tough pastry. "Seven this evening. Be on time."

"Yes, Mama."

Elena fended off a kiss on the principle that kissing after line dancing was O.K. but not before business. Amiably, Connie accepted rejection, started the car, and drove away, saying, "We get to call the big private water users. The water utility provided the list, but they say they can't make the calls till Monday when their office staff comes in. I didn't think it could wait until then."

Elena agreed. "What are the others doing?"

"Perry's directing a team combing the wilds of New Mexico for people who might be rude enough to substantiate Brazlitt's alibi. He's also got agents checking out the prolifers in case they were the ones targeting Morrison. G.'s in church. Say, did you see the papers this morning?"

"Just the drought-in-Mexico story." Elena stretched in the car seat and yawned. "I barely got up in time to swallow some of Sarah's acid-rain orange juice and stale instant coffee when you honked. What is the fourth estate saying?"

"Nothing you wouldn't expect. The city's in an uproar. People with grass think their lives and lawns are in danger. Businesses are threatening to move. The Chamber of Commerce says we'll never attract desirable industry with bombs going off, so why aren't the police, the FBI, and the ATF doing something? People without plumbing think vigilantes are coming after anyone who ever expressed a desire for running water. Politicians are talking to anyone who'll listen and avoiding questions from anyone who asks. The mayor says the Republican governor should call out the National Guard and won't because Los Santos votes Democratic. And there are letters to the editor from people who think Mexico is sending over agent provocateurs to set off the bombs and then stir up trouble afterward. They want the border closed."

Elena sighed. Even though the FBI had taken over as the primary investigating agency, Lieutenant Beltran was going to expect her to come up with a viable suspect, not to mention reporting to the stress management firm contracted to treat stressed-out LSPD officers. And Elena *was* stressed out— wondering when the next flashback or nightmare would hit, when and where the next bomb would explode. "I think, once we've warned the water hogs, we should start revisiting Water Now members—especially the creepier ones."

"O.K. I choose Celestina Ortiz and Sister Gertrudis Gregory. I'd like to look around that convent, see if there's any evidence she sent those notes."

"Wonder if we can get a warrant? I choose Father B. and those two weird farmers. Oh, and I've got to be home by six-thirty. If I don't show up for Sarah's dinner party, she'll make me pay for my catered plate."

Connie laughed heartily. "How'd you ever end up rooming with an engineering professor?"

"It all started with an exploding snail," said Elena and told him the story of Sarah, the exploding snail, and Gus's accusation of attempted culinary murder.

34

..

Admitted to the offices of the water utility by a guard and presented with a list of private water users with astronomical bills, Connie and Elena began their phone calls. They talked to hysterical women who said they'd never sleep again if people were going to bomb them for keeping their landscaping attractive. They talked to defensive men who said they paid their bills and expected the local authorities to protect them from crazies.

After several such calls, Elena remarked to Connie, "Have you noticed that Morrison wasn't, even with his outrageous bills, the worst water hog by any means? So why did the bomber choose him?"

Connie thought about her question. "Maybe he was picked by someone who was in a position to see his sprinklers going and his green yard."

Elena nodded. "Or maybe a disgruntled patient saw the bombing as a way to get even with the doctor and make it look like the water bombers did it."

"A patient?" Connie looked doubtful.

"He's an obstetrician. When people lose a baby or have one with birth defects, they sometimes sue the doctor. Maybe there are some who'd consider killing the doctor. After all, the bomb

213

was set to go off when the greenhouse phone rang. Morrison is the one who spends time there."

"Oh, hell," Connie groaned. "I hope you're wrong. We don't need any new complications."

"Still, I'm going to call him. There aren't any Water Now neighbors to see how much water he's using. And ordinary neighbors are probably as guilty as he is."

"Hey, Morrison's the victim," Connie reminded her.

"And what about workmen? We want to know who works on or in his house and sees those sprinklers going. I'll ask him about workmen and disaffected patients."

"Go ahead. I'll finish this list."

Elena called the doctor. His response to her inquiry about dissatisfied patients was horror. However, he did mention two families who had sued him and lost, taking the losses badly. He accessed his patient records by computer and ran a check for the surname of every Water Now member, but without much success. There were surname matches but no absolute Water Now matches.

Reluctantly, he agreed to call back after checking his wife's household records for the names of firms and individuals who had worked for the Morrisons. While she waited, Elena returned to the water district list, and Connie went for take-out tamales—his treat. They had almost finished the green chili and pork variety when Dr. Morrison called back to give her a list of names and telephone numbers. No Water Now matches at first glance.

The two spent another hour on the telephone pursuing business owners and sole proprietor contractors at their homes, their relatives' homes, and their recreational and other weekend activities. "Dead end," Connie finally pronounced after the last call. "So who are we closest to among the Water Now people we picked to visit?"

"Sister Gertrudis Gregory. The rest are Upper and Lower Valley," Elena replied, and they left the deserted water utilities offices to seek out the nun.

They were again referred to the Reverend Mother, who told

them that Sister was attending a migrant workers' rally down-town, but was expected back within the hour. "Have you decided about your subscription to the *Holy Name Gazette*?" she asked Elena.

"Ah—I—ah—haven't had time to read it," Elena stam-mered.

"Perhaps you'd like to wait for Sister in her office."

"She has an office?"

"She publishes the *Holy Name Gazette*. You're welcome to wait there and read back copies. I'm sure she'd be delighted with your interest."

"Great idea," said Connie. "Of course, being law officers, we need your permission. No one wants us anywhere without a warrant these days."

"My dear Agent Amparan, we at the Convent of the Sacred Chamisa have nothing to hide. Feel free to look at anything that takes your interest." The Reverend Mother gave him a beatific smile, which Connie returned.

Elena had to restrain herself from clapping her hands. They'd just received permission to search Sister Gertrudis Gregory's office. Would that hold up in court? As she under-stood it, the sisters didn't own anything, or they owned everything in common, or the church owned the convent. Whatever. If anyone could give permission to search, it was the Reverend Mother. "I certainly won't pass up that opportunity, Reverend Mother," said Elena. "I know reading back issues of your gazette will be an inspiration." —to solve the case, if they were lucky.

They were shown to Sister Gertrudis Gregory's office by a novice with a tendency to giggle. Left to their own devices, they were successful almost immediately and without prying open locked cabinets or drawers or peeking behind sacred pictures and under uncomfortable-looking seat cushions. A table by a window on the courtyard held an open box of gazette scraps with words cut out. Beside the box lay a pile of issues from which the key words could be cut. Next was another pile containing copies of *The Bishop's Newsletter* in various editions. By thumbing through and comparing words to those in the photocopies Elena carried in her purse, they found all the elements of the message, Turn off the Water or We Will, not to mention the airplane leaflet, which evidently had been constructed, then photocopied in volume.

"I can't believe she just left the evidence sitting out here," said Connie.

Elena shrugged. "She's convinced that everything she does is the will of God. If you can believe what she says, she's looking forward to going to jail. I think we should call Perry. Or is he with the agents in New Mexico?"

"Just in phone contact. He himself is probably in his office." Connie used the telephone on the nun's messy desk to make the call. "Hey, Melon. Amparan here. Elena's got news." He handed the telephone to Elena, who explained the evidence they'd found.

"I'm on my way," said Perry. "We'll get a warrant to take possession of the evidence and her and get her bail revoked on the clinic violation charges. I know a federal judge who'll agree that she's a danger to the public."

"Wow," said Elena when she'd hung up. "He's really enthusiastic. Plans to have her back in jail by the end of the afternoon. I wonder if he lost Brazlitt to a verifiable alibi." She swiveled in the sister's chair to face Connie. "There's no way Sister Gertrudis Gregory, even in drag, was the sprinkler company man or the state water resources man or the greenhouse man."

"What are you doing in my office?" The nun in question loomed in the doorway, looking like the epitome of the church militant.

"Reverend Mother invited us to wait here for you," said Elena.

"And while we were looking at back copies of your publication, we noticed that you'd been clipping out words for the Water Now messages to heavy water users," said Connie.

"So what?"

"You actually sent the messages?" Elena couldn't believe the woman was admitting culpability so easily.

"That's right. The water situation is critical. Those who choose to ignore it need to be warned to pay attention."

"And bombed if they don't?" asked Connie.

"I know nothing about the bombings."

"Everyone who's been bombed got a note."

"And most of the people who got one weren't bombed," said the sister with smug logic. "If Water Now got the names of the heavy users, so could someone else. The information is public knowledge."

Connie winced. "I'm not splitting hairs with you, Sister. You look guilty to me."

Elena, however, silently acknowledged that the sister had a point. Most of the recipients of her notes hadn't been bombed. And the last victim, Dr. Morrison, wasn't the most obvious choice if they wanted to make an example of a private water hog.

"What's going on here?" asked the Reverend Mother, peeking into the office, her old-fashioned wimple all but filling the doorway.

"At your invitation, they've been searching my office, and they've decided that I'm the water bomber," said Sister Gertrudis Gregory.

Reverend Mother turned reproachfully toward Elena. "You misled me as to your intentions, Detective."

Embarrassed to be rebuked by the kindly, wrinkled old nun, Elena escaped a response when Perry Melon, with three FBI colleagues, arrived to take charge of the situation.

35
..

Sunday, May 26, 7:05 P.M.

"I can't believe you did this to me," Elena whispered.

"You object to the Fongs?" Sarah asked pleasantly.

"I object to Dr. Samuel Parsley, the post-traumatic stress expert. I told you I'd get my own help."

"But you haven't done it," Sarah pointed out. "Anyway, you don't have to become a patient of Sam's. Just see how you like him."

"While he's analyzing me over the hors d'oeuvres?"

"Telephone for you, Elena," said Paul Zifkovitz, entering the dining room and interrupting the argument. He handed her a portable phone.

"Even if someone bombed the local orphanage, you're not getting out of this dinner," Sarah hissed.

"There are no orphanages anymore," said Elena, "only foster parents and juvenile detention facilities." She answered and received the news from Perry Melon that Sister Gertrudis Gregory's bond had been revoked by a federal judge. "She's back in jail," said Perry.

"Congratulations," said Elena. Then on a mischievous impulse, she asked, "Does that mean you're free tonight?"

"Well, I—" Perry sounded startled.

"Sarah's having a dinner party. If you hurry over, you won't miss the first course." Sarah looked horrified and shook her head energetically. "Wonderful," said Elena. You'll love the group. Three psychologists, an artist, a hostess with a good caterer, and me." She punched the off button and handed the phone back to Zifkovitz.

"I can't believe you did that," said Sarah. "I've only ordered for six. What am I supposed to feed this man? And who is he?"

"A very presentable FBI agent. You met him. As for the food, we'll take a little off each plate to feed him. No problem."

"No problem!" exclaimed Sarah, but Elena had sailed back into the living room and plopped down beside Dr. Parsley. "O.K.," she said, "let's get it over with. How stressed do you think I am?"

Dr. Parsley, a large, amiable man with beard, mustache, fluffy haircut, and a rumpled, tweedy look, smiled and said, "You tell me, Detective. Not too stressed to pass that plate of Greek olives, I hope."

"Police work must be very stressful," said Dr. Fong. "My subject, Detective Weizell, shows many peculiarities, even on short acquaintance. For instance, I visited the home where the children will be raised, and the father began to dance in the living room and complained to his spouse about the carpet, which mutes the sound of his dancing."

"Perhaps the dancing is a sign that he is wishing to be a dancer and suffers occupational frustration," suggested Mrs. Fong, also a Ph.D. "Perhaps his father felt such a career choice would not be a source of honor to the family."

"He has shown no signs of father resentment, Mai Liu," said Dr. Fong.

"Have you considered that in his ethnic group dancing may be an expression of joy, perhaps over the fecundity of his wife or the power of his own masculinity?" suggested Mrs. Fong.

"Only two of the five children were males," said Dr. Fong. "That is not such a matter for celebration."

"May I ask why not?" demanded Sarah.

"Can you reach that plate of eggplant pâté?" Dr. Parsley asked Elena. She plunked the plate in his lap and headed for the front door to answer the doorbell. Perry was duly admitted, introduced, and seated within reach of the disappearing hors d'oeuvres.

"I still think the dancing is a reaction to stress," said Millard Fillmore Fong. "Tell us, Agent Melon, do you dance when under stress?"

"Dance?" Perry looked confused and very grateful for the drink Elena handed him. She then sat on the arm of his chair, making him blush and earning a scowl from Sarah.

"You're wanted in the kitchen, Elena," said Sarah pointedly. "A matter of portions."

"I prefer large portions," said Dr. Parsley, who had finished off the eggplant pâté.

"Sorry, Sam," Sarah replied. "Elena's chosen minimalist cuisine."

Parsley groaned. Perry was trying to explain to Dr. Fong that he seldom danced, even on dates, never spontaneously.

"So this is not a characteristic of American law enforcement persons?" asked Mrs. Fong. "As I told you, Millard, it must be an ethnic manifestation, or perhaps Freudian." The Fongs fell into argument; Samuel Parsley, having been threatened with minimalist cuisine, attacked the predinner tidbits with greater urgency; Perry gulped his drink and accepted a second from Paul Zifkovitz, who asked him if the FBI ever bought nonrepresentational art for their offices; and Elena, grinning, allowed an angry Sarah to drag her into the kitchen.

"I don't know why you think Dr. Parsley can help me," she whispered to Sarah as they took two tablespoons from each bowl of green lentil soup to make up the seventh bowl. "The man's got an eating problem."

Sarah ignored her and said, "This has to be the smallest portion of soup ever served at a dinner party. What am I going to do if Sam asks for seconds?"

"Microwave one of those frozen cups of soup you keep in the freezer?"

"One does not serve two different kinds of soup."

"So set a new style. And don't you seat me by Parsley. I do not want to talk about my dreams during dinner."

"Let's just hope I don't drop anything," said Sarah slyly. "Think how embarrassed we'd all be if you panicked and dived under the table."

"You wouldn't," gasped Elena.

36
··

The dinner guests stared at the dessert, served by Sarah on crystal plates. The original had been four petit fours for each person, colorfully layered with alternating strips of cake and jams and charmingly frosted. The cakes were to sit in an attractive pool of artistically swirled raspberry and vanilla cream. With the unexpected addition of Perry Melon to the party, Sarah had solved the portion problem mathematically by serving each diner three whole cakes, one half and one quarter.

Zifkovitz studied his portion and said, "Nice color contrast, Sarah. I like the juxtaposition of the horizontal stripes on the cut pieces with the solid-color whole pieces." Sarah glared at him. Parsley popped a whole petit four into his mouth and chewed appreciatively.

"This is all because of me, isn't it?" Perry whispered to Elena. Before she could answer, the doorbell rang. Sarah flung down her napkin, muttering about the awkward hour for calling, and went to the door, from which Elena could hear a resentful male voice, saying, "I've come to talk to Elena."

Michael. What was he doing here? Instead of sending him away, Sarah led him into the dining room. For spite, Elena imagined, but the ploy backfired, for Michael, staring at Perry sitting on Elena's left and Dr. Parsley on her right, said angrily to Sarah, "I see you're doing your best to keep us apart."

"I don't know what you're talking about, Dr. Futrell," Sarah retorted.

"Which one did you fix her up with? Sam? Or—I don't even know him." He scowled at Perry.

"Perry Melon, FBI," said Perry, rising, looking very official, as if he might demand Michael's identification and a list of any subversive organizations he belonged to.

"You just won't give me a chance, will you?" Michael said to Elena. "I've apologized, but you—you just keep picking up new boyfriends. Psychologists, FBI agents. Did you gentlemen know she's dating some Hispanic guy, too?"

Did he mean Connie Amparan? "Are you following me, Michael?" she demanded.

The doorbell rang again.

"What now?" muttered Sarah.

"I'll get it," Elena offered, "while I show Michael out."

"I refuse to leave," said Michael. "It's unfair to punish me because I was upset about my brother's death. It's unfeeling." He had trailed her into the living room, talking.

Elena looked through the peephole, spotted Gus McGlen-levie, and opened the door. "Gus," she said, "I'm pretty sure Sarah doesn't—"

"Gentlemen!" he shouted, and a blast of noise sent Elena into shock. However she looked at that moment, it was symptomatic enough to bring Sam Parsley to her side, carrying his last portion of petit fours. She felt the firm grasp of his hands on her shoulders while Gus McGlenlevie and a complete mariachi band pushed by into the living room, trumpets blasting, guitars and violins strumming, a brass-lunged tenor bursting into a traditional ballad of love.

"Are you having a flashback?" Parsley asked. He pinched her arm, and the vision of the mountain lion faded.

"Elena, what's wrong?" Michael pushed between her and Parsley.

"Can't you see that she's suffering from post-traumatic

stress?" Sarah demanded. "Why do you think I'm inviting psychologists to dinner?"

Elena was shivering, Dr. Parsley holding her in one substantial arm, murmuring something about the startle response into her ear. While the mariachi band sang, Gus attempted to embrace Sarah.

"What you need," said Sam Parsley, "is to start talking." He offered Elena a bite of his dessert. "To me. To someone. I'll bet you haven't talked this out."

"I was debriefed," Elena mumbled.

"Did I hear something about revolution?" Gus asked the leader of the mariachi band. "I told you, only love songs."

The leader swept his sombrero in a deep bow, which put an alarming strain on the embroidered seams of his tight pants and short jacket. Then he signaled to the band and burst into a song about a lovesick mariachi.

"Telling it once isn't enough," said Dr. Parsley. "You've got to describe the event so many times, you're bored with it."

"Gus, if you don't get these men out of my apartment, I'm calling the police," said Sarah.

"I didn't realize things were so bad with you," Michael said to Elena. "If only you'd told me."

Elena turned into Dr. Parsley's shoulder, tears dripping onto his sports jacket.

"Coo-ca-roo-coo-coo," sang the mariachis, their sequined pants and jackets glittering.

"Did he do something to you, Elena?" asked Perry Melon, glaring at the psychologist, obviously shocked at the sight of her tears.

"Butt out," said Michael. "I was her lover."

"You sound like a bunch of roosters," Gus complained. "If you're not singing love songs—"

Trumpet blasts drowned him out.

"Think about something nice from your childhood," Dr. Parsley suggested, using a cracker to scrape leftover eggplant pâté from a dish on the coffee table.

"Don't you talk to her," snapped Michael.

The mariachis broke into a ranchero song about driving cattle on the waterless plains. Elena started to giggle, controlled herself, and said to Michael, "He's trying to help me, which is a lot more than you ever did."

"Dr. Tolland, this is really too much," said a portly man, appearing at Sarah's door. "The noise is dreadful."

"I'm serenading my love," said Gus proudly.

"I might have known. Orgies upstairs, serenades downstairs." The complainer glared at Gus.

"Hi," said Elena, wiping her tears away with the back of her hand and smiling at the cello professor who played bass in the H.H.U. jazz band, of which she was a member.

"An interesting manifestation of ethnic courtship," said Mrs. Fong. "However, the lover does not appear to be Mexican."

"True," agreed Millard Fillmore Fong. "Nor is our hostess. Ethnic customs enforced by location rather than familial history, do you suppose? I must ask Detective Weizell if he courted his Hispanic wife with a mariachi band."

The mariachis, at Gus's insistence, returned to romance in their choice of repertoire, but two H.H.U. policemen arrived at that moment, evidently in response to a telephoned complaint.

"I demand that you remove these musicians from my premises," said Sarah.

"Officer Hermosillo, ma'am. You didn't hire them?" asked one of the lavender uniformed officers.

"I hired them," said Gus. "And I know under that rigidly scientific exterior, Sarah, that you are touched by my romantic gesture."

"Say, it's a mariachi band," said Officer Hermosillo, looking a lot more touched than Sarah. "That's real romantic." He beamed at Gus. Then he turned to the tenor. "Do you know the one about the burro? It's one of my mother's favorites."

The leader bowed and obliged with a song about a burro.

"You're a police officer," Sarah said to Elena. "Can't you arrest them?"

"I love mariachis," said Elena. Against the comforting shoulder of Dr. Samuel Parsley, she had recovered her equilibrium and appreciated the quality and volume of the band, all of whom sang and played their various instruments with talent and enthusiasm. They had drowned out the terrifying snarl of the phantom mountain lion. "I think this is the Jalisco Mariachi Band," said Elena. "They don't come cheap."

"No expenditure is too much for the mother of my future children," said Gus proudly.

More residents of the faculty apartment building crowded around in the hall and the entrance to the living room. "This is absolutely the last straw," said Sarah, who whirled and went off to lock herself in her bedroom.

Perry received a signal on his pager and went looking for a phone. Dinner guests and neighbors were now perched on furniture or sitting on the floor for the rest of the serenade. Managing to draw Elena aside, Perry relayed the information that Connie had a new lead.

"Tough," said Elena. "These guys are really good. I'm not leaving."

Looking shocked, Perry departed. Gus dismissed the mariachis himself, paying them for ten songs, although they protested that they had only sung eight and it wasn't their fault that the *patron's novia* had disappeared.

"I'll have to think of something else," Gus said sadly, then cheered up. "Fortunately, I'm an imaginative person, especially in matters of love and ladies."

The campus police, both Hispanic, clapped enthusiastically for the last song and left with the mariachis, one asking what they charged to sing at a *quinceanera*. The psychologists departed shortly thereafter, the Fongs extremely upset that they hadn't been able to thank their hostess for a very unusual evening. Dr. Parsley squeezed Elena's hand and said, "You're a classic case, you know. Call me." He dragged a confused-looking Michael Futrell out with him, making no effort to keep his voice down when he said, "You're not helping matters any, you know."

Elena was left with the dirty dishes and an absent roommate.

Well, she wasn't cleaning up on her own. She rapped at Sarah's door and shouted, "They're all gone. You can come out."

Sarah did. "That's it," she announced. "That's absolutely the last straw."

"For Pete's sake, Sarah. It was just a mariachi band. And a very good one."

"I have had quite enough of Gus's lame-brained impulses. I am not having his baby."

"Just because he hired a band doesn't mean you have to have a baby," Elena pointed out reasonably.

"I'm not only not having a baby, I'm moving out."

Elena gaped at her. "Where?" She thought a minute. "I guess we could go to my house," she said dubiously, thinking that she wasn't really ready for that. On the other hand, she owed Sarah for taking her in, and for introducing her to Dr. Parsley. Despite her objections, she'd found him reassuring. Maybe she would call him when she got through with the case. She remembered, conscience-stricken, that Perry had said there'd been another development. And she'd refused to go along. What was happening to her? Her job was the one thing that had usually gone well in her life.

"We don't have to go to your house," said Sarah. "I'll buy one of my own. And I won't tell anyone at the university where it is. So Gus can't harass me anymore."

"Houses are expensive," said Elena. "Why don't you just get a restraining order?"

37
..

Monday, May 27, 8:30 A.M.

Irrigation District Issues Warning

Farmers and other holders of water rights along the
Rio Grande were warned by the irrigation district that
there will be no September allotment.

Spokesperson Laura Chatam of Los Santos Water
Utilities, which gets its water from the river during
irrigation season, assured Los Santoans that they will
not go thirsty. However, with temperatures already
soaring over the hundred-degree mark and continu-
ing heat predicted, Chatam said that more stringent
rationing might have to be initiated sometime during
the summer. She urged the utility's customers to curb
water usage both inside and outside their homes and
businesses.

Los Santos *Times*, Monday, May 27

Elena took the elevator down to the ground floor of the
faculty apartment building, thinking about the water allotment
article. Would the farmers in Water Now freak out because of
the expected cutback in irrigation water? Did the problem mean
more bombs? She shuddered.

And all the crazy citizens attacking each other over lawn watering—if rationing was tightened, would they get meaner? She imagined the police run ragged while the temperatures got higher and higher; the air conditioners in departmental cars breaking down, overworked, stressed out, sweaty cops snarling at one another and the public. The elevator doors opened and she stepped out, wondering if this kind of alarmist thinking was a symptom of post-traumatic stress or a result.

Sam Parsley's big, hairy, rumpled, reassuring person flashed into her mind. Maybe that's what she needed. To talk to him, lie on his couch telling him her troubles while he ate everything in sight. Did he have a couch? Did he eat during therapy sessions? Did he share snacks with his patients?

She peered toward the doors of the lobby. Where the hell was Connie Amparan? Although she had refused to pursue the case last night with Perry, Connie had called that morning to relay information from the night before. Celestina Ortiz, unemployed Lower Valley *colonia* dweller, and the two Upper Valley farmers, Efren Maruffo and Ollie Ray Ralph, had all acquired explosives in recent months. The ATF agent suggested that he and Elena reinterview the three suspect members of Water Now.

Instead of seeing Connie, Elena started nervously when Michael Futrell jumped from a lobby chair and rushed toward her, words tumbling out as if he were afraid she'd silence him before he could get it all said. "Elena! Elena, I want to apologize. I saw what happened to you last night. I mean when that mariachi band came in. I guess I never realized how much my brother's death had affected you. I know something about post-traumatic stress—nightmares, flashbacks, overreaction to innocent stimuli. If there's anything I can do—"

The phrase "overreaction to innocent stimuli" pissed her off. But then he was a professor; he talked like that. Otherwise, he seemed to be playing nice for a change. Elena studied him. This was the kind and thoughtful, if stuffy, Michael she had known and felt so much affection for in the early months of their relationship, as opposed to the jealous and judgmental Michael she had seen in the month before they broke up. "I appreciate your concern, Michael, although I don't know what you could do."

He took her hands hesitantly. "That's the first civil word you've said to me since March. You don't know how happy it makes me. I've really missed you, Elena."

She nodded but said quite honestly, "I've been too angry to miss you, Michael, and too—I don't know—whatever's wrong with me."

"You are going to get help, aren't you? I promise, I won't complain if you decide to see Sam Parsley."

Elena felt her eyebrows rising, her irritation reasserting itself. Whoever she went to for therapy, if she decided to do it, was none of his business. Where did he get off? "I'm working the bomb case," she replied stiffly. "I don't have time for personal indulgences. If you've been reading the papers, you know that the whole city's in a panic."

"And with good reason," said Michael somberly. "No one knows where he'll hit next."

"Including me," agreed Elena grimly.

"I wonder—do you have *any* free time? Maybe we could go out tonight, perhaps see a movie. Something light and amusing to take your mind off the case and—other things."

Elena sighed. "You're twelve hours too late," she said. "The cellist—you remember? He came to complain about the noise last night? He mentioned that the jazz band's meeting tonight. Frankly, I jumped at the chance." Then she wondered how good an idea it was to mention the jazz band, of which Michael had always been jealous, particularly the trombonist, Rafer Martin.

Michael, with obvious difficulty, tried to look cheerful and sympathetic. "I understand. Maybe on the weekend."

She shrugged. "I don't know, Michael. Let me think about it."

"Hey, Elena, I've been waiting out in the parking lot for fifteen minutes."

She turned as Connie Amparan walked through the door,

looking eager and enthusiastic. Michael's face flushed with anger, and Elena thought, *He hasn't changed at all.* "Michael, this is Connie Amparan. ATF. We're working the bomb case together. Connie, Michael Futrell."

Michael nodded stiffly and said, "Perhaps we could talk later in the week, Elena. I've got a class to teach."

"As soon as you said ATF, your friend there got that constipated look on his face," said Connie, holding the lobby door for her, sounding bitter. "You wouldn't believe how many people respond that way since Waco."

They walked to the parking lot where Connie caught a campus cop trying to ticket his ATF car. Still grumpy, he was so curt that the lavender-suited officer backed off, alarmed. Elena was surprised. Connie was usually as even-tempered as you could expect from anyone with natural testosterone.

"Let's take the farmers first," he suggested.

"O.K. What kind of explosives did they buy?"

"Dynamite," said Connie. "Got it legally from a dealer here in town. For agricultural purposes, according to the form." They were talking over the roof of the car.

"The well bombs were dynamite," Elena mused.

"Right. It's a good lead."

They climbed into the car and headed for the two farms in the Upper Valley. "How's Perry doing with Brazlitt?" Elena asked. "Anything new there?"

"One of the spotted owl buddies now says he was actually in the forest with Brazlitt. But hell, it's been long enough that Brazlitt could have talked him into providing an alibi."

"Aren't his calls from the jail being monitored?"

"Well sure, but anyone from Water Now could have started putting pressure on his alibi witnesses. Actually, I think the case is coming together. We got the nun for sending the threats. Brazlitt, with a history of environmental terrorism, is in jail with an almost nonexistent alibi. Now we've got three members of the group buying explosives. Of course, they'll come up with some half-assed reason they needed dynamite, but the important thing is we know now that they use explosives and they have connections to buy."

Thinking about the case as they drove out of the city, Elena concluded that she didn't yet have any instinct that they were closing in on the bombers. As they entered the rural road system, she remembered Sarah's mariachi serenade. What a blast that had been! Not that Sarah had appreciated the gesture. She'd been furious.

But you had to hand it to McGlenlevie: obnoxious as he was, he was really pushing the courtship. Elena found it hard to believe that Sarah would actually leave her comfortable faculty apartment and buy a house to get away from Gus.

To ask questions about Maruffo's dynamite purchases, Connie and Elena had to pursue him into the far reaches of his fields, where they found him bending over a cotton plant talking in Spanish to one of his farmworkers. Before they could get out of the car, his wife, who had followed them, rolled down her van window and shouted, "Hey Efren, those two agents are back."

Maruffo looked up, spotted Connie and Elena, and scowled under the brim of his dusty Stetson. "Listen," he said when they were within speaking distance, "I already told you everything I know. I got nothin' more to say. *Comprende?*"

"What about that dynamite you ordered?" asked Amparan.

Elena was watching Maruffo closely and saw a flicker of unease cross his face. Then it was brown and bland again, and he said, "Like I told the dealer, it was for the farm."

"You still have it?"

"I used it."

"On what?"

"I—ah—used it to knock down a barn. Cheaper than taking it down piecemeal."

"O.K., let's see the barn," said Connie.

"It's gone."

"The foundation will be there. Some debris. Let's see it."

"Listen, I bought that dynamite legally. I got a permit for it. I don't have to—"

"Mr. Maruffo, I'm an ATF agent. Anyone buys explosives, I got a right to inquire. Maybe I'll get a team out here and search every nook and cranny on this farm to see what else I can find."

"Sure, you do that, an' I'm callin' my lawyer," blustered Maruffo.

"Estupido," said his wife. "That whole business was Ollie Ray Ralph's idea, not yours. Why should you—"

"Shut up," said Maruffo.

"It was Ralph's idea to blow up your barn?" asked Elena. "Or did he use his share of the explosives for something else? Maybe he's hanging on to them for some future project you and your gang are planning."

"What gang? I don't know what you're talking about."

"Reckon we'll have to visit Ralph, too," Connie said to Elena, as if they hadn't been planning to anyway.

"See what you did," Maruffo snarled at his wife.

"Put a crimp in those two-week hunting and fishing trips?" his wife retorted and stamped back to her van, her husband shouting after her.

"Settle with her later," said Connie. "We want to see this barn you blew up."

"Get a warrant. I'm not saying another word."

"We'll be back," Connie promised. He and Elena trudged to his car, then bumped along the rutted farm road between cotton fields. "What do you think?" he asked her.

"I think we saw all the barns he had when we were here before. They're still standing. So where's the dynamite? Be interesting to see what dumb story Ralph tells."

"You can bet Maruffo will have called him before we get there. I saw him head for his truck."

Efren Maruffo had called. "O.K.," said Ralph before Elena and Connie had crossed his threshold. "We've decided to come clean."

"We who?" asked Elena, excitement rising. Maybe Connie was right. Maybe they *were* closing in.

"Me an' Efren. I read about dynamite an' fish. I wanted to try it."

"Fish?" Connie scowled at him. "That's an even dumber story than Maruffo telling us he dynamited his barn."

"It's the truth," insisted Ralph. "You want to see the fish? Works like a charm. You set off the explosives, and the fish all float to the surface. I got enough we had to buy a second freezer. Wife's fit to be tied."

Connie scratched his head. "I'll take a look at the fish," said Elena. Ollie Ray Ralph had, as he said, hundreds of fish in his freezers. Gutting them must have been an interminable job. Probably he'd made his workers do it. Since the heads had been left intact, she examined the fish mouths and could find no evidence that they'd been hooked. On the other hand, some looked pretty battered. "Dynamiting fish, that's against the law," she said. "Far as I know."

"Why you think Efren stalled you?"

"But you didn't mind telling us about it?" said Elena.

"Better than being accused of those bombings in Los Santos," said Ollie Ray Ralph. "We knew what you were thinking."

"Where did you do this fish bombing?" asked Connie. Even looking at the victims, frozen and scaly, he obviously didn't believe the story.

"New Mexico. In the Gila."

"When?" asked Elena.

"February, March."

"Real sportsmen, aren't you?" She dialed information on an old black telephone and asked for the number of the ranger station in the Gila National Wilderness.

"Hey, that's long distance," Ralph objected.

"Send us the bill," she retorted and embarked on a three-minute conversation with a forest ranger, then gave the names and addresses of the culprits.

"What the hell," complained Ollie Ray. "I help you with your case, and you turn me in."

"That's right. They'll be taking you to court, Mr. Ralph. The guy I talked to said you can expect a big fine. And don't try to get rid of the evidence. I'll testify against you."

Connie followed her out of the Ralph ranch house, shaking his head. "I never heard of dynamiting fish."

"I have," said Elena. "And it sucks. They'll never in this world eat all those fish. Six months to a year from now, his wife will insist on throwing them out. Meanwhile, they screwed up the fishing in a couple of good lakes."

"You a fisherwoman?" asked Connie with the surprise of a city boy.

Elena shrugged. "I went fishing with my dad when I was a kid. To put something on the table. You know?"

"Not really. We bought it in the market for fast days, but more likely we made do with cheese enchiladas. Wonder if Celestina Ortiz is gonna tell us she's a fish dynamiter, too," mused the ATF agent.

38

"I was gonna use it," said Celestina Ortiz. "To drill myself a well." They'd found her in her backyard trying to repair a broken pipe that led to her cesspool. "You own property in Texas, you can drill a well. That's the law," she said defiantly.

Connie escorted her around the side of the house, away from the broken pipe and the odor. "You'd have to be pretty expert to make a well with dynamite," he said.

Celestina eyed him disdainfully. "I was in the army," she retorted.

"Were you?" Amparan looked interested, and Elena wondered if he'd missed that in the report.

"A lot of the shallow wells are contaminated," Elena remarked. "With that cesspool so close and the lot so small, you'd be asking for—"

"Hey, I wouldn't have to drink it."

"So where's the well?" Connie demanded.

Celestina's round face sagged with disappointment. "Nuthin' works out for me. You see that pipe? I can't afford—"

"So show us the dynamite," Connie interrupted.

"If I had the dynamite, I'd a done the well," she snapped, standing mutinously on stout legs in her dirt yard. Beside her grew a scraggly bush with yellow flowers. "The damn gang-bangers must a stole my dynamite."

"You reported the theft?" Elena asked.

"Yeah, right. Like if I say where I got the dynamite, my friend's ever gonna get me any more."

"We know where you got it," said Connie. "When did it disappear?"

"Last Wednesday night. Gone Thursday morning. Listen, I didn't set off none a them bombs. I didn't own none of that stuff that exploded—well, dynamite, but it wasn't my dynamite in the wells across town."

"What other stuff?" asked Connie.

She stared at him defiantly. "You think I can't figure out what the bomber used by hearin' the news on the radio?"

"So tell us about—"

"I'm not tellin' you nothin'. Anything I say, you're gonna use against me, right?"

"Right," Connie agreed. "First off, you didn't have that dynamite legally."

"Like I said, I bought it from a friend."

"We can arrest you for illegal possession."

"You do that. I got six kids here." Some of them were peering fearfully from the front door and the one front window, cracked and repaired with masking tape. "The county's gonna have to take them, 'cause my worthless husband went down to Jalisco to visit his brother, an' I ain't heard from him since."

"We're not arresting you now, but we've got our eye on you," said Connie. "You're a suspect. *Comprende?*"

"Sure. Hispanics always are," said Celestina bitterly. "Hispanics who ain't got runnin' water or toilets or—"

"I'm Hispanic," said Elena. "He's Hispanic."

"Maybe you should have stayed in the army." Connie turned and strode toward the car. Elena took a last look at Celestina Ortiz, a woman too big to have planted the bombs at H.H.U. or in the doctor's greenhouse. She probably couldn't have climbed the tower at the stonewashing plant or, with all that bulk, snuck into the water utilities office to leave the pipe bomb. But she knew how to get explosives. She could be supplying Brazlitt, or whoever had actually put the bombs in place. She could have made them. Maybe she'd learned in the army. But, Lord, where would she do it? In the house with her kids? Bombers got blown up by their own bombs, taking those in the house or apartment with them.

"All the stuff that was used in the bombs," said Elena to Connie. "Could Maruffo and Ralph have got it through their contacts with dealers?"

"Not legally," said Connie. "You need a permit and a good reason to have pyrodex, plastique, or detonating cord. Black powder's easier."

"She's been in the army. She had a dynamite contact. Maybe she knows where to buy the other stuff under the counter, how to build a bomb."

"Hell, you can buy army explosives manuals all up and down Dyer in the surplus stores," Connie replied.

"Seems to me I heard that in some class," Elena agreed. "She can't be the person who planted the bombs; she's too big. But she sure could have supplied the materials and even built the devices."

"Possible," Connie agreed. "We need to find out more about her. I'm going back to the office to get hold of her military records and check my sources to see who knows her in the underground explosives market. The two farmers, too. What about you? You want me to drop you back home?"

Elena thought a minute. "No, take me to headquarters. I can catch a ride home with someone at the end of the shift." She fastened her seat belt as he started the motor. "I haven't done any paperwork in days. If I don't start filing reports, my lieutenant's gonna cut off my epaulettes."

Connie laughed. "And break your sword, huh?"

"You got it." He turned onto the interstate and headed for the Piedras-Raynor exit, which would take them to LSPD headquarters.

The only item of interest in a long, dull afternoon of report writing was a visit from G. Washington. They had coffee together and talked over the case, Washington interested in Celestina Ortiz as part of the bomb plot. He grinned at her and said, "So which one of the feds are you workin' with tonight?"

Elena laughed and said, "I got a date with a Dixieland band."

"Listenin' or playin'?"

"I'm their singer, but I have to tell you they could do better. I've done more rock, folk, and Hispanic stuff than I ever did Dixieland up to now."

"You oughta hear my wife Sharana sing 'St. Louis Blues' or 'Georgia on My Mind.' That woman's got a voice like to make a grown man cry. Fell straight in love the first time I heard her sing in church."

"No kidding?" Elena perked up. "Why don't you all sit in tonight. They'd love to have a real singer. Do you play?"

He laughed. "Not a lick, but yeah, Sharana'd like that. Where and when?"

39

Monday, May 27, 8:30 P.M.

Child Drowns in High Water

Ofelia Canales, who lives in a small *colonia* on the banks of the Rio Grande, today mourns the death her daughter Viola, five. The Canales home is without water or sewer hookup; it was a hot day, so they decided to take a cooling dip in the river. Because water had just been released from the dams upstream, the river was high and running with great force. Viola ventured out a little too far and was swept away, her horrified family unable to rescue her.

Ofelia Canales says if they had water in their house, it would never have happened. She looks across the river to San Ysidro in Mexico, a neighborhood with running water, and asks, "Who lives in the Third World country? I think it is me."

Los Santos *Herald-Post*, Monday, May 27

Sharana Washington was a handsome woman, smooth milk chocolate skin, a face that glowed with goodwill and warmth, tall with a full-bodied womanliness, and she could sing! Her rich contralto bounced off the walls of the rehearsal room,

241

which had arched panels with murals of black-coated musicians playing jazz in twenties clubs. Elena liked the room and loved Sharana's voice. She expected to see pages fluttering on the music stands when that voice soared. The H.H.U. jazz band, students and professors, was thunderstruck. At the first break, they crowded around Elena to thank her for producing Mrs. Washington.

"With her singing, we could get a recording contract," said the portly classical cellist-turned-bass.

Elena's feelings might have been hurt if she hadn't agreed so wholeheartedly. Sharana's voice was a miracle. So what was she doing teaching chorus at Pancho Villa High? Elena put down the list of Water Now members she had been studying during the break and asked just that question when G. Washington's wife returned from the ladies' room.

Sharana's full-throated laughter turned heads in the room where the males of the band were emptying spit valves and performing other musical tasks Elena didn't care to witness. "Ah've got everything Ah want, honey," the black woman replied. "Lovin' family—all in good health, God be praised—a fine church to sing in, an' years worth of teenagers to herd toward decent lives. Ah do love children. You see that article about that poor little girl that drowned? But 'specially Ah love teenagers. No one in the world with more energy an' promise than a girl or boy on the threshold of life.

"An' best of all, Ah got mahself a man among men. Now if Ah'd gone off lookin' for big money an' big audiences, Ah wouldn't a been here to meet G. when he came to town an' joined mah church. Ah took one look at that man in his uniform with that nice, big, male body underneath, an' Ah knew Ah'd found what Ah'd been waitin' for. Had mah mama invite him home to dinner the first Sunday."

"Oh, really?" Elena grinned. "He says he heard you sing and fell in love."

Sharana laughed. "So he say. That man like the body in the choir robe 'fore ever he heard a note outa this mouth." She looked down at Elena's list. "You workin'? One thing G. knows is to leave it behind when he's off duty.

"You need a man, girl. Get yourself married. Now Ah know some teachers—" She glanced again at the list. "You got one right on your paper there. Philomeno Reyes. Real nice-lookin' boy. Must be about your age, give or take a few years. Teaches political science at Pancho Villa. Give him a month or two to get over his brother's death, an' Ah'll fix you two up."

Elena stared at G.'s wife, who wanted to fix her up with someone on the suspect list. Just her luck. Of course, they'd pretty much written off the grief-stricken Reyeses, who'd been spending all their time at the hospital when the bombings started and who no longer belonged to Water Now. "I'm sorry to hear about his brother. I did meet Mr. Reyes briefly at the hospital, he and his sister."

"Now there's a beautiful woman. She teaches computer science. All the nerdy kids love her to death. Nothin' she doesn't know about computers. In fact, all the males love her to death. You can watch 'em moonin' after Magdalena in the halls, their poor teenaged hormones dancin'. They're twins, you know—Philo an' Maggie. Not identical. Poor lambs—haven't got anyone left but each other now. That's about the saddest story Ah ever heard. Lost their whole family. Mama, papa, brothers, sisters. Makes me count mah blessin's. They say the Lord never gives you a burden too heavy to bear, but Ah wonder how they carry on."

"Tell me about them," urged Elena, thinking it wouldn't hurt to garner some information, even if the Reyes twins were way down on the suspect list.

"Oh, well. Must be a typical Los Santos story. Only sadder than most. They grew up in the *colonias,* Sparks Addition, Ah think. Big family, no money, an' they worked their way all the way up to teachin' degrees. Philo tole me once, he an' Maggie, they picked chili, onions, an' cotton with the migrant workers. Pickin' cotton, that's hard work—stoop labor. Mah grandmama picked cotton back in Mississippi when she was a girl. Talked about it to the day she died. Ah don't envy the Reyes twins that cotton pickin'. Or all their loved ones dyin'. Cancer took every one of 'em. Makes your heart turn cold to think of it."

G., who had sat in listening while his wife sang, strolled over with Rafer Martin. "Honey, you're talking this young detective's ear off."

"Well, you weren't here, G. An' you know Ah do like to talk. Sorry, honey," she said to Elena. "Your turn if you want to say something."

Elena smiled at her. "Not at all. You're an interesting conversationalist, Mrs. Washington."

"Sharana, child."

Elena nodded, thinking that Sharana Washington wasn't that much older than she, probably about midway between Elena and G.

Rafer Martin was laughing when he put his arm around Elena's shoulders. "You feel like talking, this is the lady to come to. She's a good listener."

"Detectives are supposed to be," said G. "Likely, Sharana, you're about to be arrested. What did she get you to confess to?"

"Likin' teenagers," Sharana replied promptly.

"Well, that is a crime," said G. "Spent three-four hours today chasing down some gang members. Heard they had dynamite, an' sure enough, we found it. They wouldn't say where they got it or what they were goin' to do with it."

"Which gang?" asked Elena, remembering that Celestina Ortiz had claimed gangbangers stole her dynamite.

"Fatherless—Lower Valley."

Elena sighed. "You may have cleared Celestina Ortiz."

"Can't believe you're talkin' bombs, G.," said his wife. "This is a music session, not a crime session."

"Sorry, honey." G. looked genuinely contrite.

"She's got him trained," Elena said to Rafer. "My ex never shut up about narc business. Not that he wanted to hear about my adventures, but—"

Everyone in the room turned toward the shrill, angry voice of Rafer's wife, Helen.

"There you stand with your arm around her, too busy with your affair to take me to that gallery opening, but you say nothing's going on. I didn't believe you before, and I certainly don't—"

Rafer's arm dropped from Elena's shoulders. "Knock it off, Helen," he snarled back. "I'm sick to death of your accusations."

"Oh, mah," breathed Sharana Washington and glanced at Elena, who could feel her cheeks warm with embarrassment.

"You're making a mistake, Mrs. Martin," said Elena, thinking, on the one hand, that she shouldn't dignify such an unfounded accusation with a defense, on the other, that she didn't want the Washingtons to think she had a thing going with a married man. "I never see your husband when he doesn't have a trombone in his hand."

"The only thing in his hand when I came in was you," Helen Martin shouted. Her face had turned a blotchy red, her usual attitude of disdainful hauteur vanished in a cloud of jealousy. Her clothes, however, were expensive and well cared for, as was her makeup. She'd obviously taken her time dressing for this ugly scene.

"Figuratively," Elena muttered. "And I don't like being slandered."

"Isn't that too bad?" Helen Martin whirled under the disapproving eyes of the band. "I'll see you at home, Rafer, and you'd better not be gone much longer."

"Right," muttered Rafer. "One more set, and I'm going out to find a divorce lawyer."

Great, thought Elena. *Now the Washingtons will think I broke up the marriage.*

The trumpet player cleared his throat. "Shall we start?"

"Let's hear both of the ladies singing together," said the student banjo player.

"Good idea," Sharana agreed. "You want me to take the harmony?"

"No, I will," said Elena, hoping that Sharana didn't believe Helen Martin's accusations. Rafer whispered an apology, and

the band reassembled, but Elena had a hard time keeping her
mind on the music. The story of the Reyes twins kept nagging
at her mind.

When the session ended, Rafer said, "She rattled you, didn't
she?"

Elena thought he was talking about Sharana.

"Helen. She rattled you. I'm really sorry."

"Oh. No, Rafer, don't worry about it." Elena hurried after the
Washingtons, leaving Rafer looking hurt, but she didn't have
time to placate the embarrassed husband. She had to talk to G.

"Get Sharana to tell you about the Reyes twins," she said
when she caught up. "Then see if you don't think we should
look into their activities lately."

Sharana looked horrified, G. surprised.

40
· ·

City Should Fear Drought

Rio Grande Compact Commissioner Paul Manfred said yesterday at a meeting on water rights that the area is overdue for a drought. He explained that droughts occur in twenty-two-year cycles, tied to low sunspot activity and El Niño. Both the fifties and seventies brought drought to the area, and the nineties can be expected to produce the same conditions.

A severe drought, said Manfred, could be ruinous. With an annual rainfall of less than nine inches and the disappearance of groundwater supplies from the Hueco and Mesilla Bolsons, Los Santos and Dona Ana Counties depend on the river for irrigation and drinking water seven months of the year.

Several winters of low snowfall in the San Juan Mountains and the Sangre de Cristos would lower the water levels at Elephant Butte and Caballo Reservoirs to the point where little or no water could be released. In that case, the river would be reduced to a "toxic trickle," composed of returned water from irrigation canals and sewers.

Los Santos *Times*, Tuesday, May 28

Elena pushed the drought story away and finished her coffee, which, in self-defense, she had perked herself. However, the cereal was Sarah's purchase: instant oatmeal, lumpy and tasteless. If Elena had had the time, she'd have made *huevos rancheros,* not that Sarah liked spicy food.

Sarah was laughing over the letters to the editor. "Did you see this message from the bishop?" she asked.

Elena shook her head. She had to be at headquarters at eight so had settled for a quick look at the front page, which hadn't been reassuring. Would hearing that drought was inevitable set the bomber off again?

"The bishop says the federal government is persecuting a nun."

Elena had to laugh. "He obviously doesn't know Sister Gertrudis Gregory. The woman admits to sending the threatening letters that preceded the bombs."

Sarah looked horrified.

"And she was out on bond at the time for harassing clinic patients here on campus."

In her tailored robe, blond-gray hair short and neat—Sarah never came to the table looking sleep-tousled—she clicked her tongue disapprovingly, sipped Elena's coffee, and continued to read. She claimed that the irritation quotient of the letters to the editor served to wake her up and sharpen her mind for her day in the electrical engineering department. Absently, she reached for the ringing telephone behind her on the buffet, answered, and handed it to Elena without taking her eyes from the paper.

"G. here," said a deep voice. "Had a call from Perry."

"Another bomb?" asked Elena.

"Not yet. He's rattled because a bunch of Catholics showed up at the federal building at seven this mornin' to protest FBI discrimination against the Church."

Elena whistled softly.

"He called from the county courthouse. Couldn't even get to his own office. They've packed the waitin' room so no one can squirm through, an' none of the agents or staff can find the key to the night door." G. sounded amused.

Elena had the sinking feeling that the bomber was destroying the whole social and political fabric of the city. He'd set the waterless against those who had plumbing, the poor against the middle class, Church against state. Citizens were alarmed, as was Elena herself.

But would she have felt that way if she weren't so stressed-out? Under better circumstances, surely she'd have been ignoring the uproar, going about her business, which was catching the bomber. "What did you think about the Reyes family?" she asked G.

"Sad story," the sergeant replied. "What do *you* think they have to do with the case?"

"They grew up in the *colonias*—really poor, according to Sharana. Everyone died of cancer. Maybe it was the water. Maybe—"

"Who-ah. Cancer can be genetic."

"Or environmental. People in the *colonias* store their water in whatever containers they can get. Maybe the Reyeses used—I don't know—toxic waste barrels or something. We ought to at least look into it."

There was the usual silence while G. considered her suggestion. "Well, the feds are chasin' down everything else. Connie's traced the dynamite from my gang bust to Celestina Ortiz to the guy she got it from, which doesn't mean she didn't plan to use it for another Water Now attack, but—well, we could spend a mornin' on the Reyes twins. Hate to hassle someone who looks as miserable as they did when we talked to 'em at the hospital."

"Grief can be a motive for violence," said Elena. "Fear, too."

"Fear?"

"If everyone in your family died of the big C, wouldn't you be afraid you were next?"

"Or maybe you know you're next. Maybe you've already got it," mused G. "So you want to do as much damage as you can before you go down."

"I had a case like that," said Elena. "One of the scariest people I ever arrested. No remorse."

They made arrangements to meet at headquarters.

• • •

G. and Elena agreed to find out what they could about the twins before talking to them again. However, they did call Pancho Villa High to be sure the suspects hadn't skipped town. The office secretary said both teachers had taken compassionate leave because of a death in the family. In their absence, Elena went to the high school and talked to teachers who worked with the Reyeses, all of whom thought well of them, felt sympathy because of their tragic history, and wondered why the police would be interested in Philo and Maggie.

Elena replied that all Water Now members, present and former, were being questioned because of the bombings. Some of the reactions to that remark were interesting. A shop teacher said, "You can forget Water Now. Philo quit because they were a do-nothing bunch. All talk, couldn't get them out to protest more than once a month. Me, I think the bombers are one of those hard-nosed national groups. Like a militia. We've got militias in Texas. I'd look into them."

So Philomeno Reyes thought Water Now wasn't militant enough? Did he know about the threatening notes Sister Gertrudis Gregory had sent? Had he started his own campaign, using the nun's list of the guilty? But what would a social studies teacher know about making bombs? Elena had taken college chemistry at UNM in Albuquerque. They hadn't taught bomb-making. She doubted that UTLS did, either.

A possible answer to her question came from a young woman who taught remedial math. She said, amused, "Magdalena told me once that you could learn to make a bomb by surfing the Net."

Elena laughed companionably. "Did she take notes?"

"Download and print out, you mean?"

"Right." Was that what she meant?

"I don't think so," said the math teacher wryly. "Magdalena loves the Net, but she was more into the health pages and the grief groups."

"And her brother?"

"Philo?" The teacher shook her head. "No interest in

computers at all. Philo's a tinkerer. In his garage workshop. Projects for the house he bought last year."

"Do they live together?"

"Mag has her own apartment."

Elena reflected that a garage workshop could be used for bomb building, although such activities wouldn't endear you to your neighbors. She went from the school to the neighborhood, where people admired Philomeno Reyes for taking much better care of his property than you'd expect of a bachelor. The scraggly lawn, for instance, had been replaced by nice rock work and desert plants, and the garage, which had been falling down, now looked good enough to live in. They teased him about hiding an illegal maid in there. Elena listened to all this while she studied the neat yard and nicely painted garage, which stood at the end of the driveway, separate from the house and, she thought, alley accessible.

She went over to the next street and talked to the woman in the house behind his. Mrs. Castillo said she wasn't one to complain, and she knew poor young Mr. Reyes was grieving for his brother, but she did hate his coming and going at all hours of the night in that truck of his.

Elena got a description of the truck, which wasn't in his driveway. With some doctoring, it could be the truck driven by the man who had turned up at H.H.U. and at the doctor's house. And Philomeno Reyes could be driving around at night and in the daytime planting bombs when he was supposed to be at the hospital or sublimating his grief on the highways and byways of Los Santos. He could be putting fake signs on his truck in the privacy of the garage, where the neighbors thought he planned to hide an illegal maid. One lady said Reyes claimed to be putting in a shower during his weekends behind closed garage doors, but maybe he was making bombs instead.

She returned to headquarters where G., in pursuing information about the family, had turned up a strange coincidence. Until the previous year, the brother who had died most recently had worked for Pan-American Stonewashing. "He got laid off because of his health."

"And lost his insurance," murmured Elena. "Remember Philomeno saying that poor, unemployed Hispanics on Medicaid didn't get liver transplants?"

G. remembered. "And Sharana said a sister died before that. Ovarian cancer," said G. "I tracked down all the deaths. Had the death certificates faxed over." He passed them across the aisle of cubicles on Homicide Row. G. had commandeered Leo's desk, Leo having taken family leave after the birth of his babies.

Elena studied the fax. "Oh, boy," she whispered. "Did you see who signed the certificate on the sister who died of ovarian cancer?" G. stopped in the middle of another call to glance in her direction. "Dr. Bates Morrison—whose greenhouse was bombed."

Looking grim, G. called a number he didn't have to look up. "Connie?"

Elena called the office of the doctor, whose nurse said he was out of town. She denied having a Maria Reyes Tomillo in the patient files. "This might have been a charity case," Elena suggested. "Do you keep those in a different cabinet?"

"May I ask why the police want patient information?" asked the woman in a voice as starchy as a nurse's cap. "The information in such files is confidential."

"We're trying to find out who bombed the doctor's greenhouse," said Elena. "Maybe you'd better cooperate before they hit his office."

There was a shocked silence. Then, "You think a patient did that? I never—all Doctor's patients *love* him."

"What about the ones who die? Do their families—"

"He volunteers two days a month at Casa de la Familia. It's a free clinic near—"

"Sparks Addition," Elena finished for her, feeling the adrenaline shoot into her bloodstream. She was beginning to see the trail to an arrest opening up in an underbrush of unconnected information. "What about malpractice suits? Any by people named Reyes or Tomillo?"

"No," said the nurse sharply.

Elena called the clinic, but their records from the time of Maria Tomillo's death had been lost in a fire-bombing.

"Tell me about it," said Elena, excited. "Do they know who did it?"

"Sure," said the volunteer receptionist. "A guy named Moreno. We treated a kid of his with a broken arm and reported child abuse. He got out on bail and threw a cherry bomb through the window of the room where we keep the records. We lost them all."

G. remembered the incident. "Gasoline in a mayonnaise jar. Connie's going to run a check to see if the Reyes twins had access to explosives. Perry's checking for military experience with explosives."

"I think we should go out to that clinic," said Elena. "The receptionist told me that a volunteer will be in this afternoon who's been working there for seven years. That covers the time of Maria Tomillo's death and then some. If we can't get any information, we'll try calling Morrison in Maine. Oh, and we could check out Sparks Addition. See the old family homestead, talk to any neighbors left from the time the Reyes family lived there."

"Hope they don't blow up anyone else while we're fumbling around in the dark," muttered G.

"Hey, this is the first time I've had that feeling I get when I'm closing in," said Elena.

41
..

The clinic was a long, plain, cement-block building, white paint peeling off the rough surfaces, a flat roof covered with gravel, and an unpaved parking lot filled with old cars and trucks, some of which looked as if they'd been abandoned rather than driven there by patients. G. and Elena found Coe Matterly, the volunteer they were seeking, behind a scarred metal reception desk facing a large, spare room full of tired women seated on ancient folding chairs, old men leaning against walls, and children either sprawled lethargically in parents' laps or playing between the crooked rows of chairs. Elena thought this was the last place she'd want to be if she were sick. But then, for these people, it was probably the only option available.

Mrs. Matterly was a gaunt woman with iron-gray hair pulled into a practical bun. She wore a faded, flowered dress with a hand-knitted sweater over her shoulders, surely unnecessary in May in a building with only ceiling fans, no air-conditioning. "Take a number," she told them. G. flashed his badge and introduced Elena.

"We haven't lost any drugs, we don't rat on our patients, and you earn too much to qualify for free care. Anything else I can help you with?" She stood to tap the head of a little boy who

255

had snuck up and kicked her desk. He burst into giggles and rolled away.

"We're looking for information about Maria Reyes Tomillo," said Elena. "A patient of Dr. Bates Morrison."

"Maria Tomillo is dead," said Mrs. Matterly.

"We know," Elena replied. "And her files were lost in a fire-bombing."

"Abusive men should have Beware the Dog signs branded on their foreheads," said Mrs. Matterly. "It took us three years to replace the equipment we lost because of that vicious coward. And the files—they're gone forever."

"But the receptionist this morning said you might remember Mrs. Tomillo," said Elena.

"*Silencio!*" shouted the volunteer into the raucous hubbub of the room.

"Tell you what," said G. "I'll take over as receptionist and bouncer. You go talk to Detective Jarvis. Before any more bombs go off."

Coe Matterly squinted at them suspiciously. "You think Maria's death has something to do with our fire-bombing? You're wrong. It was—"

"No," said Elena, drawing the woman away from her desk. "We're investigating the bombing at the doctor's house."

As they headed toward a room so small Elena took it for a former closet, a hush fell over the waiting room. G. had taken the receptionist's chair and was moving his eyes from one patient to the next, as if memorizing faces with a view to making an arrest.

"Could anyone in Maria's family have blamed the doctor for her death?" Elena asked.

"Ovarian cancer is hard to diagnose. She'd had symptoms, but they slipped by the doctors. By the time it was caught, nothing could be done for Maria. You think her husband—"

"We don't know," said Elena. "We're running down a number of leads."

"Tomas Tomillo was devastated when she died. It's a hard death. And her so young. Maybe if she'd had a private physician, the cancer might have been caught earlier. But here—we're a stopgap between sickness and death." Coe Matterly sighed. "Our patients see whatever doctor's volunteering that day, not that she didn't make an effort to come on days when Dr. Morrison would be here. Poor Maria was so sure he'd save her, him being doctor to rich women over on the Westside, the mayor's wife and such.

"He operated on her, took out everything. That broke her heart. It meant no more children. Morrison told her he'd got it all—they always say that—and he didn't charge her. But the cancer had spread and she died. Six months later, I think it was."

"And the family? How did they take it?" Elena asked.

"Well, as I said, Tomas was heartbroken. Both of them had been hoping for a miracle. But I don't think he would do anything violent. The angriest ones were her brothers—but one of them's dead now, and the other's a schoolteacher—not a likely person to bomb a doctor." Mrs. Matterly smiled dryly. "No, I think you're barking up the wrong tree, Detective."

"What did the brothers say or do?" Elena asked as casually as she could.

"Fernando—he's dead—just swore. Said the gringos were killing them all. I'm not sure what he meant. He was probably in the early stages of his own illness." She rubbed her forehead wearily. "I hope you're not going after poor Philomeno. He's had so much grief already."

"What did *he* say?"

"He said Maria died because the doctor didn't pay attention when it would have counted. Which is unfair. The doctors come here free. There are so many patients, they have practically no time with each individual—five minutes maybe. We have little diagnostic equipment. We're a quick-fix institution. But Philomeno blamed the doctor. And other people. Names I didn't recognize and don't remember."

Elena shivered. If Philomeno Reyes was the bomber, those names Mrs. Matterly hadn't recognized and couldn't remember might be people who needed to be warned.

When they returned to the reception area, every child was sitting quietly beside a parent, conversation had disappeared, and Sergeant G. Washington was reading *Peter Rabbit* to the waiting patients while a reluctant teenager in a gang jacket translated into Spanish. Elena and the volunteer receptionist had to wait for the end of the story.

"Anglo," said one mother, nodding when the reading ended. She was talking about Mr. MacGregor, the farmer who was after Peter Rabbit in the story. Elena perceived the comment as a sign of the split the bomber had rent in the fabric of the community. Hispanics did well in Los Santos; they were part of the power structure, but now the poor Latinos felt threatened, as did the middle-class Anglos.

G. passed the battered storybook to Mrs. Matterly, said, "Ma'am," politely, and nodded Elena toward the door. They climbed into the departmental Pontiac that Elena had checked out and headed for Sparks Addition, where the Reyes family had made their home before death began to overtake them all. Elena told G. about the tragedy of Maria Tomillo, née Reyes, and the reaction of her brothers.

In the poor environs of Sparks Addition they found the Reyes home, which stood empty, decaying, and forlorn. Elena marveled that parents and six children could have lived in the small structure. When she looked through the broken windows, she saw floors littered with the debris of overnight transients and partying teenagers looking for privacy. A broken pipe ran aboveground to a depression at a back corner of the small lot.

"Cesspool," G. guessed. A lingering stench rose from the ground.

Under the lean-to in back where the family must have congregated, maybe slept to catch a breeze on hot nights, two barrels still sat, fading letters identifying them as the property of Olmos Chemicals, Inc.

Elena studied the containers. "That's the drinking water supply," she said. "Probably the cause of the cancer."

"You don't know that," G. protested.

"You saw that guy out on the street selling barrels. People

think if they wash a barrel out, it's going to be safe, but no one knows what's been in them, or whether it's dangerous, or whether it can be washed away. It's a problem on both sides of the border. You ever looked at the statistics on birth defects in these areas?"

They were walking to the front of the house when an old man hobbled over from the next yard. "The Fargo brothers trying to sell you this place?" he demanded in Spanish. The man was looking suspiciously from her to G., and she wondered if he thought he was about to gain, as neighbors, an interracial couple.

"Bad luck house. You won't live to pay it off. Nobody worked harder than Paco Reyes, but he died before he could pay off the last year. They all died, and the Fargos took the house back." The old man cackled. "But the sons of whores can't sell it. It's haunted."

Had the Fargo brothers been among the names cursed by Philomeno Reyes when his sister Maria died? "Do the Reyeses ever come back here, *abuelo?*" she asked.

"No more. They left to avoid the curse on the family. The youngest ones, they maybe could have paid the house off for their mother, but they took her away. It did no good. They're still dying one by one. Even the cousin who lived with them—I hear he's got the cancer in the *cojónes.* Big-time businessman with his store on Dyer, guns and—"

"Ammunition? Explosives?" Elena interrupted.

"Sure. Anything you want. Jesus Reyes. His father died in the mines in Mexico, so he come here to his uncle, who married a good girl from Juarez so he'd have a mother for the boy. Jesus shoulda stayed in Mexico where there wasn't no curse on the family, but he come to the U.S." The old man looked around bitterly. "We all did. An' look what we got. Houses with curses. Land we pay on, an' then they take it back after we've built our homes. Like they done Paco when he died."

"Do you know Philomeno and Magdalena?" G. asked in his broken Spanish.

The old man backed away. "Who are you? You're not looking to buy the cursed house."

"Sir," Elena called, but the old man tottered to his own home and slammed the door. "Jesus Reyes," she murmured.

"Wonder if Connie's turned his name up?" G. mused. They walked to the car, now surrounded by children trailing fingers through the road dust that coated the hot metal.

Sweating, G. looked up at the glaring blue of the cloudless sky and said, "Think it's ever gonna rain again?"

42
..

Wednesday, May 29, 4:05 A.M.

They stood around the smoking remains of the car. Elena had
been awakened by a call from G. just as the mountain lion
sprang at her from under the dining room table. When its snarl
had turned shrill and strange, she struggled out of the nightmare and answered the telephone.

The driver was dead, the car blackened. When Elena arrived,
the firemen were cooling down the hot metal with hoses.
Shortly after that, EMS removed the partially charred body and
took it away. Neighbors, robes thrown over their nightclothes,
still stood in the cool air of the desert night gawking at this
unbelievable spectacle in their quiet, affluent neighborhood.
No one knew whose car it was or who the driver had been.

Since any bombing might be connected to their case, the task
force had congregated for the investigation. Logic and evidence convinced them that the bomb had been wired to explode
when the engine was turned on, but every car owner and car on
the block was accounted for. Elena wondered aloud if the
deceased might not have been stealing the vehicle. "How many
practitioners of grand theft auto are unlucky enough to choose
a car with a bomb attached?" Connie asked wryly.

That theory might have worked, but car bombs didn't usually
hang fire until the driver was well on his way. Ignition

triggered them. G. guessed that the vehicle had been a Jeep Grand Cherokee, which was popular with thieves, but there were no reports of one being stolen. I.D. & R. had tried for a serial number from the shattered remains. They had a few digits, not enough.

"Maybe the thief rolled the car down the hill and started it once he got away from the house," Elena suggested. God she was tired. "Or the owner. Maybe he let it roll downhill. Sneaking out on his wife. Kid sneaking the family vehicle out in the middle of the night. Something like that." She yawned, covering her mouth after the fact. Grandmother Waite, who hated yawns, would be incensed.

The others looked up the long hill—four blocks to the end where the street gave way to wild mountain arroyos. They fanned out and began knocking on doors. Irate homeowners, once they had ascertained that their vehicles were safe in driveways and garages and their family members safe in bed, objected to being awakened. In the four blocks, six houses were empty, no one answering after repeated knocking and ringing. Elena called headquarters to get the names of the missing householders, just in case they were identifiably someone who might have been targeted by the bomber. The yards of the empty houses weren't overly lush; the names didn't ring any bells. By then the sun was rising over the mountain, light blooming delicately on the hills, the cool, dry freshness of early morning invigorating the sleepy investigators.

"I'm for an egg and chorizo burrito," said Connie, stretching. "Let's meet at Casa Veracruzana for breakfast? I'll tell you what I found out about this Jesus Reyes."

"You've got information you didn't mention?" Melon still looked and sounded grumpy.

"We had another bombing. Another guy died," said Amparan. "I thought we were concentrating on that."

"Yeah, sorry," said Melon. "Not enough sleep lately. Don't know how you keep looking so great, Elena. You make being dragged out of bed in the middle of the night almost a pleasure."

"Doesn't she?" Amparan agreed. G. grinned.

"Not for me," Elena grumbled. "So are we heading for breakfast? I need about ten cups of coffee."

"An' pancakes," said G. "If all they've got is stuff with chili on it at this place, let's meet somewhere else."

Elena grinned. "I'll bet you'd like some grits. And fried ham. And turnip greens."

"Only if they come with pancakes an' bacon," G. retorted, grinning. "An' I never eat greens before midday."

Perry took a call on his cell phone and told them the medical examiner, after a closer look, thought the corpse was Hispanic, young. Nineteen or twenty. No I.D. But he did have a tattoo of a dripping knife inside a heart with the word Rosa on the knife handle. The tattoo decorated his left pectoral area. Having thought about this information, Elena went to her truck to radio for a computer check on the tattoo. As she made the request, a reporter from Channel 7 stuck his head through the open window to ask about the bombing. Until then, no media representatives had shown up at the scene.

Elena waved him off because her information was coming through. She climbed back out and said to Perry, "The deceased is probably Jose "Mako" Teran, car thief from across the border. He's been on our books for six years. Served time for grand theft auto, got swapped for an American in a Mexican jail and released."

Melon turned to the reporter and said, "There's your story. Car owners have found a new deterrent to auto theft."

"Can I quote you?" the reporter asked.

"No."

43
..

Water Cop Attacked

Bert Margolin, a water conservation inspector who fields complaints against those who flout the watering rules, says last year he and his colleagues issued 121 citations and 882 warnings. Although the recipients were not happy, not one threatened him.

Last week Margolin was directed by an anonymous caller to the house of Parker Chasefield, 85, of Copper Street. Chasefield was watering his yard on Monday, when watering home lawns is not allowed. When Margolin issued a warning to Chasefield, the householder hit him with a sprinkler. Sonia Chasefield, the 83-year-old wife of the attacker, then struck Margolin with a trowel.

Mrs. Chasefield and her husband were charged with assault. Margolin suffered bruises to his cheek and chin. His toupee was washed off by water from the hose and landed in a petunia bed. Mrs. Chasefield said, "He deserved it. You can't grow flowers without watering."

Los Santos *Times*, Wednesday, May 29

The pancake house was filling up, but Elena and the explosives men had secured a round table in the corner overlooking the traffic on North Mesa. Connie had grumbled because there was no chorizo on the menu, no breakfast burritos. But the coffee was hot and plentiful, and Elena didn't much care what else they served.

"Jesus Reyes," Melon prompted his ATF counterpart, who, in the absence of burritos, had settled for the He-Man Breakfast: eggs, steak, pancakes, hash browns, toast, juice, and coffee.

Amparan laid down his fork. "Jesus Reyes. Gun dealer, but he's also a licensed explosives dealer."

Elena held her coffee cup out to the waitress for a refill. "Can we tell if he's been providing explosives to a relative?"

"Or to Brazlitt?" asked Melon.

"We'll have to visit Mr. Reyes and comb his records," said Connie. "In the meantime, I plan to finish my steak."

"Can you do that?" Elena asked. "Don't we need a warrant?"

"For the steak, no. But hey, I'm ATF. Any explosives dealer is in my jurisdiction." Connie grinned. "Wanna come along?"

"Absolutely," said Elena. Her beeper went off, and she headed for the cashier's counter where, cranky from lack of sleep, edgy from overdosing on coffee, she reached over the counter and plucked up the phone when the cashier suggested that she use a public telephone outside. The call provided Elena with some very interesting information, which she took back to the table.

"Auto Theft says one Benjamin Fargo has reported the theft of a Jeep Cherokee," she told her colleagues. "The ID number matches the four digits we got off the vehicle that was bombed."

"Fargo?" G. looked thoughtful. "The *colonia* neighbor said the Fargo brothers owned the Reyes plot and got it back when the father died."

"Bingo." Elena grinned. "There's just one hitch. Benjamin Fargo claims it was in his driveway in Santa Teresa, nowhere near the street where we found the bombed-out vehicle with Teran's body in it."

"I think I better go talk to this Mr. Fargo," said G. "Push him a little on where he really was last night."

"Maybe he was visiting a lady friend at one of the houses where no one answered the door," Elena suggested. "Or maybe one of those houses is owned by drug dealers, and he was making a buy. Want me to call the narcs?" She felt wired, full of ideas. "Maybe he murdered someone in the neighborhood, then came out and found his wheels gone and the street full of police. That would shake him up."

"Maybe we should talk to Mr. Fargo first," said G. dryly, "before we go rushin' off in twenty different directions. Anyway, you're interviewin' the explosives dealer with Connie."

"Right," said Elena. "Let's go."

"He doesn't open till nine," said Connie.

"You better talk to the other brother, too," said Elena. "If the bomber went after one, maybe number two is next."

"We'll take care of it," Perry assured her.

"So you think we're right about the Reyes family, Perry?" Elena laughed exuberantly. "You've given up on Brazlitt, right?"

"One bomber in jail is worth two maybes running around loose," said Perry. "But the Reyeses look good. They'd be easy recruits for Brazlitt."

"They quit before he came to town," said Elena.

Melon and Washington paid their bill and left in pursuit of the Fargo brothers. Elena and Connie bought newspapers and settled in to wait until Jesus Reyes opened his establishment.

"Oh, wow! Look at this!" Elena passed her paper to Connie. The car bombing was plastered across the front page in an eight-column banner headline. "Bomber Strikes Again."

"Well, it's no surprise they'd feature it," said Connie. "It's the biggest story of the year, and people are getting pretty nervous."

"No, no. Look in the lower right hand corner. About the Mexican Consul."

Connie folded the paper and read the story. "Can you believe that?" he exclaimed, and read the statement aloud. "'A vicious attack on a Mexican citizen, comparable to, but worse than, recent attacks by U.S. law enforcement officials?' What does he think? We're booby trapping cars? And he doesn't mention what Señor Teran was doing in the car. Look at this. 'A dangerous precedent in border relations.' Shit!"

"And they arrest and jail any cop from the U.S. who sets foot over the middle of the bridge wearing a gun. I knew the last guy they put in jail for taking hot pursuit across the border."

"The moral of this story is never make jokes with a reporter. Remember Melon talking to that TV guy, something about car owners coming up with a new deterrent to auto theft? They probably put it on the six A.M. news, even though Perry said no to a quote. Then some illegal getting ready to go to work heard it and called the consulate. Bingo! We've got an international incident."

"I hope Perry doesn't get in hot water," said Elena.

"The consul didn't mention the FBI."

"Oh, boy," she said, having turned to the local section. "Now golden-agers are attacking the water cops."

"It's getting pretty hairy," Connie agreed.

Ten minutes later, Connie rose and glanced at his watch. "We oughta get there just when Reyes unlocks his door."

Elena nodded. "This should to be interesting."

"He's definitely got cancer," said Elena. She and Connie were in the glass-windowed office of Jesus Reyes, Connie at the computer, Elena on the telephone making calls. But she was staring out at the owner, who looked gaunt, gray, and inexplicably indifferent to their activities.

"O.K., here's a pyrodex order." Connie read off the name and telephone number of the buyer and the amount purchased. Elena wrote it down. "Why do you think he's got cancer?" Connie asked.

"Look at him. He looks like death in cowboy boots. Even his hat's too big. And the old man who lived next door to them said the cousin had *cojónes* cancer." She dialed the number Connie had given her. He went on searching six months of Reyes's orders, looking for the types of explosives that had been used in the bombings.

The purchaser of the pyrodex told Elena that he'd only ordered and taken delivery on half the amount recorded in the Reyes computer file. "If you're trying to hang that bombing at H.H.U. on me, forget it. I can prove what I did with the stuff, and I'm calling my lawyer right now."

"Thanks for your cooperation, sir," said Elena. "O.K., we now know where the sprinkler system pyrodex came from," she said to Connie.

"I've got three detonating cord purchasers for you." He dictated the information. Elena made the calls. Outside in the store, Jesus Reyes showed a 9-millimeter Glock to a customer, but he didn't seem to have his heart in the sale. Sweat dripped off his face in the cool, air-conditioned store. His mouth opened, and he gasped in air. *Against pain,* Elena thought. Was he another victim of those chemical barrels at the deserted Reyes homestead, the boy who had come to live with his uncle in the land of promise after his father died in a Mexican mine?

Two of the purchasers of detonating cord verified their orders as recorded in Reyes's computer. The third hadn't purchased as much as the record showed, nor paid as much as Reyes had entered. "No big sales of black powder," said Amparán, "but he's bought plenty. We'll have to check what he has stored."

Reyes never even turned to look at them. He sold the Glock, then sat down at a desk with another customer—hard-hat type—and began to write. *Taking an order?* Elena wondered.

"Here we go," said Connie. "A slurry order. Four containers." He gave Elena a name and number.

"I don't use slurry," said the owner of the business indignantly. "You ever see any oil wells around here? Why are you wasting my time with dumb questions?"

"That one's a complete fake," Elena told Connie. "Four slurry canisters, four wells." Reyes was gulping down pills. *For pain? Chemotherapy?*

Connie began to dictate a list of eight dynamite purchases. Elena called construction companies until she found several that denied ordering as much as Reyes's invoice showed. "There's the car bomb and the well dynamite," she said.

"One order for plastique," said Connie. He gave her a number.

The president of a small construction company said he wouldn't know what to do with plastique. "That's the greenhouse," said Elena.

"And that's as much as I can find in the last six months. All the altered orders date from before the relevant bombings."

Elena sighed. "Let's hope our bomber doesn't have any more in the works."

"Wonder why he hasn't tried hand grenades or Molotov cocktails? He's used everything else." Connie shut down the computer. "Time to talk to Reyes." The two walked into the sales area. Reyes was sitting at his desk, head thrown back, eyes closed. His clerk eyed him anxiously.

"Sir," said Connie loudly, "we've found discrepancies in your records. Customers who claim they never ordered as much or any of what you claim."

Reyes opened his eyes. "So my record keeping is shit. So sue me."

"You know the ATF rules. What you're doing is against the law."

"What am I doing?"

"You tell us," said Elena. She noticed a picture on the desk of a young man running, his upper body turned to pass a football.

"I'm being eaten alive by prostate cancer," snapped Jesus Reyes. "That's what I'm doing. So who's surprised my records aren't any good? What do I care?"

"You can go to jail," said Connie.

Elena picked up the picture of Philomeno Reyes. As Bonnie

Murillo had said, he had great buns. Or else both he and the bomber had great buns.

"You're going to have to explain what happened to every single item on this list." Connie leaned across the desk and snapped the paper in front Reyes's nose. Reyes took the photograph out of Elena's hand and turned it facedown on the desk.

"Who is he?" Elena asked, sure she knew.

"None of your business." Reyes took the list, his sleeve drawing up as he reached for it. Elena could see the bones in his arm. He looked like a photo from a concentration camp. Deep-set and dark-rimmed, his eyes ran down the notations Connie had made of discrepancies. "Don't know where the stuff is."

Connie stared at him. "It doesn't bother you that you're already an accessory to two murders?"

Reyes shifted in his chair. "I don't know what you're talkin' about."

"We're talking about your cousin Philomeno," said Elena. "Playing football in the picture." She nodded toward the frame where it lay facedown among papers.

"If you knew who he was, why'd you ask?"

"And your cousin Magdalena."

"They're schoolteachers. What about 'em?"

"We're going to get warrants to search their premises," said Connie.

Elena wondered if they could. Melon evidently had some special in with a federal judge. He'd got the nun's bail revoked without any trouble, and no one had jumped them for searching Sister Gertrudis Gregory's office.

"We're going to compare what we found in the bombs with what we find in their places—your cousins'—with what we find out about the lots you handled," said Connie. "Then we'll build a case against the three of you. Domestic terrorism. Murder."

Elena let Connie talk while she watched Reyes. The man's eyes darted to the phone on his desk, then back to the ATF agent. "By the time you get all that lab work done, I'll be dead."

"We're taking you in right now," said Connie. "You've got enough federal violations for us to hold you until we catch up with your cousins. And the only phone call you'll get is to a lawyer."

Reyes was sweating again.

44
..

Connie had taken his notes, Elena's notes, the computer printouts, and Jesus Reyes. Leaving the booking and further interrogation of the cousin to the ATF agent, Elena took the picture of Philomeno and went in search of Bonnie Murillo, whom she found working at a Good Times convenience store near the Lyndon Johnson Elementary School. After selling a package of generic cigarettes to a customer for an exorbitant price, Bonnie studied the picture of Philomeno playing touch football. "Would I forget a pair of buns like that?" she asked. The woman obviously had a phenomenal memory for male buttocks. Turning back to business reluctantly, Bonnie rang up a tank of gas, a bag of low-fat chips, and a can of bean dip for a customer in a lime plaid maternity blouse.

"What about the face?" Elena asked, not sure how a jury would respond to eyewitness bun identification.

With less interest, Bonnie studied the face. Philomeno's mouth was wide open as he leapt to pass, either sucking in air or shouting at his receiver. "Could be him. No braid, though."

"Forget the braid," said Elena. "That could have been a fake."

"Well, yeah, the face looks right," Bonnie decided. "Must be right, 'cause I'm positive about the buns. I looked every time

273

he bent over those sprinklers." She filled a cup with Pepsi for a customer. "Think he's the bomber? Wow! What a turn-on! You can tell I haven't gotten any in a while. Dating is hell with two kids at home you gotta set an example for. But yeah, he looks right."

"Thanks," said Elena, figuring that was as good an identification as she was going to get. Bonnie was already ringing up a carton of milk and a Twinkie for a man in overalls and a Diablos baseball cap when Elena said goodbye and left. Once outside, she called Perry to report Murillo's semi-identification of the bomb planter at H.H.U. "If she saw him in a backside lineup, I think we'd have a positive ID."

Perry laughed with what, in him, passed for exuberance. "Never heard of fanny ID."

"Why not?" said Elena. "I've run bicycle lineups."

"Did it help your case?"

"Oh, yeah. The witnesses ID'd the bike of a cop's daughter."

"I think I'll have the search warrants in an hour or so. Why don't you head for my office. We'll hold an interdepartmental meeting in the conference room, then tackle his house and her apartment. They're both still on compassionate leave, though I have to say, he's not at home. We don't know where he is, which makes me nervous. I've got two men staked out at his place."

"They need to watch the alley, too," Elena warned.

"Right. I sent them over as soon as we got word whose car blew up last night, but Reyes was gone already. How soon can you be here?"

"I wanted to show the picture to Billy Roy, the H.H.U. well attendant who originally identified Brazlitt as the well bomber. Do I have time?"

"We won't start the meeting till you arrive."

Elena marveled at the cooperation. It was now officially Perry's case, but he was keeping all the original officers informed and involved. Was it because he had the hots for her or because of the brotherhood of bomb guys, of which she now seemed to be a member? Either way, it was sort of nice. Not that she wanted anything more than a casual relationship with Perry. Of course, maybe he'd grow on her if he continued to ask her out. He or Connie Amparan or both. Why not? Being a one-man woman hadn't worked out. She just got a load of jealousy and efforts to control from Michael. From her ex, too, now that she thought about it.

She obtained the number for the well house and called Billy Roy, who said he'd be glad to look at a picture, although it had been a while since the bogus water inspector planted the bombs and he'd already identified the guy.

"Are the wells repaired and running yet?" Elena asked.

"You're kidding. My boss is practically in tears over the state of the shrubbery on campus. I guess you haven't been there lately."

"I live on campus," Elena replied, "but I'm not home much. See you in fifteen minutes."

When she arrived at the well site, reconstruction was in full swing. Billy Roy said the contractor would have crews working seven days a week in two shifts until the wells were pumping again. Then he looked at the picture of Philomeno Reyes and said, "Hey, that's not the one. He doesn't have a beard. The other man—"

"And you call yourself an actor." Elena glared at him. "Haven't you ever heard of a fake beard?"

"Well, sure, but a beard changes your appearance. How am I supposed to—hey, wait a minute." He stared hard at the touch football player. "Maybe—yeah, look at the ears. He's got Mr. Spock ears."

Elena looked, too. Philomeno's ears did look sort of Spock-ish. "Did the bearded guy have alien ears?"

"Absolutely. That's him," said Billy Roy triumphantly. "Guess I was wrong the first time. And to think, I was almost fooled by a fake beard. Let's draw a beard on this picture."

"Let's not," said Elena, and whipped the picture into her purse before Billy Roy could deface it in his anxiety to be a helpful citizen.

A huge clang from outside sent Elena ducking down against a wall, trembling.

"Hey," said Billy Roy. "You're really jumpy. They dropped a pipe down the well. No big deal." He helped her up. Elena fought off the incipient flashback by aggressively picturing Grandmother Portillo in her mind's eye. No mountain lion could compete for attention with a personality as forceful as Elena's paternal grandmother.

45
..

Magdalena Reyes paled when she saw Elena and the others at her door. "I told you, we don't belong to that organization anymore," she stammered. "We were at the hospital when—"

"We have a warrant to search your apartment and vehicle, miss," said Perry Melon.

"My brother just died. Can't you—" Tears filled her eyes, catching in her lashes and glittering like prisms in the sunlight spilling onto the balcony that fronted her second-floor apartment. Elena thought Magdalena's distress looked as much like panic as grief, but then maybe she was seeing what she wanted to see.

"Where's your computer, ma'am?" asked Agent Masters, the FBI computer expert they'd enlisted. When Magdalena's eyes widened with escalating fear, Elena decided that they might actually get a confession from this young woman before they went after the brother. But the possibility that he might be planting another bomb while they talked to his twin made Elena shudder. She took the young teacher by the arm and drew her toward a sofa by the window.

"We have a few questions, Ms. Reyes," said Elena. It was hard to believe that a woman so pretty, so fragile-looking could be a conspirator in a serial bombing case. "You told a colleague at your high school that anyone could build a bomb by studying certain Web pages on the Internet."

"Is that what this is about?" Magdalena tried to look relieved. "I'm a computer teacher. I was expressing my astonishment over the kinds of things you find on the Web. Why there's—there's even pornography. I didn't mean I'd *build* a bomb, or even that I could. But it's my job to familiarize myself with new technology in the field. If I don't keep up, how can I teach the subject?"

"Bomb-building?"

"No!" she cried. "I'd never say anything about the bomb pages to a student. I was talking to a teacher—marveling that—the—the government would allow—"

"The doctor whose greenhouse was bombed—Bates Morrison—he was your sister Maria's gynecologist."

A spasm of pain flashed across the suspect's face. "He's had thousands of patients," Magdalena protested.

"The vehicle of the developer who sold your parents land in Sparks Addition was bombed last night."

"It was?" She looked surprised.

"Are you saying that only your brother is responsible for the bombings?"

"I don't know what you're talking about." She now looked confused.

"You have only one brother left," said Elena, "and he's been identified as the man who planted the bombs at H.H.U."

"You're lying. We don't even belong to that group anymore."

"What group?"

"Water Now. We quit. If anyone—"

"—could be made to look guilty, it would be Water Now. Right?"

Perry and the FBI computer expert waved Elena into another room. G. remained, his huge frame bulking in a delicate little tub chair. He stared at Magdalena Reyes silently, making her very nervous, Elena imagined.

Elena followed the agents down a hall and shut the door to Magdalena's bedroom. "Find anything?" she asked.

"You name it; we found it," said Agent Masters. "Printouts from the Wizard, Jack the Ripper, Vandal Pyros."

"But just the recipes, no ingredients," said Perry. "We also found Catholic publications filed under Business Correspondence in her file cabinet." He handed copies of *The Bishop's Newsletter* and the *Holy Name Gazette* to Elena. "Odd place to put the material. How are you and G. coming?" he asked as she leafed through the files.

Elena recognized the headlines. These were the issues from which words for the water warnings had been clipped. "She says the remark about bomb information on the Net was made in passing to show what weird things were available, that she has to explore the Web to keep up with new technology, and she said about four times that she and her brother don't belong to Water Now anymore. Hoping we'll zero in on them, I suppose."

"Which we have been, up to yesterday," Perry admitted. "I'm going to be embarrassed if it turns out that Brazlitt really was either planting owls in New Mexico or in jail here in Los Santos when all the explosions occurred."

Elena felt a bit smug because she'd never been that stuck on Brazlitt as a suspect.

"The material we found is good evidence for bombings that have already occurred, but she also has material on letter bombs. That worries me. God knows what they've sent through the U.S. Post Office to people they've got grudges against."

Shaking her head, Elena returned to G. and Magdalena Reyes to confront her with the computer information the FBI had turned up and the church publications they'd found.

"That doesn't mean anything," said Magdalena. "I'm Catholic. Why wouldn't I—"

"—have many copies of two particular back issues of *The Bishop's Newsletter* and the *Holy Name Gazette*, issues in which the words 'Turn off the Water or We Will' occur?" Elena shot back.

"I'm sure neither publication said anything like that. Why would they?"

"And printouts of Web pages on bombs, especially letter bombs."

Magdalena swallowed. "I wanted to show them to a friend at school. What with the Unabomber—"

"Which friend? Your brother?"

"He's not interested in computers."

"Which is why you had to get the information for him."

"I didn't—"

"Where is he?"

"Home, I suppose. I haven't talked to him today."

"He's not home. What's he doing? Mailing the letter bombs?"

"No!"

"I'll need the keys to your car, miss," said Connie Amparan, coming in from outside where he had been checking the car in its apartment parking space.

"I assure you, there are no bombs in my car," said Magdalena stiffly.

"We want to make tire prints. Those Michelins look like the tread marks we found at the Pan-American Stonewashing plant the night its water tower toppled."

"I wasn't there."

"Maybe your car was," Connie suggested.

"Her purse is over on the buffet." Elena pointed toward the end of the living room, which held a small dining room set. "Now, Ms. Reyes, let's get back to your family. Your cousin's already under arrest."

"What?"

"Jesus. We arrested him this morning. He can't account for all kinds of explosives, types that were used in the attacks here in Los Santos. His records have been seriously compromised."

"Jesus—is sick. If anything's wrong with his records, it must be carelessness."

"A mistake that's going to send him to jail," said G., "or so ATF Agent Amparan tells us. Even if we can't charge him as an accessory to murder, which will likely be the charge against *you,* he's broken federal regulations."

"Both of you will undoubtedly end up in jail," said Elena. "The length of the sentences may depend on how cooperative you are."

"You'd better tell us where your brother is, Ms. Reyes," said G., "before he kills anyone else."

"I don't know where he is, and I don't have to talk to you. I—I want a lawyer."

Elena nodded. "As soon as you're booked. Once we've searched your place, we'll be taking you in. And of course, we'll be searching your brother's place."

"I'll have to change my clothes," said Magdalena Reyes, looking frantic.

"You look fine, ma'am," said G.

"I want to change," she repeated stubbornly.

Connie returned in time to hear her demand. "I'd be willing to swear we've got a match on the tire prints." He glanced at the telephone on the coffee table, then called out loudly. "You guys through with the bedroom?"

"All through," came Perry Melon's voice from the kitchen.

"Go ahead, ma'am," said G.

She scurried off, never looking back. G. nodded toward the telephone, and Elena, understanding, slid her finger onto the hang-up button as she lifted the receiver. She gave Magdalena a few seconds, then eased the button off and listened to Philomeno Reyes saying he wasn't home, asking the caller to leave a message. There was a worried pause after the tone, then Magdalena's voice saying, "Jesus has been arrested. They're taking me in now. It's almost two. And they're going to your house next."

Does the woman really think we don't have anyone watching her brother's house? Elena wondered.

When Magdalena returned, in a prim dress instead of the jeans she'd worn to answer the door, Perry Melon was rearranging machine-embroidered letters on the coffee table. "Isn't that the name of the company that planted the pyrodex in the H.H.U. sprinkler system?" he asked Elena once he'd formed the words.

Magdalena Reyes's eyes widened as Elena nodded.

"I found these in a box of Blueberry Morning cereal," said Perry.

"Weird place to keep sewing stuff," G. remarked. "Care to explain that, ma'am?" He looked toward Magdalena, whose hands were twisting nervously.

Elena said, "Warning your brother when we could listen in wasn't very smart, Ms. Reyes. You'd do better to tell us where he is. Before he kills again. And exposes you to another charge of capital murder. Or blows himself up by mistake."

Magdalena shivered.

46
..

Perry Melon, with the search warrant, took Elena, G., Connie Amparan, and one other FBI agent into the empty Reyes house with him. He felt they had waited as long as they could for the presumed bomber to return. Every law enforcement officer in the county was on the lookout for Philomeno Reyes. Every means of public transportation out of Los Santos was covered: buses, planes, even the three-times weekly Amtrak passenger train that stopped on its journey between Los Angeles and New Orleans, not to mention the more frequent freight trains.

Customs was stopping people at the international bridges. The border patrol had been alerted in case Reyes tried to swim the river. The highway patrol and the LSPD were on the lookout for his truck. But no one had any idea where the man was, and his sister wouldn't talk. Neither would Jesus Reyes, who was under guard at the county hospital, having collapsed during the first half hour of interrogation.

Outside the Reyes house, on the street, in the alley, plain-clothes agents and officers in unmarked cars or on foot were stationed to give warning if Reyes appeared, to trap him if he tried to disappear. Everything was covered that could be covered when they went into the house and garage to search.

It was a small house built from uncut chunks of native stone

cemented together like a jigsaw puzzle, like the ubiquitous rock
walls that surrounded backyards all over Los Santos. Wooden
porch rails, doors, and window frames showed, through their
bright blue paint, the ravages of blowing sand and temperature
extremes. The garage, sitting on the back of the lot at the
intersection of two alleys, was a twin in material to the house,
but less well kept and much more securely locked. Reyes had
equipped the little building with heavy padlocks and an alarm
system.

Elena was assigned to the house and told to be careful if she
came across anything that might conceivably be an explosive.
Unnerved by this warning, she called G. in to examine such
finds as a suspicious crystalline substance in the kitchen, which
he identified, to her embarrassment, as rock salt.

However, she also found on a kitchen bookshelf *The
Anarchist Cookbook, Improved Explosives,* and *The Poor
Man's James Bond* lurking behind battered copies of *The New
York Times Cookbook, French Cuisine for Beginners,* and
Vegetarian Menus from Southeast Asia. Reyes must have
bought the nonbomb cookbooks secondhand for camouflage,
she reasoned. The man was no gourmet chef. His refrigerator
and cupboards held practically nothing.

She found military field manuals behind books on Mexican
cooking and *Seasoned with the Sun,* a local Junior League
contribution to good eating. She found a computer printout
from Anarchy Today and a bundle of handouts from gun shows
at the Civic Center and the Shrine Temple stuck inside a
loose-leaf binder entitled, *The Housewife's Favorite Recipe
File.* The gun show literature concerned explosives, not guns.
Philomeno Reyes had even gone to a national show in Alabama
the previous year. Bombs were not an impulsive, recent, or
openly manifested interest with him.

Pleased with Elena's discoveries, G. himself found a braid, a
beard, and a mustache in the bedroom, stuffed into a radio from
which the innards had been removed.

"Funny place to store your hair collection," said Elena when
G. showed her. She'd finished with the kitchen and moved to

the bath while G. continued to go through the drawers and closet. In a laundry hamper she found a uniform with stitching picked off the back. The color was right—olive. The missing letters were probably those they found at Magdalena's apartment, letters spelling out the name of the nonexistent irrigation company that had allowed Philomeno the opportunity to mine H.H.U.'s sprinkler system. The trousers had no doubt covered the enchanting backside spotted by Bonnie Murillo. Or maybe it was the uniform of the man who put slurry canisters in the wells. They also found the grubby white coveralls of the fake gardener at Morrison's greenhouse. Everything they found they bagged.

The living room yielded nothing, nor did the second small bedroom which Reyes used as a study. It was filled with books on the social sciences: history, sociology, even criminology. There were a few books on water usage, law, and problems in the Southwest. Elena bagged those, too, but she wasn't sure they'd do much for a court case. Reyes could say they related to his teaching, whereas *The Anarchist Cookbook* could hardly be claimed as a subject for instruction at Pancho Villa High School, not unless the school's namesake miraculously returned to life. The hero-bandit would probably have been interested in bombs and urban terrorism.

"You finished?" asked G.

The searchers from the garage had just slipped in the back door. "We won't have any trouble convicting him," said Perry.

"What did you find?" G. asked enviously. It had been obvious to Elena that he'd rather have been assigned the garage, but the feds had co-opted the juicy stuff.

"A cut end of detonating cord," said Connie, grinning. "Pyrodex we can compare to the unexploded stuff at H.H.U. Radio fuses. You name it, we found it."

"It's a wonder he didn't blow himself up." Perry radioed the men watching outside. "We're moving the evidence out. Don't panic when you see us coming."

"What about the yard?" Elena asked. "And the attic?"

"We don't want to stay too long," said Connie. "We got

plenty of evidence. Now we need to get him, so the sooner we leave, the less likely he'll catch us here and run."

They began gathering the evidence and carrying it through the front door to a nondescript van parked at the curb. When they trudged through with the last lot, a neighbor came bursting from his house, waving a shotgun. "I seen you robbin' Philo. I called the cops. Don't move a step." He pointed his shotgun at them.

Perry sighed. "We *are* the police, sir. In a manner of speaking."

"Yeah, sure. Like I believe that," said the belligerent neighbor, a short, skinny, balding man with a reddened face.

"I'm going to show you my identification," said Perry.

"Don't move," snapped the neighbor.

"Agent Perry Melon, FBI. Shooting an FBI agent is a federal offense. No parole." Perry had set down the plastic bag he was carrying in order to reach carefully, slowly for his pocket.

"FBI?" The neighbor's belligerence waned. Then he saw the shield in its leather holder. "Well, how was I to know?" he mumbled.

"He's wearing a suit, isn't he?" said Connie wryly.

Melon produced his photo ID. "Now, sir, what is your name?"

"Anastasio Porto," said the man reluctantly.

"You'll have to come with us, Mr. Porto."

"I'm under arrest?" the neighbor cried indignantly. "I was just being a good citizen."

"Damn," muttered Perry.

Elena had never heard him curse.

"The whole neighborhood's looking out their windows or standing in their yards," said Melon. "The rest of you drop your loads at the van, then get these people into their houses as fast as you can."

Elena deposited the books from the kitchen with the van driver, then realized that she'd left the water books in the study. She turned to Perry. The rest were fanning out down the street. "Did you leave the front door open? I forgot three books from the study. At least one looked like a radical environmentalist thing about water."

"It's open, but hurry. And throw the lock behind you. We don't want to tip him off with an open door."

"If he comes back," said Elena.

She glanced up and down the street where arguments and explanations were proceeding on various doorsteps. If Reyes chose to return now, he couldn't help but know something was afoot. Then she looked up at the sky, hot blue, not a wisp of cloud. It had been months since she'd even heard rain predicted, much less felt its cool touch on her face. You wouldn't think that the threat of drought would mean much in the desert, but it did. The snowpack had been low this year. Therefore, the reservoirs were emptying. What would happen if the snow failed next year, and the next? And the rain never fell in spring and summer? Frowning, she trudged to the house.

Once in the living room, Elena headed for the short hall off which the bedroom, study, and a bath opened. She had just reached the study door when she heard a woman's voice. Elena paused, having taken a second step into the room, realizing that the voice was Magdalena's message on the answering machine. At that instant, the open door swung violently and slammed into Elena's head, stunning her, making her stumble and fall. When she tried to scramble to her feet, reaching for her gun, she was looking into the barrel of someone else's, a handsome man with Spock ears.

"I was in the doghouse," he said.

"You still are," she replied, dazed.

"No, I mean while you people were searching my house, I was waiting in the doghouse. Pretty lucky. The last owner had a big dog."

Oh shit, she thought. She could see the passport in his hand. If only she hadn't come back for the water books, he'd have been trapped in the house. Or even if he'd escaped, he'd have been caught at the bridge. Now she was trapped with him.

47

Water Attack Spreads to New Mexico

Vandals chopped down 25 cottonwood trees that were part of a 200-tree beautification project along the Rio Grande. Painted on the picnic tables in the riverside park were the words, Cottonwoods Suck up Water.

The United States Fish and Wildlife Service, which partially funded the project in an effort to provide nesting and roosting places for migratory birds, has offered a $200 reward for information leading to the arrest and conviction of the culprits.

Anna Moppet, a spokesperson for the Bunyan Society, said in a telephone interview, "Chopping down trees should be a capital offense. The aura of a tree or plant being destroyed is a scream for help."

Los Santos *Times*, Wednesday, May 29

He pressed the gun against her forehead while she was still on the floor. Elena thought how little pressure on the trigger would kill her. "I want you to put your gun on the floor and give it a shove," he said. "If you try anything, you're dead."

289

Elena would have nodded, but she didn't want to jostle the gun. Carefully she drew her Glock from its waist holster and gave it a shove.

"Scoot away from the door," he ordered, stepping back to pick up her weapon, keeping his trained steadily on her head. "Into the room."

She thought of diving the other way but knew it wouldn't work. He had two loaded guns; she had none.

"Do it."

"Sorry," she mumbled. "I'm a little dizzy." She edged into the room, away from him. He closed the door and stared at her as if considering his options.

"What the hell did you come back for?" he muttered. Because he didn't really seem to expect an answer, Elena made none. "Get up. Go sit on that chair." He pointed to a straight-backed chair, probably the last survivor of a battered dining room set. The chair stood against the wall adjoining the living room. The front wall of his study held a window that overlooked the street. The wall across from Elena, framed in bookshelves that had held the three books she returned for— how she wished she hadn't done that—contained a window on the side yard with a desk in front of it. The fourth wall, to her left, was adjacent to the bath with the hall door at its left corner. As she pushed herself off the floor and took the hard chair, the house plan flashed through her mind. Although the hall door wasn't going to help her much, the two windows, to her right and across the room, were to her advantage.

"The neighborhood is crawling with police," she told him. "FBI, ATF—"

"I know that," he snapped. He went to the window and lifted one slat on the venetian blinds to peer out. "As I see it, I can blow up the house with both of us in it, or I can try to get away with you as a hostage."

Someone shoot him, she prayed, then had to wonder if her colleagues had even missed her yet. They probably thought she'd stopped to put on lipstick or something. "Do you want to die?" she asked, afraid he'd say he didn't care.

"If you know anything about my family, you know I don't have much choice," he replied, dividing his attention between her and the front yard.

Someone could slip up to that side window and get him, she thought. *Maybe.* The blinds were closed, but there was a gap where one had broken.

"Even if I die, I've started something. Maybe it'll continue without me."

"I don't know what you mean," Elena replied.

"In the paper this morning. Someone chopped down a bunch of trees in New Mexico because they suck up water. It's spreading."

She stared at him, thinking that he looked so innocuous. It was hard to believe that he might kill her. Philomeno Reyes was a nice-looking man, not as beautiful as his sister, but handsome enough, medium height, as the witnesses had said, good build, although she couldn't see the buns that had caught Bonnie Murillo's fancy. His female students probably suffered from crushes. Or maybe not. He wore lightweight pleated slacks, and a pale green golf shirt. Maybe he was too conservative for today's high school girl. Conservative? That was a laugh! A serial bomber—conservative?

"There's a black man coming up the walk. Who is he?" Reyes demanded, his voice ragged.

"Oh God, G." She couldn't let Reyes shoot G. "Let me warn him off. I know his beeper number." She was afraid Reyes would refuse, would wait till he got a good shot at the sergeant and take it.

Without saying anything, Reyes moved away from the window, plucked a cordless phone from the desk, and tossed it to her, cracking her on the wrist because she'd been taken by surprise. He was back at the window before she could lean forward to pick the telephone off the floor. Elena punched in G.'s pager number.

Frowning with irritation because she was taking so long when they needed to hurry, G. had his hand on the doorknob when his pager beeped. Impatiently, he dragged it from his pocket to look at the screen, then froze. He recognized the number of the house he was about to enter. He'd called it several times before they went in. Knowing that something was wrong, he turned and walked toward the van, his back tingling. If she was playing some joke on him—

"Where is she?" Connie demanded. "Don't tell me the house is empty? I didn't see her come out."

"He's the head of the bomb squad," said Elena in answer to Reyes's question.

"Appropriate. When he calls, which I presume he will—" Reyes was looking between the slats again, gun on Elena, his own body carefully poised to the side of the window. "—tell him if they try to come in, I'm going to blow up the house and take you with me."

"I'm sure they found all the explosives," said Elena, hoping against hope.

"Not the ones on me." He patted his shirt just above the waist.

So much for that idea. Did he have dynamite strapped to his body? "You don't know you're going to die of cancer," she said.

"Sure, I do. And if I'm taken alive, I'll be sentenced to death. Then it'll be a race to see who gets me first—the state or the big C."

"You'll be charged under federal statutes. No death penalty there, and federal prisons aren't—"

"No parole," said Reyes. "The black man's climbed into that van. Some other guy, Hispanic, is staring at the house."

That would be Connie, Elena thought, wishing she were out there with him. The telephone rang.

"He's got her?" Connie looked horrified. "How'd he even get in the house? We had it covered on all sides."

"He must have slipped in while we were repositioning," said

Perry Melon. "How did she sound?" Perry spoke to G., but he was making a call at the same time.

"Controlled," said G., who was on another line, "but I don't want to think about how long she can keep a handle on herself. We all know what kind of shape she's in."

Amparan was gnawing his lip. "We should have—"

Melon waved the ATF agent to silence. "I need a SWAT team," he said into the telephone. "The serial bomber's holding a female police officer hostage. He's threatening to blow up the house, himself, and her. . . . Hell, yes, he means it." Perry hung up and said to his colleagues, "Fifteen or twenty minutes."

G. had made the same call but to the lieutenant in charge of the LSPD Tactical Unit, his lieutenant, who also managed SWAT teams.

"Why did you come back?" Elena asked.

"Passport," said Reyes.

"The bridges are being monitored."

"There's always the river. That's how my dad got here, may he rest in peace."

"What about Magdalena? And Jesus?"

He gave her a sharp look. "What about them?"

His tone was so hard she wished she hadn't mentioned them. It might just make him angrier to know that his sister and cousin were already in jail.

"What about them?" he demanded. "Why are you asking me about my sister? And who's Jesus? There are a hundred Jesuses in Los Santos." He stalked over and put the gun to her forehead again. "So what about Magdalena?"

"She's in jail," Elena whispered, then took courage. "Looks like you figured on running out on her. I guess you still do. Killing yourself and me leaves her to face the trial, jail, maybe a death sentence if they try her in state court for murder."

"She didn't do anything."

"Tell it to the undertaker," Elena snapped. "You can't clear your sister or your cousin, not if you're dead."

"Which cousin?"

"The gun dealer. He's in jail, too. We arrested him this morning, her this afternoon. Then we came over to wait for you."

"I ought to shoot you right now."

"Well, they'll storm the house for sure if they hear a shot. I imagine the SWAT teams are arriving."

He went back to the window and looked through the blind slats again.

"There's probably a sharpshooter sighting in on you."

He drew back quickly, a thin veil of sweat shining on his forehead and upper lip. Elena wondered if she was doing herself any good.

"Magdalena didn't do anything."

"You're not worried about Jesus? Well, I can understand that. We had to put him in the hospital." Reyes' head snapped toward her. "Maybe your cousin will die before you have to feel guilty about deserting him. You grew up with him, didn't you? I guess he's the closest thing to a brother you've got left."

"Shut up!"

"Sure." She slouched in the chair.

"How bad is he?"

"Jesus? The doctor said he was good for a couple more months, maybe a half year."

Reyes sighed. "So they'll shoot him full of painkillers and dump him back in jail."

"Probably. Hell of a place to die, especially if you could clear him. And your sister. If they really weren't in on this."

"If you think that, why did you arrest them?"

"The FBI did. They're calling it domestic terrorism."

Reyes laughed. "Good term. That's what I grew up with. Anglo terrorism, domestic variety. Money-grubbing terrorism, Anglo variety. Slow killing terrorism—"

"You and Magdalena look pretty healthy to me," Elena broke in before he could work himself into a fury.

He threw the phone to her again. "Call your buddy. Tell him if they want you back alive, they're going to have to give me

Jesus and Magdalena, safe escort to the airport, and a small plane, fueled up. You'll go with us. If they keep their word, we'll set you free somewhere. If they don't, you're dead. We're all dead," he added bitterly. "But then we probably are, anyway."

Elena imagined them pushing her out of the plane once they left U.S. airspace. Her heart was drumming, her palms cold with sweat. "Call them yourself," she said. Elena wanted him to connect with a hostage negotiator from the Crisis Management Team. Those guys might be able to talk him out; she'd never manage. "I'll give you the number." She held out the phone.

He shook his head. "It's your life we're bargaining for here. Us Reyeses—no matter what happens, we haven't got that much time. I'm just doing this for my sister's sake. She won't get a fair trial if I leave her."

Elena made the call, stated the terms.

"Tell him we'll need approval," Perry said. "Are you all right?"

"For now," she replied, knowing they'd stall and stall, knowing they wouldn't want to let Reyes out with her in tow. They'd want to contain the situation until they could slant the odds in their favor, and hers.

"They need approval from higher up," she told Reyes.

"Yeah, sure. I've seen how it works on TV. Well, it's your life they're screwing with."

"They won't sacrifice me," said Elena. "That's not the way it works." She hoped she was right, hoped they felt the loyalty to her they felt for each other—Perry, G., Connie, and the rest of them.

48
..

"Has he said how he plans to blow the house up?" G. asked. As instructed, Elena had called G. again. "We went over the whole place."

"You're betting my life on that?"

"What are you talking about?" Reyes demanded.

"They don't think you have a bomb."

"They didn't think I was anywhere around, either. Anyway, I've got two guns. I don't care how we go. I'd just like to take some of them with us, and a bomb would do that."

"He says you didn't know he was here, either," she told G.

"Is he listening?" Perry asked, his voice coming from the background.

"To me," Elena told G. "He says he has the explosives on him, plus the two guns."

"Let me talk to him."

"You talk to them," she said to Reyes, holding out the telephone again.

"No. I don't want some hostage negotiator trying to trick me. Tell them to either get me that plane or admit they don't care what happens to you."

"He won't talk," Elena said into the receiver. She knew G.'s lieutenant had arrived, plus SWAT and CMT units. They'd be hanging out in the big white van with its incongruous ruffled curtains at the windows, hovering over the equipment, studying the boards, doing all the right things, except that Reyes wouldn't give them the time of day. "He wants the plane," she told G. wearily.

"And my sister," said Reyes. "And Jesus. We're not leaving without them."

"He wants his sister and cousin, too. And the plane. Or he kills me and himself."

"Do you believe that?" G. asked.

"I don't know."

"What don't you know?" demanded Reyes.

"Why you won't talk to them yourself," she answered.

"No," said Reyes.

"How does he seem?" G. asked. "Dangerous?"

"Of course." Here she was, stuck in a little rock house with a serial bomber, and G. wanted to know if he was dangerous.

"I mean does he seem ready to blow? Losing it? You know what I mean."

"No."

"He doesn't?"

"No. Maybe. I don't know."

"What?" demanded Reyes.

"Whether you're hungry," Elena improvised.

"Yeah, right. Like I'm going to let someone in here with food."

Elena sighed. She was hungry. And thirsty. How come Reyes wasn't?

"I'm putting Perry on," said G.

Great, thought Elena. *Now the official bullshit starts.*

"Tell him Chief Gaitan and the Special Agent in Charge are negotiating for the plane, but we need federal approval if he plans to leave U.S. airspace," Perry told her.

Elena looked toward Reyes, who had rolled his desk chair between the two windows. It was dark outside, but he'd turned on only a desk lamp, which he moved to the floor so that he could keep his eye on her without highlighting himself to sharpshooters. "They need federal approval if you plan to leave U.S. airspace."

"Bullshit!" he muttered.

His eyes were red-rimmed, his black hair mussed. Probably he'd had as little sleep as she lately, although for different reasons. He'd been making and exploding bombs; she'd been having nightmares. And getting called out in the middle of the night because of his bombs.

"What'd he say?" Perry asked.

"He said bullshit."

"Listen, Elena, you sound as if you don't care any more. You've got to stay alert, hon."

Hon? Since when did Perry call her hon? "I am."

"You don't sound it. I didn't want to tell you this but he got the Fargo brothers and one other guy."

"What? How?" She sat up from her slump, alarmed.

"Letter bombs. First we heard about Christopher Olmos."

She glanced at Reyes, remembering Olmos Chemicals stenciled on a water barrel under the lean-to porch of the abandoned Reyes place. A shiver went up her spine.

"Fifteen minutes later, Morris Fargo. Dead. When we heard that, we checked on Benjamin, the one whose car blew up. By the way, we found out what his Cherokee was doing on that street; he was spending the night with a lady, not his wife."

So that's why Benjamin Fargo had lied about where his vehicle was when it was stolen. Out of consideration for his tootsie, or for himself; maybe he had a wife who objected to adultery.

"Anyway, he's alive," said Perry, "but he's in bad shape. So be careful. We're gonna get you out of there, but you've got to be careful with Reyes."

"Jesus." Elena felt her heart speed up.

"What?" demanded Reyes.

She didn't want to tell him about the Fargos or Olmos. He might celebrate by killing her. Or get mad because one was alive and, in a rage, kill her. "They need permission from Mexico if that's where you're going," she said.

"Tell them they've got an hour. That's it."

"He says you've got an hour."

"Tell him we can't—"

"Hang up!" Reyes sighted down the gun barrel.

Elena hung up.

"We're not talking to them again. I get what I want in an hour, or we're both dead."

Evidently, he'd forgotten about the letter bombs. "How'd you ever start down this road, anyway?" she asked. She needed to get him talking, so he wouldn't notice the passage of time, so he stopped looking out the window to check on the SWAT teams, stopped listening for someone sneaking up on the house.

49

Wednesday, May 29, 9:30 P.M.

"I'm not even sure how many babies Mama had," said Philo Reyes.

He was sitting against the wall, wrists on bent knees, the gun held in both hands and pointed at Elena. She could see, by the light of the desk lamp on the floor, the dull gleam of the barrel, the neatly pressed crease in his slacks, his fingernails, bitten ragged, but his face was in shadow, and his voice seemed disembodied and numb with sadness.

"Miscarriages, stillbirths, some of the babies deformed. And they kept having them, mourning every one they lost. Only five of us lived long enough to go to school. And they were so proud of us. Neither one of them could read or write, but their kids could. Except for Fernie. He's the one who just died."

Elena nodded. "Liver cancer," she said. He frowned at her. "You told me," she reminded him. She ached all over from the long hours on this hard chair, longed to get up, stretch, walk around, yet she was careful not to move, afraid if she startled him, he'd shoot.

"Oh. Well, Fernie had a learning disability. They asked my mother if she smoked during her pregnancy." He laughed bitterly. "Like she ever had enough money for cigarettes if she'd wanted them. Couldn't even afford prenatal care. A

301

midwife delivered us all, the quick and the dead, as they say."
He fell silent.

"So Fernie was dyslexic?" Elena asked. She dared not look
at her watch. He'd been talking, but she had no idea how long.

"I guess. He just couldn't learn to read. Alfredo read better
than Fernie, and Alfredo died of leukemia when he was eight.
Fernie, poor *hermano,* he lived longer, got a job. He was a good
worker."

"What'd he do?" There'd been no more calls. What was
happening outside? Elena carefully lifted one buttock off the
seat, hoping to ease the ache.

"Worked for Pan-American Stonewashing." Philo's smile
was bitter. "Worked for them nine years. Then he got cancer,
and they fired him. They used more water than hundreds of
families and fired a man who was dying from bad water, from
no water. He lost his health insurance, his salary, his self-
respect, and then he lost his life. Just this month."

"I'm sorry," said Elena. Were they going to provide a plane?
Let Philo escape? She eased her weight onto the other side.

"Sure you are. You want to hear about Maria? My father?
My mother? My father died before he even got that rotten
house paid off. Worked five years to get the down payment for
the land; then he sent for my mother and married her. He met
her at a dance across the border in Zaragosa. He and Jesus built
the house. He loved to tell us about how the Fargos paced off
the land, said it would be his in twenty years. All he had to do
was make the payments, didn't even have to pay the taxes. He
thought he was so lucky, my father. His own land. They said
the water would come, but it never did, and they knew it
wouldn't."

Elena thought of the Fargos and shivered. They'd paid for
the lies. Or had they thought they were telling the truth? She
had to keep her mind off how uncomfortable she was, off what
was going on outside, concentrate on Philo, keep him talking.
But if he got his plane, she couldn't let herself be forced
aboard. She just couldn't.

"They told him the same lie for almost twenty years. That

the water was coming. By then even us kids knew it wasn't. Papa died two months before the land was paid off. And the Fargos took it back—their land and our house. We couldn't make the second to last payment, because of my father's funeral."

"They never resold it," said Elena. Would the feds try to rescue her on the way to the airport? They were probably in charge.

"What do you mean?"

"The Fargos couldn't sell it. The neighbors say it was a bad-luck house and no one would buy."

"It was. Bad luck. Bad water."

"Your parents must have been very proud of you and Magdalena. First generation to finish college." No need to worry about a trip to the airport. There wouldn't be a plane. So what were they going to do? Let him blow up the house with her in it?

"My father, he never knew we went to college. Two years after him, my mother died, living in the projects on welfare. Humiliated. Too poor and too proud to see a doctor. The cancer was everywhere by the time we dragged her into a free clinic. She never knew how we turned out either."

"She'd have been proud," Elena whispered, wondering whether the talk was making him more or less dangerous, beginning to understand, at least somewhat, how he felt.

"Maria, my eldest sister, went next. In agony with her third pregnancy, and the doctor didn't pay any attention. Said she was eating too many chilies. Morrison. All I got was his damn greenhouse." He stared through Elena, and she wondered whether she should try to make a break for it. She might never have a better chance. What were they doing out there? Had they left? No, they wouldn't do that. They'd have the SWAT teams deployed. They'd—

"By the time they did an emergency cesarean on Maria and found the cancer, it had spread."

Too late to run, she thought. Philo had refocused on her.

"Too late then," Reyes said. "She got some chemo, some

radiation, lost her hair. She was really proud of her hair. It looked like yours." He peered at her in the gloom. "So she died. Now her husband's trying to raise their two kids. And grieving." He pulled his knees up closer to his chest, as if in protection against his own grief.

"Maybe her kids are gonna die, too," he continued. "What if it passes through the generations, the poison in the water we drank? Maybe it went from her womb to her children."

"I've never heard of that," said Elena. The SWAT team. Her life depended on a bunch of guys who translated their acronym Several Wackos Armed to the Teeth. Pretty funny—as long as your life didn't depend on those wackos. "Maria's kids ought to be O.K.," she said reassuringly. "They weren't born in Sparks Addition."

"What do you know? Fernie and Jesus were diagnosed with cancer about the same time. Jesus could afford a doctor and went. Fernie got scared and went to a free clinic. Both of them with the kinds that spread like brush fires. So we buried Fernie. *Where the hell are they?*"

"Who?" Elena asked, startled.

"They're supposed to bring Jesus and Magdalena here. Why haven't they come?"

Elena didn't know what to say. She couldn't suggest that the feds hadn't been able to find his cousin and sister because she'd already said they'd been arrested.

"They're lying, aren't they? There isn't going to be any plane."

"Did you mean to kill people?" she asked quickly.

He seemed confused at the change of subject, then mumbled, "I don't know. Not at first. The injuries at the university—those were a mistake. They were warned."

"You sent the notes?"

He laughed, a croaking, funereal sound. Was that her imagination? Or the fact that neither of them had had anything to drink for hours? God, she was thirsty. And it was hot! He hadn't turned his swamp coolers on. Maybe he never bothered with them, having grown up without air conditioning.

"Sister Gertrudis Gregory sent the notes," he said. "But I helped make up the list before we quit Water Now."

"Clever," said Elena. She was sweating. She felt as if the heat was pressing down on her, stifling her—like an electric blanket turned too high.

"I didn't mean to kill the guard, either. Everyone was warned."

"So you just wanted to—what?" Unthinking, she wiped her arm across her forehead, and he jerked up, scaring her. But then he subsided.

"I wanted to get their attention."

"You did that." She couldn't help the dry note in her voice and hoped it wouldn't set him off.

"Yeah, but it didn't do any good. Ordinary people are attacking each other, but no one's promised any water for the *colonias.*"

"You're wrong," Elena disagreed. "The Lower Valley Water District's having a bond issue in June. If people vote to put up the fourteen million, the state will kick in fifty-eight."

"You think those people have the money to pay higher taxes?"

"They probably won't have to. Population growth—"

"No one believes that bullshit."

"Well, I think they'll vote for it." She probably couldn't run, anyway. Her feet were asleep. She moved them surreptitiously and winced at the prickling sensation. "It's too good a deal to pass up—the bond issue. And then—"

"And then the water will run out before anyone predicted. Some guy said so in the paper. So do you think when that happens, anyone but the rich will get water when there's not much left? Or it costs so much the poor can't afford it? Nothing's going to change."

"But you kept on setting off the bombs? Even when you didn't think—"

"I'm going to die," he interrupted, leaning forward, staring at her, his eyes gleaming in the lamplight that shone up dimly into his face.

"You don't know that." If they used a sharpshooter, he'd have to make it a head shot—so Reyes died instantly, without having a chance to shoot her.

"Sure I know it. Magdalena and I are going to die. Because of where we grew up. Because we drank water from contaminated barrels."

"So that's why you kept on? Even when you doubted it would do any good?" She'd dive off the chair, in case the head shot hit him somewhere else. She'd get out of the way, so they had a chance to shoot twice.

"I don't know," he said. "God, I'm tired." He raised the gun, but as if it weighed a hundred pounds. "Maybe I ought to just—"

"What about the people in New Mexico who chopped down the trees?" she said quickly.

"That's not gonna help anyone like my family." He turned the gun sideways and stared at it.

"So you kept up the bombing for—for revenge?"

"It's power," he said, looking up at her. "You find out you can do it. All that destruction, and you can control it. Direct it."

"As a teacher, you had a kind of power. For good. Over the lives of people who need you," she pointed out.

He leapt to his feet. "What do you know?" he cried. *"Your* power is in a gun. If I never do anything else, I'll have killed the people who hurt us."

So it had been for revenge at the end. But he didn't know for sure that he'd succeeded.

"And it's too late for you to stop it. I've set in motion things you don't even know about." He was standing, his upper body above the light line, but she could see the gun. Pointing at her. His knuckles white around the grip. "There's not a thing you can do to—"

Two gunshots followed each other in rapid succession. Elena, for all her plans, froze, cowering against the chair back until she saw him go down, a look of childlike surprise on his face. His gun fell and skidded from a hand gone limp. She could see the blood spreading in a red blossom on his knit shirt, seeping from his mouth. In shock, she flashed back, and his face turned to the face of Michael's brother, gouged and gnawed, one eye gone.

"I'm shot," he whispered. There were tears in his eyes, glinting in the glow of the desk lamp that sat on the floor a few feet from his face.

"No, it was the lion," she whispered. How could Mark speak? He was dead.

Then he said something else, but Elena couldn't understand and inched toward him, shivering, afraid that the mountain lion would get her too. She could smell the feral reek of it here in her bedroom. "Please," he said.

Elena blinked her eyes, shaking with fright, trying to understand why Mark was speaking. That was wrong. He hadn't . . . but he wasn't Mark, and she wasn't in her house. She looked again at the young Hispanic face. Not Mark at all, but the bomber, who had held her prisoner for so many hours. She should get his gun. And hers. Where had he put it? Because he was trying to speak again, she forgot the guns and leaned close.

"Hear my confession." The thready voice bubbled with blood.

Confession? Elena frowned, trying to remember the words of the sacrament for the dying. She had been in the room when her grandfather died. What—

"Forgive me, father, for I have sinned," Philomeno Reyes whispered. He was looking into her eyes as his own glazed over. They went blank, for the spark of his life had flickered out before he could name his sins.

She heard the shouts of her colleagues, the pounding of their feet in the house. Before they threw open the door to the room, Elena made the sign of the cross over his face and chest.

Epilogue

They sat around a table in the corner, drinking margaritas and talking boisterously—G., Connie, and Perry Melon—pleased that they'd caught the bomber and stopped the terror. Elena was on her second bowl of peanuts, having had nothing to eat for hours.

Before the four of them went off duty, Philomeno Reyes's body had to be searched, then sent to the morgue; they searched his house for bombs they might have missed. As for the bomb he'd threatened her with, there was none.

She'd shaken hands with the sharpshooter who got him, an LSPD SWAT team member who had been crouched by the side window, squinting through a broken blind into the room, listening, waiting for Reyes to stand up and present a target. She'd had to be debriefed, repeating everything Reyes had said, how he'd hid out in the forlorn, dogless doghouse no one had bothered to check, the family story, the narcotic effect on him of the power his bombs had provided, everything but the fact that for a few seconds she'd thought he was someone else.

Now they were celebrating the end of the case, talking about how amazing it was that an amateur could have executed that many bombings with so many different types of explosives without getting caught or blowing himself up.

"Saves the government the price of a trial," said Melon, sounding satisfied.

It was closure of the most final sort, Elena thought. And she was alive, for which she was grateful. So why wasn't she feeling as jubilant as the others? She took another gulp of her margarita, cold and tart on the tongue with the bite of the salt edging the rim. Connie had said this bar, the Kit-Kat Club, made a terrific margarita, although the management didn't appreciate female customers. But that was O.K. because Elena would be his guest. She didn't care about the management, but the name of the club—anything reminiscent of cats made her shudder.

"You did great," Connie said to her for the twentieth time. "Keeping him talking like that until Ramsey could get a shot." The ATF agent beamed at her. "I'll be happy to partner you any time."

"So will I," said Perry.

"Thanks," Elena mumbled. Her problem was that she felt sorry for Philomeno Reyes. She'd been heartbroken when her Grandfather Portillo died. She'd been messed up ever since Mark Futrell was killed in her house, and she hadn't even liked him. But Philomeno had watched almost his entire family die, knowing that any day, any month, he'd be next. That was a terrible thing, enough to make anyone crazy. Yet maybe he was glad to be dead. Quickly. Without too much pain. With just enough time to begin a confession. Would that attempted act of contrition count with God? she wondered.

Magdalena, who hadn't actually killed anyone, would be the person left with the guilt and the blame, and no one of her generation to console her because Jesus wouldn't last much longer, not if he was lucky.

"Hey, hon, don't look so down," said Connie. "How about going to a Diablos game with me this weekend? You like baseball?"

Perry was staring at him as if Connie had just suggested something shocking.

"What's wrong?" asked Connie.

"Maybe you two aren't aware that you're both dating her," said G. dryly.

The federal agents exchanged nervous glances, then looked toward Elena. She shrugged. "It's not like any of us are going steady."

"I didn't know," said Connie, not to her, to Melon.

"Me, either," Perry assured him. "It's not—ah—"

"—a very good idea," Connie finished for him.

"What's the problem?" Elena asked.

"I told you that we're like a brotherhood," G. explained. "Competition's a mistake with people who have to count on each other in life-and-death situations."

"Not something any of us can afford," said Perry.

Elena looked from one to the other, realizing that they were both dumping her. For the brotherhood.

"Sorry, hon," said Connie.

"Sure." Elena smiled around the circle of embarrassed men. "I think it's my turn to buy the round." At this particular point in her life, maybe what she didn't need were romantic complications. What she did need was help.

"Hey," said Connie. "We're not letting you buy. I'll get the next round."

"Would you say that to one of the guys?" she asked.

"No," he admitted.

"So you're saying I don't belong?"

"Damn right you do, Miss Elena," G. assured her. "Hey, Rosa, this lady wants to buy the next round."

The waitress switched her short skirt over to their table and said, "That'll be twenty bucks, honey. And since when are they letting girls into the Kit-Kat Club?"

"It's almost the millennium," said Elena. "Anything can happen. Women drinking with bomb techs, the Second Coming. I might even make sergeant."

The temperature had dropped into the sixties by the time Elena left the bar, having refused an escort to her car. She wanted to enjoy the quiet, the solitude, and the blessed coolness of the desert night. Now that she had no boyfriends to hang out with, maybe she'd drive around for a while, put off going to bed, where the nightmares inevitably crept up on her.

She'd parked her truck in the lot of a convenience store on the corner, the bar having no parking facilities of its own. The store had closed at midnight, but the lights of the outdoor telephone booth shone onto the blacktop with a warm, yellow glow. There'd been a moon when she first stepped out of the bar, but its light blacked out abruptly, and she looked up in surprise to see dark clouds, back-lit, scudding across the sky.

Then the realization hit her; the case was over! On impulse, she reached into her shoulder bag, searching for a card she remembered putting into the inside zippered pocket. Once she found the card, she inserted her quarter and punched in the number, tilting her head back to look at the stars to the east. They shone as brightly and looked as close as those little Christmas tree lights the state university draped all over the cactus and desert trees on campus.

"Sam Parsley," said a voice at the other end of the line.

His phone had only rung twice; there'd been no time for her to realize how rude it was to call him at this hour. But he didn't sound either sleepy or irritated, just friendly and warm. It was a nice voice, just as she'd remembered. "This is Elena Jarvis."

"Uh-huh. You decided that you're in trouble?"

"Are nightmares and flashbacks trouble?" she asked.

"I'd say so, yes. Why don't you come over?"

"Now?" She hadn't expected an instant appointment.

"Sure. I'll make some popcorn."

"O.K." She was asking for help from a therapist who was going to eat popcorn while she told him her dreams? Well, why not? As long as he was willing to share the refreshments.

The crack of thunder rolled across the city, and lightning flashed in the darkness to the west, revealing for just an instant the mysterious hills and valleys of a towering black cloud. When Elena raised her face to the sky, a buffet of sudden wind caught her braid, and she felt the wet, welcome coolness of rain. Maybe they weren't facing drought after all, she thought. Not this year, anyway. Not in Los Santos.